ROGUE WAVE

Crime by Design, Book 1

Jane Thornley

For my husband, the original River Rogue, who has supported me in all my dreams.

CHAPTER 1

My boots scrabbled over scabs of ice as the nor'easter shoved me downhill. I couldn't feel my fingers inside my intarsia mitts. Once, the package slipped from my hands and slid two feet downhill, forcing me to stop long enough to retrieve it. Only then did I risk checking behind me. Nobody followed except office workers diving for cover.

I kept moving head down through the icy shrapnel until I reached my Jeep. I popped the lock, tossed the box along with my bag onto the passenger seat, and dove inside just as the squall whipped up a fury. For a moment, I sat suspended in the center of a snowy vortex. Turning on the ignition with the heater blasting, I blew onto my fingers while the adrenalin percolated through my bloodstream like jolts of espresso.

I was a thief adrift in a frozen sea. Or, maybe I was Dorothy swirling in an arctic maelstrom on a trajectory to nowhere.

The whiteout continued while I stared out towards Halifax Harbor, everything beyond the windshield bleached and bitter. Were humans really made to exist in an ice box. Seeking relief, I gazed at the rich reds of my battered Turkish carpet bag, well-padded by my latest knitting project, before plunging my hand into its innards seeking my cell phone. With the phone to my ear, I pressed my best friend's number and waited.

"'Nancy Mahoney, Attorney at Law. Sorry I missed your call. Please leave a message—'"

I stabbed a key and jumped to voice mail. "Nancy, it's Phoebe. Please call me as soon as you get a chance. I just committed a misdemeanor. I—"

She picked up before I made it to the next sentence. "What misdemeanor?"

"Petty theft, only I'm not sure who was pettier, me or Julie. She's divorcing Bob and closing Global Threads, but forgot to mention it until today. I've been amputated like a spare limb and tossed out on my ear after ten years. No warning, no heads-up, just a 'get-out-of-my-face-I'm-upset' attitude." I slowed myself down with a deep breath. "So, being the adult I am, I took it badly and, in the end, just took it." I sighed. "Am I making sense?"

"Yes and no. The 'it' being *Tide Weaver*, I presume?" said my friend in a voice of melodious calm.

"Exactly."

Nancy, always my anchor and source of reason, replied. "Put your emotions aside for the moment and think. So, you've been laid off, hit the rage button, and reacted without thinking. You're human. Rise above it. Remember that Julie's in chaos herself. Divorce can do that to anyone. Go back to her, apologize, and return the tapestry. I understand it's important to you, but we can go after it through legal means just as efficiently."

"Just not as quickly." Waves of calm emanated from the phone, but my fractious energy sealed in my fury and grief. "Time is running out for Dad. That doesn't make a shred of difference to Julie. She's all about money now. No, I'm taking the hanging back to Dad today. He needs to see all that color, a little piece of Toby and Mom, to keep his spirits buoyed, especially now. He needs it to ease his pain, Nancy."

"And maybe you need it to ease yours?"

"So? My bloodline's embedded in those fibers. She could have offered it to me in lieu of severance pay but refused."

Nancy took a deep breath. "Forget severance for a moment. We'll get that tapestry for you, just not like this. Take it back. It's stolen property. You know the law as well as I do."

That might have been true once but, since I quit in the middle of my bar exam, it no longer applied. Still, a thief was still a thief. "Thanks for listening," I said. "I just needed to confess my sins. Otherwise, I'll live with my decision."

"That's not a decision, that's an impulse." Nancy had grown accustomed to providing me advice I rarely followed. "Ask yourself what you really want out of life and whether this act brings you closer."

Sometimes Nancy sounded like a cross between Oprah and Mother Teresa, the only cross-denominational, deeply spiritual, working lawyer in existence, as far as I knew. I gazed out at a seagull pecking at an upturned carton of fries in the parking lot. What did I really want out of life? Once I could answer that absolutely, though in mundane terms: an exciting career, love, maybe a great place to live. Though I still craved all of those things, now I wanted them with a hundred caveats. I watched the gull gulp a whole fry, his white neck undulating with effort.

"I want a new life," I said, finally.

"If the Universe registers that, you're in for a ride," Nancy said.

And then my phone vibrated, announcing an in-coming call from FAIRY GODFATHER. "Nancy, it's Max on the other line. Finally."

"You'd better get it, then. Talk later."

I pressed END and then TALK. "Max? Why haven't you returned my messages? Where are you?"

The familiar Australian accent rumbled into my ear. "Phoebe, love, sorry I couldn't get to you sooner but I've been tied up. You all right?"

I leaned back against the seat, my cell phone pressed against my ear. Outside, the squall was abating. "Yes, just fabulous, thanks, but it's not like you not to respond right away. I thought something was wrong. Have you been kidnapped by aliens?"

"I've been tracking down Toby, like I promised."

My breath caught. "And?"

"And I've found something ."

I leaned forward, resting my head against the steering wheel. I couldn't believe it. At last, at last. "Did you find him? Is he all right?"

He paused. "No details over the phone. It's complicated. We'll need to meet. I'll set something up."

"Is he in some kind of trouble?" Just like my brother to get snarled in something murky. Still, I'd blast him the moment I laid eyes on him for putting Dad and me through all this crap. It had been 10 weeks with no word. He rarely fell off-grid for more than a week at a time. "Are you here in Nova Scotia?"

"Nope, but I'll bring you to me. Meanwhile, got to know if you'll do what it takes to help find your brother."

I stilled, gazing at the dashboard in disbelief. "What kind of question is that? Of course, I will."

"Had to ask. So, do as I say, no questions asked."

"Is Toby into something?"

"No questions asked, I said."

"Where is he? Surely you can tell me that much?"

"Listen carefully. Go to your father's cottage and look for something Toby may have hidden there. I have no idea what exactly but you'll know it's important when you see it. I have reason to believe it could be a clue to his disappearance."

"Are you kidding me? Toby hasn't been back to see Dad for months."

"He made a surprise visit weeks before he disappeared. I know, I didn't realize that, either, until a few days ago. Go there now and poke around. Don't tell your father what you're up to. Don't even mention my name, understand?"

As if I would. My godfather's name had become a no-fly zone in the McCabe household and I had no idea why. How I hated secrets. They throttled the life out of you and left you hanging in the wind. "What happened between you two? Oh, wait, no questions asked. Right: 'INTELLIGENT WOMAN BECOMES MUTE ANDROID OVERNIGHT.' How easily I forget the headlines. Okay, so I go down and look for some unidentified hidden object that may connect to my missing brother in some unexplained way but can't tell Dad because you two aren't talking. How hard can that be? I'm on my way."

"You knew Toby as well as anyone. Use that to search, okay?"

My heart caught in my throat. "You said 'knew,' not 'know'."

"Just a slip of the tongue, darling. No worries. I'll call later."

CHAPTER 2

A bleak wash of sea and sky came along for the ride that afternoon as I followed the St. Margaret's Bay road along the ragged coastline. A grey pall had settled in behind the snow, leaving the world a seamless blur of white and grey melting into the water's churlish blue. Both the highway and my thoughts ran parallel, twisting in and out of the icy fog.

All the places where I grieved or fretted lay along that route—the little church tucked into a hillside above the cove where we'd held Mom's funeral, the stretches of beach I walked after Toby disappeared, plus this road that I'd driven countless times back and forth delivering both parents to city hospitals. Funny thing, I mused, my life to date had really been more joy than sorrow, but these days, I only remembered the murky bits.

The sun hung suspended in a sag of cloud by the time I rounded the bend to the little beach community where I grew up. My family home perched on a low rise across the one-lane highway, facing a curve of stony beach. Once a clapboard cottage painted a bright blue, its innocuous white siding now blended in with the snowy landscape. With Mom's studio off to the left and the other additions constructed over the years, the house bore little resemblance to the original holiday cottage beginning.

I parked the Jeep beside Dad's old Dodge truck, tucked the carton under one arm, and climbed the path, my boots crunching clumps of melting slush. A round woman in a maroon puffer coat emerged from the front door and waited on the steps, a laundry basket in her hands.

"Mrs. Hugli, hi," I greeted. "How's Dad today?"

Dad's housekeeper and sometime caregiver smiled. "One of his better days, overall. You're timing's perfect. I just made a big casserole, so help yourself. He's settling in with the evening news." Her round face briefly bloomed into a smile.

"Not too curmudgeonly?"

"I didn't say that," she said with a laugh. "Some things never change." As my father's next-door neighbor, she had known the family for over 30 years and I was endlessly grateful that she kept an eye on him considering the pittance Toby and I paid.

"Thanks for everything, Mrs. Hugli, for always and forever," I slapped one hand over my heart and put one foot on the step.

"Phoebe, wait."

I froze.

"I wanted to talk to you about the always and forever part. It's just that I don't know how much longer I can keep doing this. I'm not getting any younger, either. It's not the money, you know. I don't care about that."

I sighed. "Yes, of course. Dad's getting on your last nerve."

"Have you thought about having him come live in the city with you?"

"Yes, the way I consider solving world peace and finding an end to hunger; I do what I can but don't expect miracles. He refuses to leave."

"Right," she said with shake of the head. "When pigs fly."

"Exactly."

"He's soon going to need someone with him 24/7. You know that. Keep trying, that's all I ask. As long as you're working on it, I'll do the best I can." She gave me a heartening pat on the arm as she pushed past. I watched her trudge down the path, the sleeve of one of Dad's flannel shirts dangling from the basket in a limp wave.

Dad would never leave here. Removing him from this cottage would be like prying a barnacle from a rock only to find it fixed even tighter two seconds later, but could I bear to return to take care of him? How much courage did it take to face a past with no future, anyway?

Pushing the door open, I entered the little vestibule and kicked off my boots, hung up my coat, and stepped into the kitchen. The endless clash of colors from my mother's folk art-meets-department-store decorating scheme warmed my heart while the wood stove toasted everything else.

My mother had loved color and, though her works involved carefully planned and executed compositions, here the decor ran riot. FiestaWare sat stacked on organic earth mugs; jubilant floral curtains danced across the windows; a hooked rug tossed little boats among waves of cobalt blue. No cohesion, just joyous color. "Kitchens are the house's heart," she had said, "and shouldn't be designed so much as celebrated."

I smiled and stepped towards the stove, hands extended to the warmth. Despite all the modern electrical appliances like an electric stove and forced-air heating, my family always used an old-fashioned wood stove to ward away winter's freeze. It was like a point of honor with my parents.

How many times had my brother and I devoured cookies and milk after school in this very room, chattering while Mom bustled around the kitchen? We had once been so close, two siblings clinging to one another by virtue of our existence on the fringes of school life, oddballs in the adolescent game. Then four years between us stretched into empty air. After my brother moved away, traveling around the world as a talented dilettante delving into computer gaming, graphics, and who knows what else, our lives occasionally intersected but seldom merged.

I could hear the television droning away in the den. I set the package down on the freshly-wiped pine table while scanning the kitchen, taking in dishes drying in the rack, fresh-baked cookies cooling on the counter, and the underlying scent of possible lasagna. If I closed my eyes, I could almost believe that Mom still lived, Toby was only an email away, and life remained captured in the amber of perfect memory, my family intact forever. Only, reality always lay in ambush.

Now supper called, my stomach rumbling as I located the casserole cooling under tin foil on the counter. Slipping a chunk of lasagna onto my plate, I sat down to eat. I would have gobbled shoelaces coated in plastic right then, since I hadn't eaten since breakfast, but Bertha Hugli happened to be a fabulous cook like my mother, the two having traded recipes years ago.

"Dad?" I called out as I picked up my fork.

"Phoebe, is that you?" There was nothing wrong with his hearing. He shuffled into the kitchen and stopped, feigning shock. "What? You're going to stuff your face before giving your old man a hug?"

"Sorry." I got to my feet and gave him a big one, the kind the McCabes bestowed upon each other for time memorial. Dad always gave the best versions, in this case scrunching my face deep into the scratchy wool of the Aran sweater Mom knit decades ago.

"You must have ESP. Been thinking about you all day. Lord, it's good to see you. It's been so long. Why is my own daughter a stranger these days?" he said, giving me a fierce squeeze for good measure.

I pulled away, laughing. "I was here only last weekend, which happens to be only four days ago."

"What? Seems longer. So, you want tea with that?"

"Sure, but I'll make it." I moved towards the stove.

"You will not. Do you think I can't make my own daughter damn tea when she visits? That Bertha comes in here all the time cooking, cleaning, banging around here as if I can't take care of myself. Sit down and finish your supper. I'll make the tea."

I returned to my seat, trying not to watch his every move while I gobbled up the last of the casserole. He moved slowly but with traces of the old energy still visible in the way he plucked a mug off the hook or banged the stainless kettle down on the stovetop. Dad making a point communicated "I can still do any damn thing I did before and don't you forget it, little girl." Klunk. Despite a heart attack he'd suffered the year Mom died and the stroke after Toby disappeared plus all the troubles in between, he still looked younger than 85 with his gray beard trimmed neatly around a sturdy chin and blue eyes sparkling with feisty humor or just plain bad temper, take your pick.

Once he had been so witty, handsome, and sexy, in that man-at-the-helm-of-a-ship way, that he swept a certain art student off her feet and lured her to his sea shanty home. The siren myth reversed. Mom claimed she'd been smitten beyond reason.

The wall phone shook my reverie. Dad swung around, sugar bowl in hand, eyes alert and eager. "Toby?"

I reached for the phone, heart twisting with his. How many times had hope struck with the ring of a phone? Desperation and hope had conjoined in the McCabe family.

"Hi, Phoebe," Mrs. Hugli said into my ear, "I forgot to mention that your Dad's upped and locked the door of Toby's room."

My heart fell. "I'll take care of it, thanks, Mrs. Hugli."

I replaced the receiver. "Not Toby. Sorry, Dad."

He, turned his back to me. "That Bertha again?" he asked, banging a tin on the counter where he proceeded to scoop sugar into a bowl. "What does that meddling woman want this time?"

"She says you've locked Toby's room."

"Sure, I did. She has no business sneaking around in there."

"That's called cleaning," I pointed out.

"Same thing for her. I don't want her in there and that's that. You want cookies with your tea?"

When Dad locked the door on a topic, it would take heaven and the seven seas to pry it open. He'd close in on himself, boiling with emotional currents and dark thoughts he'd never share. The only one who could ever pry him open was Mom.
I swallowed hard and shook my head.

"How's your boyfriend, whatshisname?" Dad asked, moving about the kitchen tidying.

"Christian. We're done." This wasn't the first time he'd been told that. I ended the Christian thing months ago.

"Oh, good. Never liked him. Had too high an opinion of himself. What else is new?"

"As of today, I'm no longer working at Global Threads," I said. "Julie and I parted company earlier, rather dramatically."

Dad swung around. "Well, hell's bells, it's about time. I never did like her or that Mr. Big husband of hers. You should have left long ago. Did you quit?"

"Ex Mr. Big husband. They're getting a divorce. I got laid off." Axed, more like it. Blindsided. Forget all the promises for work in kind compensation.

"Those two deserved each other like two crabs at a tea party. You stayed too long, anyway. I'm glad you left."

"But staying all that time was easy." Everything else took too much effort, too much risk.

"You can do much better."

"I know that," I said with a sigh, "but I loved that job for a while. In a better economy, Julie and Bob had brought in some of the most luscious yarn from all over the world—Chinese silks, Italian blends—remember? Mom used to buy all her stuff from them." And, with my urging, they had begun adding textile art, even antique tribal rugs Max had help me source. In fact, the Fairy Godfather had magically sent a few impressive customers our way to purchase the very pieces he supplied. "Four years ago, surrounded by beautiful textiles and yarn, Global Threads had been my sweet spot. After things began unraveling, I had no idea what else to do."

Dad poured boiling water into the pot and shoved one of Mom's knitted tea cozies over all. "Don't you worry, dear. With your skills and qualifications, you'll find something better."

A half-baked lawyer with a Masters' in Art History who'd just dawdled away a decade selling yarn and old rugs didn't exactly attract headhunters. "Sure."

"You want one of them cookies with that?" He slid some of the chocolate chip goodies onto a plate and sat it down on the table across from me.

I shook my head. "First, I want to show you something. I brought you a present."

Dad's gaze swung from my face to the box and back again. "That?" he asked.

I nodded, clearing the plates and cutlery to the counter. "Hang on a minute. This needs room."

Dad had the carton open and removed the folded piece without a clue as to its contents.

"Allow me."

He passed me folded cloth, perplexed. I stepped back and carefully unfurled the tapestry across the table.

A sudden, inexplicable surge of joy stirred me, the same impact I experienced time after time. The 6'x3' piece flowed across our table in a swirl of blue-green blending with captured light. Rolling waves worked in silk and wool leaped and curled before the eye, the sea swallowing all but the top one-third where eight inches of sky melded from dawn to moonlight, left to right, burnished gold to deep silver-haloed ultramarine. Light streaming through the inner curve of the wave tops shimmered in turquoise and green silk, the threads so expertly worked, they glowed.

As the eye traveled below, the wonders only intensified. The sea of life, teaming with fish, mammals, coral reefs, and two gilded merpeople hovering over a treasure chest glinting with riches, were all fashioned in smaller thread count with surface embroidery adding richness to the tiniest detail. And the colors! Delicate yet vibrant, we had hand-dyed most of the shades ourselves, and the gilded thread came all the way from England. Nothing but the perfect nuance would do.

The Tide Weaver wove together strands of the McCabe family's inner world and our collective imaginations. Toby and I were the merpeople based on a fairytale Mom read to us as kids. We embraced the image of creatures at home at sea yet craving another dimension to which they could never belong and made it our own. Toby and I had designed the scene, Toby sketching the drawing, me painting it, and my mother, a master weaver, working it into being right here in this very cottage.

As a journey of life and art, it had taken five years with me running back and forth from university in town and Toby flying in from wherever whenever. We should never have sold it. Why had we? Because Mom had so wanted the endorsement the piece would bring hanging in a gallery and I could survive parting with it as long as it hung over my head in the place where I worked. I fingered the golden mermaid charm hanging from my neck, lost in a sea of memories.

A snuffling noise pulled me from my reverie. Dad stood wiping his eyes on the back of his sleeve.

"Oh, Dad, I'm sorry!" I ran to hug him. "I forgot how it might hurt you to see this again but—"

"Put it away," he growled, pain turning to anger or some other emotion I couldn't identify. "I don't want to see that again. Put it away."

I stopped steps away from him, bewildered. "What?"

"Get rid of it," he told me, shoving the carton at me.

"Get rid of it? Dad, this is Mom's work, Toby's, and my design, your family!"

"I don't care. Just get rid of it. Hide it if you have to." And with that, he swung around and lumbered back into the den, leaving me stupefied.

***

Even Dad's notorious temper did not explain this outburst. Tears I could understand, not fury. I expected joy or maybe relief, solace, something, anything but rage. It had to be his illness and, again, the impact of loss punched me in the gut.

Once he'd calmed down, I joined him in the den, knitting while he watched the news, my brain churning. I'd packed the tapestry away in Mom's studio until I could figure out what to do next and along the way, tried Toby's door —locked, just as Bertha said, secured by a clunky industrial padlock of questionable vintage. Bewildering. I decided then and there to stay the night, holed up on my narrow bed in my old room next door until I could get to the bottom of this, or at least, search the cottage for whatever Max sought.

I sat, deep into my memories, knitting long drop stitches into free-form waves that had begun turquoise but now brooded into a deep, moody blue. These days, I saw the irregular rise and fall of wave-like stitches as a metaphor for my life: erratic but with some mysterious rhythm I had yet to grasp. If the piece grew into a wrap or a scarf or a something else, I'd be fine with that, just as long as it kept moving forward.

"Dad," I ventured. "I hope you don't plan on keeping me out of Toby's room along with Bertha Hugli?"

Without taking his eyes from the History Channel, he said, "Why do you want to go in there, anyway?"

"Why would you ever want to keep me out? I miss him, too," I said over the moderator's voice describing an ancient Etruscan tomb.

When he didn't respond, I studied him. Yes, my father had gone under again but his face registered something I couldn't identify. Fear? That made sense since fear had garroted our emotions since Toby disappeared, but something else brewed, too. I just didn't understand what. Confusion from his deteriorating health? My poor, dear father. "Dad?"

"I love you, you know that," he muttered, still not looking at me.

"And I love you, too, but what's that got to do with it?"

"I just want that room kept locked for now."

I stabbed my needle into my wrap to anchor my stitches, struck again by how quickly things were changing. It felt as though my hands were struggling to hold onto a sandy beach while the tide hauled me further into the deep. "What are you hiding from me this time, Dad? In fact, what have you been hiding for the last two decades?"

"I'm not hiding anything."

"Why won't you talk to Uncle Max anymore?"

"He's not your uncle and don't you forget it. Your mother and I should never have agreed to let him be your godfather, either. Now, don't go mentioning his name in this house again."

I soldiered on. "Dad, a pall of secrecy has dominated this house since I was a kid. It began the day I came home from school to find a strange man in the kitchen." Max Baker, a tall Australian with a sense of foreign climes hanging off him like exotic aftershave, no more fit our little kitchen than the new stainless steel dishwasher that arrived shortly afterwards.

"I don't want to talk about that, I said."

"Dad, I need to know. It's important. Just tell me what an urbane Australian really wanted with the fisherman and why the two of you would stay up all night whispering while we kids had to stay in our rooms? Tell me what Max really wanted with a smelly workhorse lobster boat and why you eventually sold her, complete with coveted license, to buy some sleek new cabin cruiser?"

"What are you talking about?" he turned towards me, face flushed and eyes puzzled. "You know why I bought *The Merry Day.*"

"The Merry Dance, Dad, not *The Merry Day.* Right, to take tourists on supposed joyrides up and down the coast, like I believed that. There was more to it, Dad, and I need to know what."

My father just stared at me as if struggling to remember. I watched the expression in his eyes alter as if he had found something tucked deep in his memory that surfaced briefly and startled him. He looked away. "Did I tell you that there's a new cafe in Hubbards? One of those yuppie places looking to serve gourmet hamburgers?"

I sank back into my seat. Whether Dad had lost certain details of our past life or chose not to remember them, the results were the same. He wouldn't or couldn't tell me, leaving a huge vacuum in my family history I might never be able to fill. With Toby missing, the chasm yawned deeper.

As the night wore on, Dad and I bided the time making small-talk during commercials as the news ran into a sitcom followed by a string of his favorite television shows. We discussed possible job options for me, the escalating price of electricity, and the new cafe Sheldon MacDonald had opened in Hubbards. No mention of Max, Toby, or the family secret crossed my lips again.

At ten o'clock sharp, he shuffled to his feet. "I'm off to bed, Sweetheart. You'll turn off the lights, won't you?"

"I will," I said, rising to give him a hug.

"Good to have you here with me, you know. I get lonely without your mother."

That's the way it was with him: growling one minute, hugging the next.

"I know, Dad."

I sat knitting for a while with the television turned off and nothing but the subtle sound of the sea beyond. At times like these, I felt the ocean flowing in my veins, connecting me to the great beyond, the sense of being a single molecule amid a zillion, bringing the illusion of cohesion to my fractured life.

With yarns the colors of the chill Atlantic, I made long freeform drop stitches across my rows, the yarns suspended in some kind of life-line I wished reality would provide. Something rhythmic in working with fiber always soothed me in some profound way as if my hands reached deep inside the ocean and dropped an anchor of calm. I'd forget pain, loss, and survival, surrendering to a moment where only yarn and I existed in our own perfect world.

Dad's snoring began disturbing the peace at around ten thirty. It occurred me somewhere between a yarn change, that soon enough even my father would be gone. What had begun a bright, vibrant, turquoise began muting down into deep, moody blue. It was as though my life was slowly being drained of everyone I loved, all the threads unraveling, all colors blunting from joy to sorrow.

At around quarter to eleven, I reluctantly set my half-born wrap aside in a jumble of wavy patterns and plucked my cell phone from my bag. Four missed calls and many more text messages leapt on the little screen. I girded my loins and began scanning:

JULIE: missed call.

JULIE: missed call.

JULIE: Phoebe, tell me you didn't just do what I think you did? Call me.

JULIE: Phoebe, bring it back now and I promise to forget you ever took it. CALL ME!

JULIE: Phoebe, please. Let's talk. Bring it back and we'll work something out, I promise. Look, I sold it, okay? The Bank of Montreal offered a nice price so we let it go. It's supposed to be delivered later today. CALL ME, WILL YOU?

JULIE: Are you out of your —— mind?? That's theft and you can bet your ass I won't let you get away with it. Call me before I call the police!

JULIE: missed call.

I took a deep breath and let my gaze sail up to the whitewashed ceiling. She sold it. She sold my mother's tapestry and lied about that along with everything else. Could I trust anyone? I returned to my scanning.

NANCY: Are you okay, my friend? I sense darkness around you.

I texted a brief reply: You sense right but I will prevail. I'll phone today (your today. You'll be sleeping now) I'm at Dad's. XXX000 Phoebe

FAIRY GODFATHER: Any luck in your hunt?

FAIRY GODFATHER: Are you at the cottage now?

I messaged back: Max, yes, I'm at Dad's. Will text as soon as I finish searching. What am I looking for?

Slipping the phone in my pocket, the ringer still set on mute, I stood listening to my father's sonorous breathing while attempting to climb inside my brother's mind. If he tried to hide something in the cottage, that is, if he would ever do such a thing, where? And, perhaps the more fitting question would be why? What kind of trouble could my brother get into, anyway? Though an artist by nature and a computer graphics genius by profession, his inclination swerved to living on the edge mostly through imagination. The games he created, the ones that lined his pockets, featured warriors plunging into fantasy worlds populated by monsters and bizarre creatures. I could only pray the dangers remained imaginary.

Where would he hide something worth hiding? Certainly not anywhere my father regularly inhabited. Maybe his bedroom room or Mom's studio.

I left the den and entered the next room, the door creaking open into a shadowy world where a huge loom half-lit by the deck light held court. The wall on one side held bins of yarn and tools, the other three nothing but broad windows with more storage shelves against the floor. The unheated space stood chill and still, its warmth having left with its queen years ago.

Much like all the other once-owned rooms under this roof, Dad never infringed on the spaces of those dead or elsewhere. He kept every room intact as a way to keep us close. Every time I visited, I'd enter this room as a kind of homage to my mom. I'd sit and mourn, remembering the days when mother and daughter conjured some textile feat in our creative togetherness. "Phoebe, dear, what do you think of this idea?" or "Let's make a dye as rich and red as all the carpets in the Ottoman Empire!"

Dad built this studio for Mom. He used to joke that he'd made his biggest catch on his wedding day. At first glance, the pairing of an art student and a lobster fisherman may have seemed peculiar, but Ariadne Bracket had a long-standing romance with the sea and, Dad, in his youth, had been passionate, inquisitive, charming, and worthy of sweeping any woman off her land-locked pins.

I stood in the darkness smiling, running down the inner corridors of a happier life. Enough. I had work to do, but even before I began rummaging half-heartedly through the drawers and yarn bins, I knew absolutely that Toby would never hide anything here. He would see it as an affront to our mother. I left the bins and shelves and backed away.

Dad's snoring rumbled through the house as I began hunting for the padlock key. He used to keep keys and change in a jar by the wood stove but no such jar existed now. I dove into the pockets of his jackets hanging in the hall, fingering nails, rubber bands, and candy so old, they'd gummed to the wrappers. No key. I rifled through the kitchen in every drawer, box, bottle, and jar I could lay my hands on with no luck. I concluded he must have stashed the key somewhere in his room, which I absolutely would not penetrate.

Weary now, I wandered into the kitchen to make a cup of tea. Dad must have tidied up while I was off stashing the tapestry because the dishes had been put away. I stood leaning against the counter, wondering again what Max thought Toby might hide, here of all places, while the tea steeped and I ruminated.

I opened the cupboard and found all the dirty mugs shelved among the clean, went to the fridge to grab the milk and found the sugar bowl instead. A few seconds later, I retrieved the milk carton from another cupboard and fished a single key from the sugar bowl.

It was the padlock key. I broke down and cried.

***

In Toby's room later, I sat my mug on his dresser and flicked on the overhead light. My brother's teenage world jumped into high relief in posters and paintings, all his early work, many pieces of which Mom had framed. Sweeping canvases where painted sunsets sent shots of color across our local beachfront rose above many smaller vistas, some traditional, some abstract, some outright whimsical, all drawing me back into what had once been our shared world.

His talent circa age 19 hinted of all my brother would become. Even here he revealed a strong, energetic exploration of many mediums—oil, watercolor, acrylic, and mixed media which would eventually morph into computer animations. Though his strokes were bold, he could also work with amazing delicacy and tenderness, a tenderness that left him vulnerable on the schoolyard where boys measure their worth in bravado and testosterone rather than art and design.

My gaze landed on the merman, *his* merman, a three-foot high he-fish with a brawny torso, long red hair, and a blue-green tail, a merry caricature self-portrait of Toby the artist. The companion piece, the mermaid, hung in my room, my fifteenth birthday present, painted gold, ultra-female in shape, with long hair and a seashell bra. I still imagined myself that way: the queen of her domain, free to follow her heart wherever it may lead.

Those two images became symbolic for how we once saw ourselves as brother and sister in our early years: two fish out of water, afloat in our own imaginative worlds surrounded by the treacherous nets of secrecy. Just standing there almost broke my heart. Toby, where are you?

I began searching in all the usual places, in drawers and under the bed. My mother had packed many of Toby's things in boxes stashed in the closet so I unpacked all of those, finding nothing but old clothes. I looked behind the paintings, feeling around for taped keys or messages or something, anything. How did I know what to look for? I thought perhaps a key or maybe a letter might be significant, but nothing like that remained anywhere in Toby's domain.

The only thing I came across was Toby's sketch for *Tide Weaver* stored in a roll of painted white poster paper, which had once hung behind Mom's loom to serve as the "cartoon" design guide. For some reason, the piece had been stuffed in a mailing tube and wedged high over the bed in a narrow slot formed between the cottage's original rafter roof and the newer ceiling. As far as I knew, I was the only one who knew of the hidey-hole's existence, Toby having long ago made me swear never to reveal his secret place.

I pulled the tightly rolled paper from the tube and spread its stiff, watercolor-painted surface across the bed. It was an exact duplicate of the weaving and, as such, struck me anew with its vibrancy, even though the painting had suffered over the years. Despite being tucked away in a tube, it had been torn and cracked. Toby seemed to have attempted to strengthen the flimsy paper by backing it with a few additional layers, which he sealed to the original by taping the edges.

By then, I was so tired, I just replaced the cartoon in its tube and took it with me as I headed for bed.

That night, I dreamt our cottage rocked and rolled far out to sea. Huge waves crashed against the walls, sloshing through the open windows and running icy currents across the floors. I struggled out of bed, sinking up to my ankles in running water sluicing back and forth across the floor. I knew I had to find something of value but wasn't sure where to begin. I needed fins, I realized. I needed a magic tail that would propel me deeper and farther than I could otherwise travel.

When my eyes opened, I sat blinking into the dark. Home, I realized, as in childhood home, and I was sitting in bed, not standing in water. My phone's light illuminated my room. Throwing off the covers, I padded over to my dresser and plucked up the phone. Max had texted me: "Check your email. I just sent you a ticket to Bermuda. Meet me there tomorrow night."

I texted back: "I'll come providing you promise to answer every question I ask."

The response came the next morning. "A deal."

CHAPTER 3

I stood in the living room of the Astwood Cove Cottage taking in the Colonial tropical tourist decor. Rattan and bamboo accessorized by potted palms and lots of polished mahogany created a cosy "Englishman in the tropics" ambience. I missed home already. Though I appreciated the bowls of hibiscus and the fire burning in the hearth, after six hours snow-stayed at the Toronto airport followed by another four in the air, I missed authentic more. The one consolation was that, somewhere beyond those walls, I sensed a warmer sea.

I lowered my carpet bag now seconding as a knitting bag cum carryall onto an ottoman and sighed.

"Is everything to your satisfaction?" asked Ted, the Astwood Cove Cottage service elf who had picked me up from the airport to deliver me into this lush nest.

"Perfectly," I said, taking in his pink windbreaker and white chinos, the resort's uniform, I gathered.

"Any questions?" he beamed, all friendliness and white teeth as he stood there holding my battered suitcase and vintage carry-on." Mr. Baker instructed me to cater to your every comfort."

That would be just like my fairy godfather, still trying to sprinkle fairy dust after all these years. "How much does all of this cost per night, anyway?"

He laughed, as if anyone staying in a place like this had to ask. The depth of Max's pockets had always piqued my curiosity. "The bedroom's on the second floor. Here, I'll take your bags up," Ted said with another grin.

"Okay," I murmured, following behind him long enough to glimpse the four-poster bed, candlewick bedspread, and continuation of applied ambience in all the right places. I acknowledged the luxury of the en suite spa bath room with a nod, my eyes glazing over downstairs halfway through the tour of the well-appointed kitchen with its stock of gourmet edibles, the sunroom with cove views, and patio with built-in barbecue/fireplace. Just in case an ocean didn't offer water enough, the cottage even had a small pool. By the time Ted finished the sweeping parade of amenities, I couldn't stop yawning.

"If you want anything at all, just call the front office. Someone's on duty 24 hours a day to answer to your every need," Ted told me after adding more wood to the fire. I thanked him and finally he exited.

Alone at last, I sank into the cushy chair by the fire and closed my eyes. Long ago I'd dubbed Max Baker "fairy godfather" for good reason. He always came bearing gifts, treats big and small, rare and expensive, the kind that rural Nova Scotian kids rarely saw let alone owned.

Why had I come? Why did I allow Max to keep pull my strings? I should have insisted he tell me what he knew over the phone, but it's like I allowed him to spread a magic carpet at my feet to dull all the rough edges of the world. As if he could. Yet, I needed answers, I reminded myself, and I knew I'd never find them by staying home. My eyes opened. What did Bermuda have to do with Toby's disappearance? My fairy godfather had some explaining to do and I couldn't wait to grill him until his wings dropped off. Where was he?

Fishing my phone from my pocket, I released the AIRPLANE MODE function and waited until the cell signal engaged. Minutes later, a text message slipped into view: HI, PHOEBE. WELCOME TO BERMUDA. SEE YOU AT 10:00. MAX

I checked the time: 9:29. That left half an hour before facing my summoner. I strolled into the kitchen, plucked an apple from the fruit bowl, and headed out the front door.

I'd researched the island online before I left, slipping across page upon page of tourist spiel. Bermuda was served up as the epitome of British culture encapsulated in a semitropical climate. Tea and shorts, mopeds, and cottages the color of breath mints were all portrayed against a brilliant turquoise sea. Charming but why would Toby come here? He preferred his travel straight-up exotic. And he would never miss Dad's birthday.

I pondered this while following the sounds of the sea. Even on this moonless night, the well-lit paths crisscrossing the grounds found the beach in any direction, but I figured I could find water even without a guide. It called to me like a huge, beating heart, breathing in and out with the tide. All I needed to do was keen my ears and follow the siren's song.

The scent of flowers spiced the air, their velvet faces brushing my hands as I jogged down the path towards the beach. I lurched into a full run downhill. Breaking through the oleander hedges and crossing the sand, I headed straight for the water's edge. A trio of spotlights fixed on one of the fringing palms illuminated the surf's low boil.

I stood staring out to sea, the wind whipping my hair. Overhead, a spangle of stars swam in the inky blackness while, below, the sea beckoned me on with a surging, luminous, dark. How I longed to dive deep and far, as if that watery void might somehow soothe all my aching parts. I tugged off my sneakers, peeled away my socks, and rolled up my jeans, wading up to my calves in the salty bite. The chill invigorated me like a zap of body caffeine.

Thus began the old game of feint and parry between the sea and me. I always played; I always lost. Seeing an oncoming roller, I'd turn, scrambling back to shore, vying for safety before a wave grabbed my knees. I made five successful dash and scrambles before one biggie flung a mass of icy tide against my back and force me neck-deep into the absurdity of it all. Beware the rogue wave, Dad always said. That unexpected swell of invisible currents and tidal pull will bring you to your knees every time. You won't even see it coming. I never did. I laughed at my folly and struggled to my feet.

Shivering, I trudged back to dry land to don my socks and sneakers. With sand chafing my feet, I followed a stone pathway up to headland overlooking the sea. I'd scan the topography and then return to the cottage for a shower and change.

A viewing area carved into the rock formed a prime scenic spot. Two low stone benches braced a round gate that framed the dark sea heaving beyond. If I stood under that arch of that moon gate, I could see the lights winking from other cottages nestled about the property across the cove. If I leaned forward far enough, I could glimpse tropical fish shooting jolts of color in the underwater spotlights nestled into the cliffs. I squelched a sudden craving to dive in with the fishes. Maybe another time. And then my cell phone rang.

Turning my back to the wind, I plucked the phone from my pocket and hit TALK.

"Phoebe? It's me."

"Dad! What are you doing calling?'

"What d'you mean, 'what am I doing calling'? I'm your father and it's my God-given right to call my daughter. Besides, I've been worried sick. Why haven't you called? You're breaking up."

I moved to the other side of the lookout to fix a better signal. "Dad, I spoke to you only a few hours ago. Is everything all right?"

"Sure, everything's all right with me. It's you I'm worried about."

I closed my eyes. It had to be because Toby was missing that anxiety hit him over my absences, no matter how brief. Even though, to his knowledge, I was still in Halifax, beneath it all, he sensed something. "Everything's fine, Dad. I'm just out for a walk. I'd better get back home, though. It's getting late."

"You shouldn't be walking the city streets alone. It's not safe."

I hated lying to him but his anxiety was too fever-pitched to know the truth. "It's fine, Dad. I'm fine. Stop worrying. Besides, I can take care of myself. "

"Like Toby?"

Damn. "Dad, I'd better go."

"If you're worried about money, I can lend you some. I got a little put by."

Dad always thought himself well-off if he had more than a month's grocery money stashed. He didn't realize Toby and I supplemented his pension. "Thanks, Dad, really but I'm fine for money." I wasn't but he didn't need to know that.

A flashlight flickered up the path towards me. "Look, I'd better go, my battery's giving out. I'll call soon, I promise. In the meantime, mind your ticker and don't go overdoing it."

Pressing END, I dropped the phone back into my pocket and watched the figure approach.

***

He arrived at the top of the bluff, windblown, a tall, tanned man with a lean, rangy, body, lithe like a panther. Though I couldn't see his features in the dark, I had the sense of a sharp, angled face and deep-set eyes. He could have been another Astwood service elf or maybe a fellow resort resident, except this man didn't wear pink or dress in typical tourist garb. Dark jeans, a turtleneck, and leather jacket struck me as more biker dude than resort wear, even off-season.

"Hi," I greeted him.

"You're Phoebe."

"Thanks for telling me. And you are?"

"Noel Halloren. I work for Max." The accent was undeniably Australian. Another Aussie.

Well, of course, I knew Max had employees but, other than his girlfriend, I'd never met any of them before. "Really? What do you do for him?"

Halloran grinned, an unsettling flash of white in the shadows. "Anything he wants me to."

"Anything? Does that make you sort of an all-purpose dogsbody? No job description, just a blank page where he fills in the details?" For some reason, the man's presence provoked my smart-ass side.

He laughed. "Fits. In this economy, an employee's got to diversify, even a hound."

"*Dogsbody,*" I mused, uncomfortable under this stranger's scrutiny. "That's a naval term referring to a gofer, in case you didn't know."

"Hails from the early nineteenth century, and gofer is fitting enough, too, since I was sent here to fetch you. Max is waiting in the cottage."

"Oh, good." I slipped past him and made my way down the path, the dogsbody at my heels.

I burst through the door of the cottage into the lounge where Max Baker stood helping himself to the house Scotch dressed in a navy turtleneck, jeans and his signature crocodile boots. "Phoebe, my little mermaid!" he exclaimed.

"Max, my fairy godfather!"

He laughed, spreading his arms for the kind of embrace we'd exchanged since he officially became my godfather some 20 years earlier, but mine was more guarded. He squeezed me tight, regardless, as if trying to press away the years that separated us, this tall man who always smelled of sandalwood laced with foreign shores. I squelched the bittersweet memories along with an inexplicable urge to cry. "Thought we agreed you'd stop calling me 'fairy' years ago?" he said into my hair, his voice muffling laughter.

I stepped away. "Unless you stop the little mermaid reference, the deal's off. Anyway, I'd say that Dad's been asking after you, but you're persona non grata these days. Why's that?"

He shook his head. "No clue. He's been mad at me since Toby disappeared."

"Like he blames you."

"What kind of fool thinking is that? I'd do anything for Toby and your family, he knows that. Every time I call, he hangs up, and after the heart bonker, he wouldn't let me in the hospital to visit him. What's up with him, Phoebe?"

I shook my head. "I found the milk in the cupboard and the sugar bowl in the fridge, if that helps answer your question, but there's something else going on. That's why I came. Whatever Dad's hiding or can't remember, concerns Toby."

"I'm sorry, love. I truly am. If you need money for special care or anything, just ask."

I never would and sensed he knew it. I'd thrown up a speed bump along the highway of endless gifts long ago. "Thanks. How's Maggie?" Maggie being Max's longtime secretary/assistant/partner or undefined companion.

"Great. You'll see her tomorrow."

"The last time I saw you both was the night Toby didn't show for Dad's birthday bash. He fell apart that night and I've never been able to mention your name since. I tried again last night but he's clammed shut. I just don't know how much of it is due to stroke damage or to something else. The doc says he suffered a series of minor strokes that night. Did I tell you that already?"

"You did, honey."

I wrapped my arms around myself and stepped towards the fire. "I didn't even know it at first. For weeks, I put his behavior down to Toby's disappearance."

"You aren't a doctor, Phoebe. Don't blame yourself for what you couldn't have known."

I turned around to face him again, finding him standing tense, hands flexing at his sides. He ran one hand through his thick hair and tried to smile.

"I've got you covered in sand." I pointed to his sweater.

He looked down at the grit-sprinkled chest. "No worries. You go swimming with your clothes on or something?" He stepped towards me until his outstretched arms touched my shoulders. With the fireplace at my back, I stayed put. "You're soaked!"

"She was cavorting in the waves," I heard Noel comment behind me. So he'd been watching. I wished he'd leave so I could talk to Max in private.

I shrugged. "Water and I go way back. "

Max grinned, still a handsome, powerful, presence at nearly 75. He stood six feet tall, the permanently tanned skin below the silver mane suggesting either a life outdoors or months prone on a tanning bed. The latter just didn't fit. "Always the mermaid. I remember you playing on the beach when you were a kid. Your mum said she couldn't keep you dry during summer hols. You always headed straight for water."

"Speaking of which, I'm damp. I'm going up to change," I said, stepping past him towards the stairs.

"I'll be waiting."

29

I nodded, heading up without another word, my emotions boiling. It wasn't just seeing Max again that had unsettled me or the sudden transport to this otherworld island, but the whole brew of anxiety, fear, and grief I'd been living under for weeks. Seeing Max triggered everything all over again.

Hot water washed away the sand and salt, offering a little pulse-motion shower message between my shoulder blades in the process. After I'd wiped myself down with towels more plush and pink than I thought possible, I finger-curled my shoulder-length red hair while rooting through the carry-on bag for something to wear.

I loved clothes but couldn't afford much, preferring to squander my expendable income on art and yarn. Occasionally, I'd make my own or upcycle some of Julie's cast-offs into my own perverse sense of style —boho meets yahoo.

All I brought this trip was a hastily plucked assortment of jeans, tops, and knitwear, leaving an undue amount of space for yarn and Toby's *Tide Weaver* cartoon that just fit crosswise into the bottom of my suitcase. I ended hiding the tapestry up in Toby's old hidey-hole and bringing the drawing instead. I needed moral support.

I selected a green turtleneck and a fresh pair of jeans. Moments later, I investigated the damp redhead in the mirror and, keeping with the dog metaphor, decided I looked like a cross between an Irish setter and a wet beagle.

Downstairs I found Max standing in the living room with the curtains open staring out to sea, a scotch glass in hand, while Noel occupied a chair by the hearth, long legs stretched out before him. They had been heatedly discussing something. Conversation stopped abruptly when I entered.

"There you are," Max greeted, gazing at me fondly for several long moments. "That's much better. So, do you like the place?" he indicated the cottage with a wave of his glass. "Comfortable?"

"It's beautiful, thanks, but I would have been just as happy with something less grand."

"You've got to get over that. You deserve the best of everything."

"Why, if I haven't earned it or can't afford it? You forget that I'm an overeducated and underemployed—unemployed, actually—underachiever who lives in a lovely but cheap little flat in Halifax." I sighed. "Someday maybe I can afford something really nice but not now."

"No goddaughter of mine's going to hole up someplace shabby, if I can help it. Aren't you still working for Global Threads?"

"They're closing the shop."

He shook his head and took another sip from his glass. "No wonder. That pair didn't know a dog's ass about running a business. You should have let me buy it out for you long ago before they ran it into the ground."

"The economy ran it into the ground, not them." Not that I believed that, but there was no way I'd allow my godfather's largess to extend to buying me a business. Enough was enough. "A lot has changed."

"Not that, not you. Well, you have changed, obviously, grown into a lovely young woman, but you'll always be a daughter to me. I'd give you the world if you'd let me."

Okay, so maybe that was the liquor talking but he probably meant every word. "I know and thanks, but right now all I want is my brother back plus answers to this secret you and dad concocted years ago. Ever since I was a kid, certain topics were always off-limits. I'd always accept that and backed off, but no more. I'm not stopping now until I get the answers I came for."

"You may not like the answers, Honey."

"What the hell is that supposed to mean? Look," I said, raising my hands and letting them drop again. "It's like this: I have nothing left to lose so start talking. Where's Toby?"

"It's a long story, Phoebe."

"Then give me the short version. Have you found him, yes or no?"

"No, I haven't found him but I know where he was the week before he vanished."

"Here in Bermuda?"

"Right on. Why not join me in a drink while I fill you in on the details?"

"No, thanks."

"Tea, then."

I sighed in frustration. "Look, all I really want is answers but, if it will make you happy, I'll drink tea while you explain every detail. Come into the kitchen with me while I make it so you can get started." I turned towards the kitchen.

"No worries. Noel will make it for you, won't you boy?"

Boy? I turned to Noel, finding him lounged deep in his chair studying me with a morose expression. Not tanned, I realized. His skin was a naturally deep caramel color and his face a fierce combo of angles Mom would have dubbed "swarthy". Striking, not handsome, but no boy. He had to be at least 35.

Noel's lips quirked into a smile as he unfolded himself from the chair. Tall, maybe six foot four, he towered over Max by at least two inches. In two strides he was before me, bending his waist in a mock bow. "The dogsbody at your service. Milk with that, ma'am?" he said in a passably British accent.

"Yes, please, but no sugar. Look, I'm particular. I like my tea the old-fashioned way in a warmed pot rather than just a tea bag dumped into a pot and boiled to within an inch of its life. I better do it."

He looked over at me from his still-bent position, eyes sparkling. "No worries. I live to serve. Anything else?"

"Bikkies," Max interjected. "Or crackers and cheese. She must be starving."

"As you wish." He straightened, cast me a long look, and strode into the kitchen.

I turned to Max. "Who is he?"

"My 2IC. I need someone to help run my businesses. No worries about him."

"Okay. Now, back to Toby."

Max poured himself another inch of Scotch, replacing the nearly empty bottle on the side table. "I've got a lead, like I said," he said, tossing back a draw of liquor.

"But he didn't mention making a detour to Bermuda in his emails. He made it seem like he was flying in directly from LA via New York."

"No doubt wanted you to think that."

"But why?"

"You know Toby, always chasing down something. You didn't find any clues at your dad's?"

"Nothing new or different."

Max went over to a briefcase sitting on the couch and removed a folder of papers. "Look here." He passed me an eight by eleven black-and-white photo of two men on a wharf. The picture was of poor quality, taken from a distance, and obviously enlarged. "Taken by a security camera at Smith's Cove up coast one week before Toby disappeared. Notice anything?"

I brought the photo under a lamp and studied it hard. One man had his arm raised in discussion while the other faced him, hands on hips. The figure on the right could be anyone in a long dark greatcoat, since his body was turned away from the camera and had his collar up around his ears, but the one with his hand pointing skyward could be Toby. He had Toby's lithe build, though it was difficult to identify much conclusively since he wore a baseball hat and sunglasses. I could just see the outline of his face, all similar to my brother's jawline.

"I can't be sure."

"Look again." Max pointed to the upraised hand before slipping another photo on top the first, this one an enlargement of the hand. I nodded. Toby's tattoo was clearly visible on the fleshy part just beneath the thumb. "Who else you think would have a tat of a bloody mermaid on his hand?"

"Merman," I corrected. I had the mermaid but in a less public place. Toby, that had to be Toby. I turned to Max. "Who's the other guy?"

"Name's Alistair Wyndridge. Ring any bells?"

I shook my head. "Sounds familiar."

"Author, wrote all kinds of high seas historical novels, romantic stuff."

"*Thunder on the Seas* or *Brethren of the Coast*? I read a couple of those years ago." My eyes fell to the picture again, a tremor coursing through me as though some great force had just plucked my spinal cord. "He came here to meet Alistair Wyndridge, but why?" Then I turned to search Max's face. "What else do you know?"

"Wyndridge denies ever having seen him, denies even knowing who he is."

"You asked?"

"In a roundabout way. Bastard's hiding something. He saw Toby and this proves it."

"So, why not confront him with this photo and demand an explanation?"

"Do you think he'd tell me if he didn't tell the police? Besides, he's a bloody recluse. Only makes appearances for the occasional book signing or an auction or two. Used to collect rare manuscripts. Has a few screws loose." Max tugged the photos from my hands and led me over to the couch, indicating that we sit. "We need subtler methods."

Noel entered at that moment bearing a tray clinking with tea things that he set on the ottoman. Keeping his eyes averted, he carefully set a mug on the table beside me and poured milk from a crystal jug. "Say when."

"When."

With aplomb, he whisked up the botanical teapot and poured the brew into my mug, twisting his wrist at the perfect moment to avoid drips. "Biscuit with that, ma'am?"

I plucked a shortbread from the proffered plate. "I'm impressed." I smiled up at him. "You're an excellent dogsbody."

"Trained in England," he remarked with a quirky grin.

"A corgi, then."

"Corgi's a purebred. I'm too much of a bitzer for that."

"Bitzer?"

"Bits of this, bits of that."

"Cut it out, you two," Max said, unduly annoyed.

"Right, so, Max," I said, turning back to my godfather, "Define your version of subtle."

"The kind that pretends to be something she's not. We need to get inside Wyndridge's and hunt for clues."

My eyes widened as I bit into a cookie. "Which is where I come in."

"You're perfect."

I chewed less enthusiastically. "Because?"

"Because you know Toby better than anyone. You'll know a clue when you see it. We'll get you in there for a couple of days only and then pull you out. It's safer that way."

I placed the half-eaten cookie on the edge of my plate and laced my fingers in my lap, noting that Noel now sat across from me, eyes scrutinizing my face. "Just how do you propose to get me in there?"

"Wyndridge put in an advert for someone to organize his library a couple of weeks ago," Max said with a grin. "Perfect timing. He wants someone to plough through a bunch of manuscripts he's collected—cataloguing, classification, that sort of thing. Think he plans to sell his collection. It's just so damn perfect, I couldn't believe our luck. He put the ad out incognito-style using a box number but I have informants."

"Of course you do." I shrugged, the sense of unreality intensifying. "What qualifications is he looking for?"

"A Master's of Librarianship or an archivist preferred."

"Perfect. My degree in Art History plus all my stale law courses and work experience as a gallery slog ought to make me a shoo-in."

"Phoebe," Max spoke with exaggerated patience. "You wouldn't be applying as yourself. I took the liberty of submitting an application in your name."

"Not her name," Noel corrected.

"Right, not your name. Look."

He passed me a file folder. I flipped it open only long enough to scan the name SUSAN WAVERLEY neatly printed on the top page along with a list of degrees and work experiences definitely not my own. I let the folder drop to my lap to rub my temples. "Are you suggesting I assume a false identity with fabricated credentials to enter a famous author's employ on a ruse?"

"You say you're not backing down on finding Toby or unlocking your dad's secrets. I promise you, this will do both."

I looked at him. "Wyndridge and my father are connected?"

"Look, it's complicated. If you say no, Maggie would take it on, but she wouldn't be half as good as you would be here."

"You promised me answers."

"And you'll get them but I can't hand everything to you on a plate 'cause I don't have all the details. Find out what Toby was doing with Wyndridge first. Susan Waverley's been short-listed. Now we're just waiting for an interview time."

He had to be kidding. Just when I thought the prize might be in reach, he'd jerked the damn string. "Is this for real?"

"Do you want to find your brother or not?" Max asked.

I held up my hand. "Stop with the emotional blackmail. I said I'll do what it takes, but that doesn't mean I like it." But, in truth, it seemed like going forward was the only avenue open.

"Fair enough," Noel remarked.

"Glad you approve," I said without looking at him.

"Sorry, honey. I didn't want to involve you but this is just too damn good to pass up. Only you can make full use of the op. We had a man in there for a while who had all the finesse of a front-end loader. Stupid dropkick left me in the lurch." Max drained the last of his glass and stared out into space. "We need you, darlin'."

"What's with the old 'I have a man in there now' kind of thing that just rolled off your tongue like you're a godfather of another kind?"

"I do whatever it takes when seeking something important, Phoebe," he told me, eyes a little unfocused.

"And do you seek important things often, Max?"

"Often enough, and right now it's your brother. What we need to do isn't strictly legal, if that's what's worrying you."

"Everything's worrying me, Max, and let's get something straight: I know your business is somewhere south of legal. You sell antiques and objets d'art, but I always wondered how you source them and how come you make so much money doing it? I mean, how do you acquire fifteenth century Ottoman rugs and genuine Roman statues when countries have laws forbidding their sale?"

"You used to call me 'Uncle Max'". The blue eyes turned on me were blurry and reproachful.

"Don't change the subject."

"With money, that's how. Anything can be bought for the right price and somewhere, somebody else is ready to buy it for a higher one. Sometimes objects arrive at my door with uncertain providence but the world is an unstable place. Plenty of Roman artefacts are emerging from Afghanistan, for example."

"As in stolen, looted, or just purchased from the war-torn and desperate?"

Max passed his empty glass to Noel, who reached over and slid it onto the coffee table minus a refill. "I source art and artifacts for wealthy clients, mostly private collectors and museums, and—Noel, fill that bloody glass!—but sometimes I don't know the exact providence for every item." He shrugged. "I just do what I do."

"And what did you do with my father all those years ago?"

"Noel, get me another drink!"

"No." Noel scowled. "You're over limit."

"Who the hell limits me?"

"Get me one, then," I said. "I'm the one who needs a stiff drink right now."

Noel shook his head, a little smile on his lips. Attractive lips, I thought, full and sensual. Like I needed to drift down that canal.

Max turned to me, face as red as a boiled crustacean, fingers drumming on the chair arm. "I liked your dad, feisty old bugger."

"Yeah, so what does the feisty old bugger and the arts and artifacts dealer really have in common?"

Max took a deep breath. "I promised your dad I'd never tell you. He made me swear and I'm damn well going to honor that one if it kills me, but I can't help it if you find out on your own. God knows you have a right to the truth."

"Then tell me."

"Go in there and you'll probably find out. That's all I'm saying."

I stared at him in disgust, climbing to my feet. "Give me a break, Max; soon my father won't remember what day it is! If it concerns my family, I have a right to know, and from your lips, since you dragged him into this, whatever it is. We've all been affected by this secret. It's been throttling my family for years. Tell me."

"Your dad believed it was too dangerous to get you involved."

"It's my right as an adult to measure my own risks."

"And your father's right to protect his child as long as he wants. If you were my daughter, I wouldn't tell you, either!"

Noel let out a grunt of derision. We both shot him a quick glance but he kept his gaze fixed on the floor.

"Did Mom know?"

"Yes."

"But she didn't like it, did she?"

"No, she didn't like it. Or me."

"How can you even face me again and still remain silent?" I was standing now, fists clenched at my side.

"I'm protecting you, like your dad wants. It's bad enough that—" His words faded away.

I went cold. "It's bad enough what?" I swallowed hard. "Bad enough that Toby found out?"

"I was going to say that it's bad enough that I brought you here when your father told me never to contact you again."

Chapter 4

"Nancy?"

"Phoebe? Where are you?"

"I'm standing in the upstairs room of a little vacation condo in Bermuda, here at Max's request. I've come to find Toby."

My friend sighed deeply as if to steady her voice. "You'd better tell me everything."

When I explained how I ended up there, along with a few salient details, she listened without saying a word. "If you go into Wyndridge's under an assumed identity, you'll be breaking a more serious law than just stealing what we might argue belongs to you and yours," she said, finally. "But you already know that."

"I do, but, Nancy, I've backed down from too many things in my life. I just don't want finding Toby to be one of them. And now I'm afraid Dad might know more about this than he's letting on, or can remember. And Max has a lead that looks as though I may be in the best position to follow, plus I'm right where I need to be to unlock everything that's been kept hidden from me for far too long. I know it sounds crazy but what do I have to lose that isn't gone already?"

"I can think of several responses to that but so can you. Your dad's protecting you, so why not let him do it?"

"Because he lost that right long ago."

"I have court in 20 minutes but I'm going to set a little research in motion on this Wyndridge character. In the meantime, stay in touch and try not to do anything too impulsive or dangerous, as if my saying that will make a shred of difference."

After the call ended, I stood by the window watching sunshine billow through the sheers of the open casement. Nancy would enter a situation only after she'd studied all the facts and lined up the pros and cons for an educated, reasoned decision. Not me. I'd dive headlong into a situation and try swimming my way to the surface. If that failed, I'd just tread water while the world spun around me. So how had that worked for me so far?

The glinting turquoise sea surged beyond the casements. This island, I realized, was like a rough-cut jewel. Turn it one way and the polished surface sparkled with brilliance; turn it another, and the sharp primordial layers of ancient stone eclipsed the luster.

I removed my cell from the charger, realizing that the scent of bacon and coffee rode the morning air and that someone was rattling around downstairs. Donning the regulation-issue pink robe, I dropped the phone into my pocket and padded down to find a woman in the kitchen, dressed in a pink apron setting a table on the patio.

"Morning, miss. I'm Dora James, your housekeeper. Are you hungry this fine day?"

"Yes, I am, Dora, and whatever you're cooking smells delish."

"Eggs, any way you like them, with bacon, ham, French toast, home fries, the works."

"What's the occasion?" I indicated the white tablecloth, the table set for three on the adjoining patio overlooking the cove.

"Mr. Max sent me over to prepare breakfast. He and the missus will be here in a few minutes."

He and the missus? In a few minutes? Crud. I turned and dashed back upstairs, nabbing a coffee along the way. Twenty minutes later, I arrived at the bottom of the stairs just in time to open the door for Max and Maggie, who was definitely not Max's missus, much to her chagrin.

"Phoebe, hon!" The tall blonde of indeterminate age swept down upon me, wrapped in perfume and some linen designer ensemble the color of fevered coral. "Oh, it's so good to see you again," she said, air-kissing either side of my head. "I'm just so excited that we're all down here together. Last time was so upsetting with Toby missing and all."

"He's still missing, Maggie."

"Sure he is, honey, but we're so much closer to finding him. Come on, let me look at you." She stood back, one long painted nail on her chin. "You look a bit pale."

"I'm tired but fine. Besides, pale is my default position."

"Still, you need some color in your cheeks. What do you think, Max?"

"I think she looks bloody lovely, as usual," Max commented, passing me with a squeeze of my shoulder. "Come on, let's have brekkie. My head's killing me."

She rolled her eyes. "Baby's got a brain-pain today. Wonder why?"

"Over-imbibed."

"Over-imbibed—love it!"

"So, where's Noel this morning?"

Maggie waved a hand. "Off on business. Come along. Let's have breakfast and get down to work." Maggie linked arms with me as we strolled towards the patio. "I know this Toby thing has been hard on you, but we can't have you going in to Wyndridge's unprepared now, can we? You nervous?"

"About what?"

"About your role?"

"Role?" I slipped into a chair on the patio and studied her. Damn, but the woman never aged. She still pulled off the same blonde bombshell look she carried 20 years back, including the gravity-defying cleavage. The legs, I noted with a pang of envy, remained sleek, toned, and incredibly long. With the aqua sea backdrop and the intense coral of her jacket, I needed to squint.

"Hon, you all right?" she leaned towards me while Dora poured coffee into our mugs.

"I'm fine," I said, waiting for the maid to get out of earshot. Once Dora retreated, I returned to our conversation. "Are you referring to this research assistant ruse as a 'role'?"

"Sure I am. I mean, that's what you'll be doing, isn't it? Acting? I'd love a job like that. Still, our casting director here," she thumbed towards Max, "didn't think I looked the type, even though I would have gone in if you refused. Maybe I'm not scholarly looking enough, anyway." She shrugged, grinning with her laminate teeth. "I could have worn a bad wig. Still, I get to help you get ready. I'm in charge of wardrobe, too."

I stirred milk into my coffee with more care than it deserved. Max, I noted, had zoned out, sipping his brew and gazing out at to sea. "Maggie, I know you used to act once upon a time, but I hardly think pretending to be a librarian requires a wardrobe mistress."

"Oh, you're so wrong," Maggie said, sprinkling artificial sweetener into her coffee. "And, I didn't just used to act, I had supporting roles in a couple of near-hits. I almost got to star beside Julia Roberts."

I'd heard that many times before. "You were legit."

"Very legit. The thing is, you have to look the part. It so won't do to have you looking like your present state of," she paused, trawling for a word, "whatever. Toby understood that clothes matter."

"Toby can afford to satisfy his tastes, I can't. Please get to the point."

"The point is Alistair Wyndridge is filthy rich, like, as in a collector and connoisseur, and unmarried, too. He appreciates beautiful things. Like any man, he'll choose a pretty woman over not so much any day."

"So, a woman is the same as a thing."

"You know what I mean."

"No points for brains, in other words."

"Oh, please. Do you think he wanted me for my brain." She nodded towards Max. "He doesn't know I have one half the time."

I decided to leave that untouched. "Personally, I prefer to think of myself as interesting or arresting, and possibly intelligent, at least some of the time, but not pretty. Maybe attractive on a good day," I added. "And I think I could pull off amusing."

"Interesting doesn't cut it, hon, and neither does all the rest. Appearances count, and let's face it: you need work. Try not to be yourself, for once. We've got to outdo the competition."

"Ah," I said with a nod, "the competition. Of course, others must be vying for underpaid librarian to the famous reclusive author."

"They wouldn't know who placed the ad unless they have the inside track. Wyndridge gave a box number."

"Still, these things have a way of getting out, especially with the Internet. Anyway, surely no mere mortal can compete against that stellar, platinum-plated, resumé you guys concocted. I mean, the bogus Susan Waverley not only has every degree possible for an A-type librarian, but has done several stints in noted institutions and published, too. She's some kind of wunderkind bibliophile. Aren't you afraid Wyndridge will question why she'd want his little job?"

"Did you read the script I left you or not? She's taking time off, staying with her aunt here in Bermuda—that's me—and this job seems the perfect little break for a big career girl. People are complicated. They don't do the expected stuff all the time. Look at me: former actress now taking a detour in the arts and antiquities business. Who knew?" She shot a quick glance at Max. "But there are fringe benefits."

"What about reference checks?"

"*If* he does a reference check, and that's a big if, the phone numbers I gave will connect with somebody ready with a rehearsed story. Wyndridge doesn't get out much, that helps. Don't worry," Maggie flicked her right hand, sending the diamond ring on her middle finger into a sparkle-fest, "we've done this kind of thing before. Besides, those citations are real. Susan Waverley was a real person. She just happens to be a real dead person."

I lowered my mug to the table. "I'm assuming a dead person's identity?"

"Sort of. That's just in case he does an Internet search, which he probably won't. He doesn't even have a web page. Can you believe that? Imagine an author without a website? His publisher's doesn't count."

"I've assumed the identity of a dead person?"

"You'd have to really dig to find her obituary. Wyndridge isn't much for doing thorough background checks. He's stuck in his fictional world like most writers. The practical stuff he passes onto his mother, who is so old she probably still uses carrier pigeons. Anyway, let us worry about that stuff. You just ace the interview and get in and find clues on Toby."

Dora reappeared distributing bowls of fresh fruit. For a few minutes we suspended conversation while placing our breakfast orders. I decided on eggs, bacon, toast, and more fruit, while Max settled for toast with a side of Tylenol. He did appear rather yellow around the gills. Maggie, on the other hand, ordered a green smoothie and a fruit plate.

Despite the big breakfast order, I still hadn't recovered from the dead-Susan information. "How did she die?" I asked during our next intermission.

"Who?" Maggie asked, sipping her brew.

"The real Susan Waverly."

"Are you still on about that? I don't remember. I don't think the obit said. Forget that. Let's talk about the interview."

"Do I even have one yet?"

"No, but you will. We've given the cottage here as a contact number. It's all in the background sheets I prepared." Maggie dissected her fruit into tiny pieces.

"After I set Noel and Max packing last night, I went through everything—all the sheets on Wyndridge, the background info on Susan Waverley, may she rest in peace, everything. I also reviewed your character profile for the bogus Susan, if that's the right term. You have a bit of a flair for writing fiction yourself, Mags, not that any of it seems even slightly based on reality. Anyway, I've got the particulars committed to memory and will ad-lib the rest." In theory, it sounded like a fun. I doubted reality would be.

Maggie paused, her knife suspended over a wedge of cantaloupe. "You liked my writing?"

"I appreciate comedy."

"I think that's the nicest thing you've ever said to me."

I turned to her, momentarily speechless. "Mags, please don't miss my note of irony. Besides, I'm sure I've said other nice things to you over the years."

"I choose to ignore the irony and I can't remember a single other nice thing you've said since you were a kid. Toby was much nicer. You always acted like I'm stupid or something," she continued. "Your mother didn't like me so you automatically didn't, either. She thought I was a tart." She lowered her knife. "Look, hon, I always adored you. You were always such a plucky little snot even as a kid, always so smart-mouthed. You were like the daughter I never had, which is why I bought you all those presents. Yeah, maybe Chanel at a school prom was a little over the top but you looked like dynamite in those heels. Blew those junior achievers right out of the water."

"And they hated me even more afterwards."

"Yeah, jealousy. So what? Where are they now, anyway—stuck in the backwoods somewhere with a lout for a husband and twenty kids? Look at you."

"Unemployed, you mean?"

Maggie sighed. "Look, my point is you never even thanked me for any of the presents for all these years."

I stared at her dumbstruck. "But I thought they were from Max."

She laughed. "Yeah, sure. Just picture Max on Fifth Avenue picking out a Chanel dress. He could pick out car, a surfboard, and maybe a rare antique something or other, but never that. The only thing he gave you himself was that smelly old carpet bag you love so much. It figures that something so old and beat up would be such a hit."

"It's made from an original antique textile."

She picked up her knife and began slicing the fruit again. "Yeah, yeah, yeah. And Chanel is made from old potato sacks. The point is, try showing me some respect, okay?"

I was about to respond when Max interrupted. "Mags will play the aunt, if you need her." He was rousing himself from detox, not that he had been listening. "Anything you need, any back up at all, we've got you covered."

"We're not taking any chances," Maggie said. "You got to get that position and that's that." She speared a melon chunk with her fork and placed it delicately in her mouth where she proceeded to roll it around with her tongue as if she might suck it to death.

"Supposing I'm quickly revealed as a fraud the moment I try to tackle real archival work, classification, that kind of thing? I can fake it only up to a point," I said, relieved to be out of the Maggie mire.

"Yeah," Maggie said, finally swallowing, "but you won't be in there long enough to really do anything but snoop. You always start really strong and then end up a mess, so we're pulling you out after a couple of days."

"I thought I was to be pulled out, as you call it, for my own safety?"

"Same thing. Either way, I'm betting you'll waver, spill the beans to Wyndridge, or muck it up some other way." She shot me a quick look. "Don't take it personally, hon. Nobody's perfect."

"I presume you think that because I quit law at the final hour it therefore follows that I can't stick to anything? That's a faulty assumption since many young people embark on false starts. I decided law wasn't for me and hit the eject button before I ended up working in an environment that didn't suit me." Actually, I liked the idea of being a lawyer more than the reality of the actual career. Besides, I could pull out some serious diction sometimes or even debate with aplomb.

"Yeah, yeah, and then you took four more years of—what was it now, painting 101?"

"Art History," I said, fighting the desire to throw food at her. "And I stayed with my next job for a decade."

"Big whoop. All that education so you could play Cinderella for Mrs. Snotty Pants for ten years. Great move. You've got so much going for you yet you never go the distance. Just don't mess this up, okay? Anyway, I figure you can play librarian easy enough for a few days. Just look reasonably intelligent and tidy the shelves. How hard can it be?"

I stabbed a banana chunk. Listening to Max's mistress assess my character galled me. "A proper librarian knows his or her stuff. It's not like organizing papers by small, medium, and large. Skill and training are involved. That's why people take degrees. And I don't waver so much as see all the pros and cons to the point where I can't choose just one."

"Exactly." Maggie speared a cube of pineapple. "Anyway, it's easy to fake anything with a lot of confidence and a little information. You'll have me on speed-dial. The moment you need me to dig up information, say the word."

"Susan Waverley was an accomplished scholar. I doubt having you on speed-dial is going to compensate."

Max, looking slightly fortified after coffee and pain killers, looked over at me. "Look, Phoebe, you've been around libraries long enough to pull off a little confidence trick for a few days. With two degrees under your belt, you must have solid library experience."

I sighed. "Well, I dated an archivist for a few months. Does that count?"

Maggie grinned. "You bet! You must have learned a thing or two from him."

"Probably not what you need. Christian and I stayed mostly in the closed stacks for the full four months of our relationship, wedged between rare books and the conservation room. Classification never came up. Actually, neither did conversation." I popped a mouthful of fruit and smiled.

Maggie grinned back. Max scraped back his chair and disappeared into the cottage with a grunt, apparently looking for a coffee refill. "He doesn't like thinking of his goddaughter getting it on with a guy. So, was this guy good?"

"He had solid expertise in certain areas, which I appreciated, but be took up with a freshman, or should I say, fresh woman, so I dropped him. Those rare book men can be real Lotharios."

"Really? Who'd have thought. I always figured they'd be kind of stuffy. Is he why you're still not with anyone?"

How I hated this question. Why did every woman past puberty need a male accessory? "I've never found a man interesting enough to make it worth sitting through episodes of Hockey Night in Canada." Not that Christian was much of an athlete beyond the stacks but it seemed like every other heterosexual man needed a tribal game fix. His just came in the board game variety.

Maggie snorted. "For me it's been the World Cup soccer matches. Yuck."

"Mags," Max interrupted, returning. "Stop bumping your gums and tell her about Edna Smith."

Maggie nodded. "She's the one you've got to beat. We've gone through the applications. Lots qualify but she's worked for him before and she's local so we have to assume she's a serious contender. Works in the Public Library in Hamilton. Not very good-looking but she is a professional librarian. Oh, and has local history listed as an interest."

"You accessed the applications? " Would I ever get used to the way these two worked?

"Yeah, sure. Wyndridge collected them by mail, so Frank only had to get into his den and scan the particulars. No computer hacking or anything."

"Frank, I presume, is your inside guy?" I sliced a loquat in two, trying to stay cool.

"Ex-inside guy."

Dora entered carrying a tray of eggs and sides. After our breakfasts were distributed, we ate in silence for a few minutes.

"Why ex?" I prompted after a bit.

Max replied between gulps of coffee. "Useless dropkick left a few days ago. Said he wanted more money but I paid through my teeth for him in the first place. Nothing but a bludger. I wasn't paying him more. Wyndridge hired a replacement before we even knew Frank had gone, some jack-of -all-trades named Bert, but that's not his real name. Probably works for a competitor. We've got a few plans in the works."

I paused, a forkful of egg en route to my mouth. "Like what?"

"Wyndridge has had some staff turnover recently. He's looking out for a head housekeeper but has had trouble finding someone mommy likes," Max said.

Maggie sighed. "I so want that role."

Max barked out a laugh. "That's like trying to make a Ferrari look like a truck!"

Maggie scowled and sipped her smoothie. "Give me some credit. I could do it."

"Hey, that sounds like a compliment to me," I pointed out. "I'd probably be compared to some little economy number."

But Max wasn't listening to me. "You don't even know how to clean," he said to Maggie.

"Well, how hard is that?"

My cue to change the topic. "What else do you know about Edna Smith?"

"Not much," Maggie muttered, casting baleful glances at Max. "What else do you need to know except you've got to beat her for that job?"

"What if I don't get that job, then what?"

"We have a contingency plan." Maggie dabbed her lips with a napkin. "There are always contingencies."

"Like what?"

"You don't need to know the details."

"I like details. Try me."

She dismissed that with a wave of her hand.

"At least give me the gist."

"Look, hon, if you must know, we're prepared to offer her more money to take another job."

"Stop calling me hon, will you? I hate it."

Maggie stared at me. "Really? Okay, so forget about her, *Phoebe.* She's our problem."

After that, I let conversation drop and answered questions only when asked. Not for the first time, I wondered what I'd gotten myself into while I pondered all the assumptions on my character forged by Mags and Max over the years: I never followed through; I always overthought everything until stymied by indecision. The whole discussion left me irritated and disgruntled.

My instructions for the day were simple: I was to search out some kind of virtual librarian crib sheet online while waiting for the interview call. If no call came through by 2:00, I was to contact the Wyndridge estate and request a status update. Apparently, Max's vacated informant had told him that Wyndridge was fast-tracking the assignment and wanted someone in place as soon as possible.

The moment everyone exited, I checked my phone and found two text messages, one from Nancy requesting I call back and one from Julie: PHOEBE, I'M SORRY. I'VE BEEN SUCH AN ASS. DECIDED TO REOPEN GLOBAL THREADS AS A WEBSTORE. PLEASE BE MY MANAGER. WE'LL TALK ABOUT THE TAPESTRY.

For a tiny instant, a lilt of joy danced in my heart. I had a job, if I wanted it; Julie was finally taking my recommendation to broaden her reach via the Web! Then, I quashed it all. No more going backward for me, only ahead. I left the call unanswered.

I called Nancy back. "Phoebe, my researcher mined some interesting facts about Alistair Wyndridge this morning. An estate agency has been making enquiries on his behalf to purchase property in the Maldives."

"The Maldives? You mean Alistair Wyndridge is going to jump ship?"

"Possibly. The interesting point is that his finances don't appear to support the purchase of an island anywhere. Despite the relative success of his fiction ventures, he's more or less broke with all his assets tied up in his Bermudan house, which, by the way, is quite a pile. Are you still going through with the library ruse?"

"Of course I am," I said quickly. "Nancy, are you in the camp that believes I'm a quitter?"

"Whoa," said my friend. "Back up here. What's this about?"

"Maggie, in her infinite wisdom, provided me with a character assessment over breakfast today. She claimed me to be a wavering quitter who can't be trusted to go the distance. I was insulted."

"We are all on our own journey, Phoebe. Rather than paying attention to her, start listening to yourself. Have to go now. Talk later." And then she hung up.

Another riddle. I sighed, gazing around at the cozy cottage for answers and finding none. I called Dad. Besides the usual complaints about Bertha Hugli, all seemed well on that front or, at least, well enough.

Next, I paced the patio rehearsing myself as Susan Waverley, a professional information organizer, a published scholar, and the exact opposite of law school dropout, aspiring artist, and collector-of -fiber-bits, me. Susan had a stellar career once, had slowly risen in her profession of choice, to arrive at the apex of success. I rarely finished anything, more certain of what I didn't want to do than what I did. Maybe maturity was purely a physical state after all.

And assuming a dead person's identity seemed creepy, not to mention illegal. She was dead, I was not. I was borrowing all she had accomplished for my own ends. Maybe, if the dead did see beyond the grave, she'd forgive me, knowing that I was only seeking my brother.

Maggie had printed out a few pages on Susan's accomplishments, including a list of her publications, such as the obscure title Managing Rare Documents in the Modern World. Crud, she had written an entire book about that?

The more I considered the impersonation, the more nervous I became. By eleven-thirty or so, I was frantic. Could I be somebody else for an extended period? Wasn't pretense only a lie playing dress up?

Finally, I grabbed my tranquilizer of choice and sat by the pool, knitting my way to calm. Deep in the quiet world of alternating knit and purl, I breathed and loosened. I could do this. I had to do this. I held up my wrap, forming now like an amoeba in the throes of a hurricane, all long dropped stitches and waves of undulating fiber going in no fixed direction—another life metaphor—and yet it pleased me. Regularity was merely a yawn waiting to happen, whereas sudden surprises and detours were the stuff of discovery and transformation. Or so I told myself.

In the meantime, nobody called the cottage to arrange an appointment. At 2:00, I set my knitting aside and called the number Max had left for the Wyndridge estate. A woman with a British accent answered. "Good afternoon, the Wyndridge's residence. Mrs. Wyndridge speaking."

Since he wasn't married, I presumed I was addressing his mommy. "Hi, Mrs. Wyndridge, my name is Susan Waverley, and I'm calling in regard to the status of the research position that I've been short-listed for." Would Susan sound so hesitant or end her sentence in a preposition? I needed to be more assertive, polished. "I understand that interviews are to commence shortly. Please inform me as to the time and place so I can arrange my time accordingly," I added. Now, I sounded as though I had just sat on a carrot.

Silence followed. I thought for a moment she'd hung up. Or expired. "Mrs. Wyndridge?"

"Yes, Miss Waverley. I regret to inform you that the position has been filled."

"Filled?" I blurted out. "How can that be after you said I'd been short-listed? That's highly unprofessional, probably against Bermudan labor laws. I could have you cited for faulty hiring practices."

"Very sorry to have inconvenienced you. Good afternoon." The line went dead.

I stood staring out the patio door, across the table, towards the brilliant sea. Damn. Wyndridge must have offered the job to Edna Smith and she accepted. I pulled out my iPhone and texted Max: HE'S BYPASSED THE INTERVIEWS AND HIRED SOMEONE ELSE, PRESUMBLY E.S.

Chapter 5

I bounded along a flower-lined path thinking what I would do if I couldn't get into the estate. Would that mean never finding Toby? I jogged past stone benches, moon gates, hidden fountains, and two swimming pools artfully hidden in foliage, all very lovely but I was preoccupied. The Astwood office stood storybook perfect, a white-roofed pink cottage with shutters and a mass of fiery red bougainvillea rioting across one wall. Besides a few guys packing a golf cart and two speed-walking women, the property seemed deserted.

Ted, the service elf, sat behind the desk studying a computer screen. At the sight of me, his face split into a wide grin. "Well, Ms. Waverley, how may I help you this fine day?"

"Call me Susan. I need transportation. Can I rent a car somewhere near?"

Ted spread his hands, his grin wide and white. The world had become a much brighter place since teeth whiteners. "I have just the thing."

I followed him out the door and across the lawn to where a line of mopeds sat shining in the parking lot.

"Surely I'd break my neck on one of those. No car rentals?"

"Car rentals are not allowed —too small an island, so visitors use mopeds. Only residents may own a car. Care must be taken but that's the only way to get around effectively. It's what most of us ever drive. We keep a few on hand just for the convenience of our residents. Come, I'll give you a quick lesson."

He selected one from a row of identical shiny blue clones, each complete with a helmet, a lock, and a prayer. He rolled one out for my inspection. After a rundown of preliminary safety tips, he urged me to drive around the parking area under his supervision. Straddling the bike, I considered the gears briefly, tested the brakes, and practiced turning. It didn't feel half bad.

"Is this it?" I asked, pulling up beside him. "Am I now licensed to be killed?"

He laughed. "You won't be killed. Just be careful. Wear your helmet; it's the law. If a big lorry comes bearing down on you, pull over to the side, if you can, but never stop in the middle of the road, no matter how beautiful the scenery. Go slow, but not too slow. Those things won't get much faster than 50 miles per hour anyway. Take your time and enjoy yourself. Oh, one more thing," he added with a snap of his fingers. "Take the tribe roads across the center of the island to avoid the traffic. Use them as shortcuts. Here, I'll show you."

Ted unfolded a tiny, pocket-sized map and spread it across the handlebars. "Most of them cross perpendicular to the main coastal routes and cut up through the island's suburbs, like there and there." He traced the tiny lines shooting across the island. "Take those if you'd prefer to avoid the scenic routes. They can be distracting and, I won't kid you, the coral cliffs around here are deadly." He noticed my carpet bag slung over my shoulder. "And that won't do."

"You don't like my style?"

He flashed a grin. "I like your style just fine, but lock that bag of yours in the rear compartment so it doesn't go falling off on the road or knock you off-balance."

"Oh, right." I unlocked the compartment, shoved my bag in, and turned to him with a salute.

Thanking him, I scooted off, the breeze blowing in my face amid the intoxicating scent of growing things. For the next 30 minutes, I focused on the simple task of staying alive but soon morphed to staying alive at top legal speed in a glorious setting.

Astwood Properties occupied prime real estate on the south coast of Bermuda, the land of picture postcard beaches and stretches of parkland. The vistas of turquoise sea and pink sand off to my left offered endless distraction with hardly a piece of shoreline I didn't long to explore. Instead, I gripped the handlebars and kept my eyes on the road. This wasn't a vacation. At least I didn't have to fight tootling tourists, just the constant whizz of the locals passing me with what seemed like a death wish.

I travelled at a good clip, searching for a tribe road jutting off into the hills until, finally, I spied a tiny lane nested between a restaurant and a banana grove. I peeled the brakes ever so slightly when I made the turn. The moped sputtered and bit the ground up a steep incline. A thick canopy of trees shaded the road. Only when I reached the crest of the hill did I relax, letting the bike coast down into the leafy shadows towards another stunning vista before shooting out onto the highway.

By the time I reached Hamilton, the moped and I had bonded. Traffic congested the narrow streets as I wound through the town looking for a parking area with bike designations. Glancing at the other bikes for direction, I parked, locking the helmet onto the seat, and grabbed my bag. While standing in the parking lot, I checked my phone, seeing a roll of text messages and missed calls all from Max. Dropping the phone in my pocket, I slung my bag over my shoulder and strode across the street. Most of them demanded I call him back, which I would, after I completed my mission.

I walked past the Front Street shops soaking in the town's colors and bustle. A stiff harbor breeze blew against my back as I strolled uphill toward the library, which nestled on a steep street running perpendicular to the water. A renovated building of creamy stucco, it lacked the impact of the earlier British Colonial version I'd glimpsed online, but as a library, any manifestation was fine by me.

Inside, I breathed deeply the familiar scent of books and photocopiers, which brought back memories of Christian and the heady stew of lust I once called love. Man, that guy knew his stuff. I marched to the information desk on the second floor to ask for Edna Smith. When the clerk indicated a sturdy black woman in a denim suit accessorized by a pair of biker boots assisting an elderly client with pink hair, I hesitated. Now what? It's not like I had a plan. I waited until the elderly lady shuffled off to the borrower's desk with a clutch of books under arm before stepping forward. "Ms. Smith?"

The librarian turned with a smile, one of the genuine varieties that reach the eyes as well as the mouth. "Yes, how can I help?"

"Hi, I'm looking for information on Alistair Wyndridge and someone suggested you'd be the one to ask."

"You could ask anybody here and they could steer you in the direction of our local celebrity, but I'm as good as any," she grinned. "What kind of information? Maybe one of his novels? We have them all. We're expecting the final volume in his Bermudan trilogy soon but I'm afraid you'll have to wait for that one."

The elderly lady approached again, saw us talking, and settled down at the nearest table to wait.

"I don't want information, or at least, not that kind. I just need to talk to you. Could we go somewhere private? There's something I need to ask or, maybe I should say, tell you, about Alistair Wyndridge."

Edna didn't hide her amazement. "You want to speak to me in private about Alistair Wyndridge? Are you a reporter or something?"

"No way. This is personal, very personal."

"And you think I can help you with that?"

"Yes, but in confidence. This really isn't the place to get into it."

Edna put her hands on her hips, eyeing me for a few seconds, shaking her head. "Are you some kind of nutter?"

I smiled at that. "I guess that depends on who you ask. I'm joking; I'm perfectly sane. I just need to tell you something."

"Then tell me here."

"I can't. It's private but I know you'll want to hear it. This is very important. Please."

Maybe she read something in my face, something like desperation mixed with sincerity. "Well, this is a first. I have a book talk starting in 20 minutes —P.D.James, *An Unsuitable Job for a Woman*, in case you want to sit in—and then I head right home after that. I have kids to take care of and dinner to prepare."

"Could I meet you somewhere on the way, someplace private? I have a bike. I won't take too much time."

I saw her hesitate. "Against my better judgment, all right. I'll meet you at the Old Devonshire Church. Do you know where that is?"

"I'll find it."

"If you want, meet me outside the library at 5:00 — I park around the rear — you can follow me there. I live in Flatts Village and the church is about halfway. You'll find it interesting. What's your name, by the way?"

"Susan Waverley."

"Okay, Susan. See you later."

I thanked her and exited the building, not wanting to sit in for a book talk nor anything else, for that matter. Clouds scudded in from the ocean as I perched in a little city park by a huge banyan tree and called Max. The phone rang directly to his answering machine, where I left the message, relieved that I didn't have to explain anything in person. I told him I'd just taken a trip to Hamilton for the afternoon. If all went according to plan, by the time we made voice contact, I'd have the Wyndridge job.

I bided the next half-hour in a little corner bookstore purchasing tourist-issue local interest books with titles like *Bermuda Triangle: Unexplained Shipwrecks* and Wyndridge's recent *Brethren of the Coast*, which I began reading on the spot. The man favored high-seas adventures set in the seventeenth century, with dashing naval officers wresting booty from pirates while upholding Britain's mandate to go forth and conquer. Women appeared as the occasional spoils of war but rarely made an appearance on Wyndridge's brigantines and frigates, other than as a figurehead strapped to a prow. Not my reading tastes, perhaps, but I knew Toby once enjoyed them. One of the Wyndridge novels had been made into a big action film with the starring role played masterfully by one of boyhood crushes.

At the appointed time, I stuffed the books into my bag and waited, saddled on the moped in the rear parking area as Edna emerged from the library. She pointed at the glowering sky, making a face before beckoning me to follow. In a moment, I was merging into the traffic at her tail. Bikes and cars surrounded us in a steady stream of vehicles heading home after the day's work. Keeping Edna in sight demanded all my faculties.

She drove like a biker chick, legs straddled, skirt hitched up exposing those funky boots. In comparison, I gripped the handlebars like Pollyanna on a joyride through hell. The darkening skies, the threat of rain, an increasing sense of urgency, all forced me to hang on tight, gunning the engine at the first sign of clear road. Sometimes I lost her only to catch site of her moments later three or four vehicles ahead.

We followed Middle Road along the island's backbone while banana groves, botanical gardens and cottages whizzed by. The January darkness fell hard, thickening like glue amidst the shrubbery. I shivered as the cool wind bit through my hoodie. In my haste, I hadn't brought a jacket or anything but my carpet bag squashed in the seat compartment along with my new books. Gradually the traffic thinned, peeling off to the tribe roads and the cozy cottages lining our route and, when Edna finally indicated to turn, I couldn't wait to get off the road. I followed her into a parking lot, propping my bike beside hers near a path leading to a low white church.

I stood for a moment, stretching my legs, gazing around at what I knew to be a landmark. The Old Devonshire Church, a one-story cottage-like building, sat in a copse of palms on a low rise surrounded by whitewashed sarcophagi and above-ground tombs glowing ghostly in the gloom. The structure had the simple lines of seventeenth century design, practical and unfussy.

"Built by the first settlers?"

"Originally, but this is a reconstruction. The first church blew down in a hurricane in 1715, with the next rebuilt version burned to the ground by an arsonist in 1975. Who knows why? Lots of theories going around on that one. Come on, let's get inside before the heavens open up. Like I said, I don't have much time."

"Thanks for meeting me like this. I wouldn't have asked if it weren't important. The place is certainly private enough," I remarked as we walked up the path.

"Only the dead eavesdrop here, and they're not talking."

"Good thing. The living make enough noise."

"Got that right. Come on in. I've got a key."

I studied the rounded coffin-shaped mounds as Edna unlocked the door. "These are family plots, aren't they?" Cemeteries fascinated me in a morbid way but my interest preferred to flex its wings in the daylight hours.

"Yes. An island this small gets crowded below ground." Edna glanced over her shoulder across the graveyard. "Every one of these tombs are stacked six to seven coffins deep, since there just isn't enough space to do it any other way. These are all family

58

plots. Mine's on the other side. It's kind of comforting," Edna shrugged. "Together in death as in life, though I had an aunt once who always fought with her husband, my uncle Fred, so badly, she said they'd be scrapping down there, too."

I shivered despite myself. "Do you believe in ghosts?"

"I do, and you?"

"Undecided. Right now, I'd rather stay that way. This place has a sense of foreboding."

"Sure it does. It's called 'death,'" and she laughed. "Everybody ends up that way, one way or the other," she said as the key clicked into the lock. The thick cedar door swung open and she went in ahead of me to switch on the lights. "My cousin, the deacon, made me honorary assistant charged with replenishing the flowers and performing a few other custodial tasks. I kind of enjoy it. The place is so peaceful when a service isn't on and the tourists are gone."

"Do you mind the tourists?"

"Oh, they're all right as long as their well-fed and the sun's shining. When it rains, it's like we locals are responsible. I'm sorry for the weather, you know, but it's not my fault."

"It still beats Nova Scotia this time of year." I stepped into a lovely wooden church, completely unexpected given the exterior. Old cedar beams overhead took the shape of ship's knees, a construction technique used for boat building that I recognized from the old buildings back home.

"Is that where you're from?"

"It is." Since Susan Waverley hailed from Baltimore, I figured I'd better change the subject. "Wow."

"Nice, isn't it? I like that it's not pretentious. Just those rows of pews made in the days when the island still had plenty of natural cedar. Some pieces survived the fire but you can still see the scorch marks. Over there's the altar, our pride and joy, you might say. That and our candlesticks, which date from the sixteen hundreds, are about all that's left with any value. All right, Susan, tell me what you have to say but make it quick."

Edna strolled up the aisle towards the altar, me trailing behind while rehearsing my words over and over again. Everything seemed silly, overwrought, or just plain lies, especially the truth.

Damned if the truth didn't sound the worst of the lot, but that's what came out of me in the end.

"My brother is missing and his last known destination was here in Bermuda. As far as I can tell, the last person to see him alive was Alistair Wyndridge, only he denies it."

Edna stopped, swinging around to face me. "Are you kidding me?"

"No way."

"How do you know that?"

"I have a picture of him standing with my brother out at Smith's Cove. It's a long story as to how I got the photo. Let's just say for simplicity's sake that I have a private investigator on the case."

"And has this investigator spoken to Wyndridge?"

"How can he even get to him? From what I understand, the man avoids contact with the outside world."

"That he does," Edna said, nodding. "He suffers from agoraphobia and a few other afflictions. He's a bit odd to some people's thinking."

"So," I said picking up the story, "I applied to Wyndridge's research job hoping to get in to find out what's going on. I was even short-listed, but today I discovered the position had been filled. No interview required."

"And somehow this investigator found out I was the lucky applicant," Edna was gazing at me, hands on hips. "Wow, he or she must be some crackerjack."

"I have to find my brother, Edna. I don't care how reckless or crazy it sounds, but I need to get into Wyndridge's and find out what he's hiding."

"And your brother's name?"

"Tobias McCabe. You probably don't know of him since he goes by the pseudonym Tobias Thomas, but he designs high-tech computer games with award-winning graphics. He's tall, slim yet muscular, and has bright red hair, which he often wears long in deference to his latest Viking or high-seas animated characters. He—"

"Shit!" Edna slapped her hand to her mouth, dropped it to add: "Sorry, God. Tobias Thomas?"

"You've heard of him?"

"Hell, I saw him!" And she almost slapped her hand over her mouth again but rolled her eyes up heavenward and mouthed *Sorry, God,* instead. "I saw him," she repeated, dropping her hand. "I saw him at Wyndridge's."

I stared at her in hopeful disbelief. "When?"

"The last time I worked for Alistair, about four months ago."

"Two months ago?" I did a quick calculation. "That was long before he went missing."

"He was a house guest. I didn't see him around much but bumped into him one day by Wyndridge's dock when I was out for some air. Alistair didn't introduce me or anything, which I thought odd, but Toby introduced himself. Really charming guy. Said he was there on a diving holiday, but I can't say I believed that. Alistair dives but he's a pretty solitary character."

Suddenly, I felt weak in the knees and plunked down on one of the pews. "Why would Wyndridge lie? Something's going on in there and I have to find out what."

"And you're thinking to get in there as a librarian to snoop? Are you even a librarian?"

"No, but I have to get in somehow. What else can I do? He's my brother."

Edna held up her hand. "Look, I like Alistair. We get along just fine but I just go in there and do my job knowing he's fiercely private. I don't snoop. I don't ask awkward questions. I just put my head down and work. He called me yesterday to press me to take the job after I convinced him to post for a proper archivist in the first place—you should see the manuscripts and artifacts he's collected, way beyond my skills—only he chickened out. Told me he'd had a change of heart and just wanted someone he knew and trusted. That's why I said I'd take the job. Now you're thinking of going in and digging around? Bad move, bad move."

I opened my mouth to speak but she hushed me with an upheld finger. "Let me finish. Maybe he's hiding more than just knowing your brother. Something's up with him and I don't know what. I don't want to know. Well," she amended, "I do but I sense it's better that I don't. The Wyndridges go way back on this island and there's always been rumors. The more I worked in there, the more I sensed all the stuff he might be hiding. Stay out of it."

I shook my head. "But I can't just go away without knowing. The police aren't pursuing this seriously. Wyndridge is probably the only one who may have the answers. How can I stay out of it?"

"I don't know, don't know what I'd do if it were my brother, but that's my advice. You just convinced me there's no way I'm taking this job, after all. I'm going to call and say I'm not taking it. If he asks you next and you're fool enough to say yes, that's up to you."

"You sound scared."

"Let's just say that I like to read my mysteries, not live them."

"Well, how cryptic is that? Are you afraid of him?"

"Not really, though he is eccentric. I think I'm more afraid of what he might be hiding. Enough said."

"Oh, hell, I don't believe this. You saw Toby! You can testify to his being with Alistair Wyndridge. Don't you see what this means? He denied ever seeing Toby."

"That's probably not enough to get the police back on the case, if that's what you're thinking."

I dug my hands into my lap. "I don't know what I'm thinking except to confirm I'm on the right track."

Edna plopped herself down beside me. "God help you, but I think you're doing this all wrong."

"What aren't you telling me?"

She jumped to her feet. "I've got to get going. It's getting late." She reached inside her leather jacket. "I just hope you know what you're doing." A Blackberry emerged from her right pocket, along with a packet of tissues and a mini-bottle of contact cleaner. Scanning the digital screen briefly, she pressed a button and waited in silence as the phone rang while stuffing the other objects back in her pocket.

"Yes, Mrs. Wyndridge. This is Edna Smith. Yes, that one. Sorry for calling at dinner time but is Mr. Wyndridge there? It's important." A pause, then, "Yes, of course. I understand. Would you please pass the message on that I'm withdrawing my name from the position. Yes, yes, I know, but I'd rather not get into specifics on the phone. Something's come up. Yes. Thank you."

And she clicked off. "There, done. Now, I have to go. Keep in touch, okay?"

I followed her to the door. "I will, one way or the other. Thanks for everything."

At the entrance, she paused, listening. "Hear that rain?"

It was hard not to, since it pelted the building in a torrent of wind and water. I couldn't hide my alarm. Like, I was ready to drive in that?

Edna peered out the door. "Typical. When it pours here in January, it's like it rains sideways." And then her phone rang. She had it pressed to her ear in an instant. "I'm here," was her form of hello. "What? Are you kidding me? I thought I told you to come home right after school? Southampton? But I told you not to. Wait by the entrance then." She shrugged, dropping the phone back into her pocket. "My eldest kid. With all the wisdom of a 14-year-old, he decides to play cricket this afternoon with his mates. Now he's stranded on the other side of the island in this rain and guess who gets to pick him up?"

"Oh, I'm sorry. It's wild out there."

"Which way are you headed?"

"Near Astwood Cove."

"You've a drive ahead of you, too. Maybe you should head for a cafe and wait it out. I'm used to driving in bad weather here. There's one just down the road."

"No, thanks. I have to get back, too."

"We may as well travel in convoy, then. We're heading in the same direction for part of the way. You don't have a raincoat, do you?"

"No, but I'll be fine."

She pulled out a little blue plastic pouch from her left pocket. "Here, take this. It's like wearing a trash bag but it will do. I have another under my bike seat. Drop it off at the library someday when you're in town."

"Thanks." I pulled the sheath of crinkly blue over my head gratefully.

"You'd better get better prepared for this island. She's full of surprises," Edna remarked, opening the door wide. "Carry raingear wherever you go, even if the sun's shining. So, follow me up until the junction. Be careful."

Outside the wind whipped the words from our lips as we dashed for our bikes, rain stinging our faces. Edna didn't bother putting on her second rain jacket, if she even had one, just jumped on her bike and eased her way onto the road, waiting for me to catch up.

I'd planned to call Max to say that Edna had withdrawn her application, but I couldn't keep her waiting in this. I had no alternative but to clutch the handlebars and steer the bike onto the slick road. With the helmet fastened and the visor down, I couldn't see more than a few yards ahead of me, enough to fix Edna's taillights in my gaze.

***

The occasional bus, taxis, or moped whizzed past on the opposite side, stirring up a water whirl to further drench my skin. Rain jacket or not, my jeans were soaked, my hands red with cold. Plunging through the dark on that motorized hunk of metal was miserable enough, but trying to keep up with Edna took everything I had.

And once on the open road, Edna drove like a banshee. We cut across the center of the island until we reached the long stretch of road following the south coast, me struggling to keep her in sight. Not many bikes kept us company by then, most of them smart enough to stay off the road. A few cars passed while a few skilled bikers darted between Edna and me with crazy confidence. I thought I'd lose sight of her completely but managed to keep her in site.

Soon we were alone on the South Road, the glory of that scenic coast now consumed by wind and rain, the postcard views obliterated by an upstart tempest. I tried not to think about the waves crashing against the cliffs to my left. Though I had grown up with the sea, it never stopped terrifying me in bad weather. We'd had too many deaths by ocean in my family history: an uncle who fell overboard on a fishing trawler, plus many more going back down our salty family tree. Dad had regaled us with plenty of stories over the years.

After about ten minutes, I saw the lights of a solitary rider in my rearview mirror. At first, I almost welcomed the company, since Edna wove in and out of sight by then, disappearing at every bend. At least here was another human being out in this crazy night. I had slowed way down, fear of hydroplaning consuming my earlier need to keep up. The bike remained at a polite distance behind me as the thick coastal shrubbery of Warwick Long Bay hedged away to the left. I remembered this stretch from my earlier drive when I could actually see. An abrupt turn ahead would lift the road away from this mostly uninhabited range and on towards the South Shore resorts and small properties. Soon I would be at Astwood Cove.

The rear rider suddenly moved up to my tailpipe as if wanting to pass. Oh, great. All I needed was another brave or crazy Bermudan driver. I saw no oncoming traffic so slowed down, edging to one side to let him by. But he didn't take the offer. Instead, he matched his speed with mine so that we were both crawling along.

Which was all wrong. Panic hit hard. I clutched the handles. Who was this? Why was he crowding me? And then another bike came into view behind us, this one gunning quickly as if to overtake us both. Before I could form a plan or devise a response, this bike whipped past us, accelerating around the bend.

Edna! It wasn't so much a thought as a stab in my head, something bad about to happen. I knew it, I just didn't know how. I hit the gas, picking up speed, terrified of what I'd find ahead. When the crash came, I was rounding the corner. I couldn't see anything, just heard the scream. And the driver who passed me didn't stop. The taillights were a mere prick of red far ahead.

Edna had disappeared. An awful cry followed by crashing metal, and then nothing.

Nothing at all.

I brought the bike to a skidding halt. The wheels spun gravel while I ran to where tire tracks drove into the abyss. I called Edna's name, called and called until my throat rasped raw. I stumbled along through the darkness crying out until I was standing on the edge of a precipice. Only the broken foliage of sea grapes and aloes separated me from what I feared most.

"Edna! Edna!"

Hands grasped my shoulders, drawing me back from the edge.

I shook him away. "She's down there! Help her, not me."

"Wait here," he ordered. "Call 911."

I already had my phone out, numb fingers tapping the numbers.

He disappeared, climbing over the rocks to the shore below. "Can't see anything," he shouted up.

"Find her!" I cried, blinded by rain. I screamed into the phone: "There's an accident on the South Road near Warwick Long Bay. Hurry!" And then I tried following after him, the stones slippery, visibility nothing. With one hand grasping the shrubs, the other the rocks, I tried shimmying down the steep slope along a narrow path eked out between the rocks.

He clambered up, pushing me back. "It's too late. The bike, the crash—no one could survive that."

"No!" I screamed at him. "No, no, no! Someone killed her! The man who passed me drove her off the road!"

Soon there were other lights around, a police car, an ambulance, someone asking questions. Did I know victim? "Yes, we had just met. A man was following us. He passed her and then this happened. He killed her."

"Accidents happen," the officer said. "Bad weather, greasy tarmac. I assure you that we'll investigate it. Can you give me a description of the driver, the bike he was driving?"

But how could I? "It was dark. He was wearing a helmet and a visor. His bike was like all the others on this island. He may even have been a she, for all I know."

"Right. A policeman will take you back to your accommodation, miss, and ask you a few more questions. Perhaps you should see a doctor for shock."

I just shrank into my shivering self. I craved an antidote for death, not some pill to lull the pain.

Peering through the faces in the crowd, I found him, the man who had looked for Edna first. A few strands of dark hair lay plastered against his forehead under the black hood of his slicker. Noel.

Chapter 6

"Drink this."

I eyed the glass in Noel's hand, my teeth chattering. "I don't do Scotch."

"So, break a rule and drink."

"Bully." But I slugged back the contents, wincing as it burned its way down. Damned if burn didn't suit my mood. I was angry enough to ignite the world. "Edna's dead," I said, holding out the glass for more. "You and Max will pay for this."

Damp towels lay heaped in piles about the floor of the little cottage. Noel's jacket hung over a chair drying before the fire while the man himself stood dark and ragged, his black hair plastered against his head.

"We didn't kill her, I said. For god's sakes, I came along behind you, remember? I even gave my statement to the police. I was tailing you, not her. When you didn't return to the cottage, I took off to find you." He poured another inch of liquid into my glass. "That's your limit."

"Maggie said they had a contingency plan if I didn't get the job." I tossed back the Scotch. "I didn't get the job, and who made you the liquor police, anyway?"

"Max may be many things but a killer isn't bloody one of them. The plan was to offer her a better-paying job. Had she arrived home tonight, she would have found a message on her answering machine." He took my glass and slipped it onto the side table. "And I deputized myself."

"Somebody ran her off the road, I said. If not you, then who?" I got to my feet, tried pacing, but wobbly legs swerved me dangerously close to the glass coffee table. He caught my arm and steered me back into sitting. I sat there for a moment, my emotions twisting. Edna had died at the scene. I couldn't believe it; I couldn't bear it, and what was worse, I couldn't stop thinking I was responsible.

"Have you considered it might have been just an accident?" Noel remarked. "It's not like road accidents don't happen on this island."

"That bike passed me and gunned it around the bend. Maybe I didn't see anything, but I know he ran her off the road."

"You don't know anything, that's the point."

I shot him a foul look. "It's an informed conjecture. The best kinds of murders look like accidents. Don't you read?"

"Not murder mysteries, if that's what you're implying. And why would anyone want to kill her?" He tugged a throw from off the back of a chair and wrapped it around my quaking shoulders. Crouching down in front of me, he added, "Go have a shower and get out of those wet clothes." He remained too close, his face all sharp angles and inscrutable green eyes. "Now."

I stared at him. "Stop bossing me around, and why would anybody want to kill Edna, you ask? How about why would anyone want to kill Toby?"

I wished I could claw back the words as soon as they escaped my lips.

"Don't talk like that."

"All these months, I refused to believe the possibility. How could anything or anyone harm my brother? He's brilliant, an illustrator, an athlete, an artist! He took risks every day of his life but not stupid ones. He always said to follow your heart, even if it steered you into the deep because that's where the juice of life exists, in risk, in passion! I was the safe one. I was the one who stayed home, went to school, studied a conservative vocation, and then backed out. It was me who didn't have the guts to grab life by the throat. How could he die?" Oh, God, I was swerving right over the edge, coming totally undone. I'd soon be blubbering, wailing with grief and fury. It wasn't fair, wasn't right!

"You don't know what happened to Toby. Stop thinking the worst," Noel said gently. "You're here to find out. Focus on that."

"How can I focus on anything? Edna was frightened of something, Noel. Do you understand? Scared to death of something but wouldn't say what."

"Look, for all we know, tonight was a tragic accident. The librarian —"

"Edna, her name was *Edna*!"

"Edna was driving too fast, you said so yourself."

"Maybe, but she also knew things she wouldn't talk about, some secret surrounding Alistair Wyndridge. She was going to step down from the job. She called Wyndridge's place while we were together at the church, not because I needed to find out about Toby, but because she was frightened and whatever I said spooked her."

Noel went still. "What did you say?"

"I told her about Toby, said that I needed to get in there to find out what happened to him."

"Jesus, Phoebe."

"She'd seen Toby at Wyndridges two months ago. She saw him!"

"What if she had gone straight to the police?"

I lifted my head, streaming tears. "As it was, she went straight to her death."

He swore again, getting to his feet. "We did not kill her, get that? I spoke to Max. He's at the other end of the island on a yacht. He's going to dock and catch a cab to get here as soon as he can."

"Great." I said through rattling teeth as I launched to my wobbly feet. He tried to steady me but I slapped his hand away. "I'll be ready for him. I'll just take a shower."

I didn't wait to see if he left. All I wanted was solitude with lots of hot water pounding down on my head, and yet, all the hot water in the world wouldn't blast away my bleakness. To make matters worse, I was loopy from alcohol on an empty stomach and lurched around the bathroom trying to find my sea legs. In the shower, I leaned my forehead against the marble tiles, crying for Edna and my lost brother until tears and shower blurred into one torrential wash.

Finally, exhausted and spent, I turned off the water taps and towelled down. Under the whine of the hairdryer, I tried to review the whole messy business but my brain stalled. Pulling on one of the sweaters I knit long ago, I climbed into my worn corduroy pants, letting my hair curl wildly in its own wayward energy. Tonight it could go to hell with the rest of me.

When had I eaten last? Breakfast. Hunger chewed my gut. Downstairs, the fire still crackled in the hearth but the damp towels had disappeared. Hushed thumping could be heard from the laundry closet, with clinking china emanating from the kitchen. A kettle whistled. Wavering between annoyance and fury, I stepped into the kitchen.

Noel stood with his back towards me dressed in an Astwood Cove Properties pink bathrobe, long hairy legs sticking out beneath, pouring boiling water into a hibiscus-painted teapot. The table had been set for two in cheery flowered placemats and blue linen napkins with a tray of sandwiches and fruit in the center, everything a little glow of cozy in a sea of gloom.

"Hungry?" he asked without turning. "Thought you'd better soak up that Scotch with grub, though you're probably already buggered. I found enough in the fridge to feed an army of two."

Turning, he set the teapot on the table and tugged a cotton Bermudan cottage-shaped cozy down over it without looking at me.

I averted my eyes from the triangle of chest hair curling above the robe's pink collar.
"I availed myself of the downstairs shower and am in the process of drying my clothes. Do you mind?" he asked.

"Would it matter if I did?"

"Not a bit since I'm hanging around until Max gets here. Besides, I'm currently minus clothes."

"Your cottage is, what, a couple of twists and turns to the right? Did you think you couldn't walk that far?"

"I'd just get wet all over again. You wouldn't want that. How about tea? Made to your specs, I might add. I am definitely a tea man myself, but I prefer mine milky with two teaspoons of sugar."

"You're babbling now."

He stopped, turning towards me, a wry smile playing on his lips. "I'm standing in the kitchen of a glowering woman wearing nothing but a bubble-gum pink bathrobe after having just tugged a small cottage-shaped something-or-other over a teapot. Wouldn't you babble?"

I smiled despite myself. "You look ridiculous."

"I'm chronically aware of that fact. Here, sit."

Nodding, I slumped into the chair, resting my chin in my hands as he moved about the kitchen. I didn't mean to stare. At first my gaze was unfocused, landing on anything that moved, which happened to be him. Only a few moments later when I looked, I mean really looked, did I notice the tattoo curving down his right leg. I leaned over, arms on knees, for a closer look as he poured the tea into my mug. The design was intriguing, an distinctive Aboriginal sand or dot painting rich with ochers and rusts, the execution surprisingly intricate. "A snake?"

"Pardon?" he stepped back as if shocked to find my face so close to his person. He caught the line of my gaze.

"Your tat, is it of a snake?"

"Kangaroo," he said. "You're looking at the end of the tail."

"I think of you as more of a snake."

"Ah, but you don't know me."

"Snake still seems more apt. Is it kangaroo dreaming?"

He met my eyes. "What do you know about the dreaming?"

"Just what I've read. Unlike you, my reading tastes are eclectic and Max kindly gave me plenty of Australian reading material as a child. He seemed very interested in the Aboriginals."

"He would."

"Which tribe are you from?"

"Walpiri."

"But one of your parents is white?'

"How observant."

I just continued, hoping to ride out awkwardness. "I've always been fascinated by the Aboriginals, their art especially. That tat looks like a work of art. Is it from where you were born?"

"It is."

He didn't want to pursue this line of questioning but I didn't want to drop it. "Must have taken a long time. It looks large."

The corners of his mouth melted into a slow, lazy, smile. "It covers two-thirds of my body and, yes, it took three days. Should I be flattered by your interest?" He placed a flowered pitcher of milk on the table, his brows arched in amusement.

"In your tat? Definitely not. I'm only interested from an aesthetic and cultural perspective."

"It's a very beautifully rendered piece of artwork. I'd offer to show it to you in all its glory, but most women are interested in the whole package."

"Whereas I definitely am not. All-over body tats are a bit of a turnoff." Which was a lie I wished were true. In fact, I admit they emanated an irresistible bad-boy attraction, especially on this bad boy. Blame the Scotch. Pulling my gaze away, I stirred my tea.

"Too bad. I think you'd appreciate the details."

He had me wondering, though. A kangaroo? So, if the tail wound around his leg, where did it begin; what part of his anatomy did it cross? "When is Max supposed to arrive?"

"Soon. He texted me that he's hired a cab and is on his way. "Here, eat, mate. I believe the one in the middle is rock lobster salad, and the wheat versions are cheese with something green inside, not mold, I hope." He passed the tray.

"Watercress." I plucked a lobster and a wheat each onto my plate, my voice shaky. "Pink isn't your color, by the way. You're more a black leather man."

He smiled. "I've gone and ruined my style manifesto but my clothes should be dry soon."

We ate in silence, me devouring two lobster and two watercress and cucumber sandwiches washed down with mugs of tea, my eyes fixed on my plate. I checked the wall clock. Nine p.m.

"Mind if I help myself to a beer?" he asked.

"I can't believe you asked."

"Habit."

"You really were trained in England. What were you doing there, anyway?"

"Studying history and archaeology. I went to Cambridge and the University of Queensland back home, just in case you pegged me for a complete loser."

"I pegged you for a dogsbody, not a loser."

"Same thing."

When he sauntered past on the way to the living room bar, I swung around to check out that tattoo again. How long were Kangaroo tails, anyway?

He returned moments later with a bottle of Heineken.

"Why are you working for Max? He treats you like dirt."

Sitting down, he popped the cap off the beer and took a couple of deep swallows while I fixed on his Adam's apple. "The pay is good and the work's interesting. The rest is just surface noise. Besides, it suits my present needs." He held the bottle out and made a face. "I miss Foster's. Now there's a beer."

"Where are you living now?"

"I have a flat in London near Max's shop. You should come visit," he said with a slow smile. "I could show you around."

"What an offer."

"Ever been to London?"

"Yes, once, before Max opened a shop there. How did you and Max meet, anyhow?"

"You might say I looked him up." He took two more very large gulps. "So, do you like the Australian wines?"

I got it: He did not want to discuss Max or his Aboriginal roots. "Are we going to make small talk from here on in? Because I'm no good at it, just so you know."

"Small talk lubricates the social wheels."

"Mine just might fall off my axle from boredom."

And he laughed at that, a full-throated howl of mirth which, I've got to admit, completely transformed his face into something bright and devastatingly sexy. Damn.

"All right then, I'll try a more substantial topic: Why did you quit law?"

I studied the palm frond on my teacup. "I was only interested in criminal law, had this idealistic notion I could make the world a safer place by championing justice."

"So where did all that idealism get you?"

"Conflicted. I soon realized our legal system requires even rapists and murders to be defended, and that someday I had might defend the guilty. Didn't think I could stomach that, so I returned to my default position of underemployed art and textile lover going nowhere."

"Soul-satisfying but economically disastrous."

I sighed, toying with my mug. "Exactly. I'm perpetually broke."

He leaned forward, his sharp-angled face suddenly serious. "Does your definition of justice fall on the side of ethics or the law?"

74

I thought of the tapestry I'd absconded and made a face. "Some might argue the two are synonymous, but not me, not any more. I define ethics more broadly these days. What is legal may not always be just, but that doesn't mean I agree with what you and Max are up to."

He grinned. "I expected you'd say that."

The phone rang. We both turned to stare at the wall phone at my elbow.

"Answer it."

"Why me?"

"You're the one staying here."

"Right." I plucked the receiver from its cradle. "Hello?"

"Miss Waverley?"

"Yes."

"This is Mrs. Wyndridge."

"Right."

"My son has requested that I call to see if you are still interested in accepting the position as researcher, which has opened unexpectedly. If you consent, you are to start as soon as possible." The tone clipped into my ear, abrupt and imperious.

I swallowed. "What, no interview?"

"You have the necessary qualifications. He finds an interview unnecessary. Will you accept the position or not?"

"Yes. When do I begin?"

"Tomorrow afternoon. Mr. Wyndridge requires intensive research within a tight timeframe and requests that you accept room and board on the estate. This is part of your salary, of course. We will send the driver to the Astwood Properties at promptly 4:30 p.m."

"Fine but I—"The line went dead. That woman had a thing about long goodbyes. I laid the cordless phone on the table and turned to Noel. "Just like that, Wyndridge has moved on to his second choice without even waiting for Edna's funeral. I start tomorrow." Despair washed over me. "I need air."

I strode to the living room and flung open the French doors to the main patio where I circumvented the pool. Scents of salt and damp leaves mingled after the rain. The sea pounded against the cliffs below as my feet scrunched over the wet flagstones to the far side of the patio. Leaning against the stone wall, I stared out at the nightscape. Below, a dark fringe of palms, ahead, the heaving darkness of the sea. A lighthouse pulsed its steady heartbeat across the night.

An impenetrable sense of loss swallowed me whole. People died. Time eroded lives and objects, both. I leaned against the stone, resisting the pull of despair. We were all so utterly alone in the end. I closed my eyes.

Tomorrow it would begin.

I didn't hear him approach.

"Are you all right?"

"What do you think?"

"I think you're in way over your head, little mermaid."

I smiled. "But mermaids are born way over their heads. Don't you get that? So, guess we'll have to see which one of us underestimates me the most." Turning towards him, it startled me to find he'd changed back into his own clothes, the black on black completely erasing the accessibility of minutes earlier.

He plunged his hands deep into his pockets. "I've called Max and told him you've got the job. He'll be here soon."

I pushed past him. "I want another drink."

"Bad idea," he called after me.

Chapter 7

By the time Max arrived, I'd discovered the joys of Bourbon poured over ice and slurped back like toxic honey. I sat in the chair by the fire calming my nerves with alcohol-laced knitting to the point where I'd lost the ability to tell a dropped-on-purpose stitch from a long yarn-over. Everything looked the same and I was fine with that. Noel lounged in the chair opposite, legs stretched out in front of him, looking grim, his gaze fixed on the carpet. We'd stopped speaking after he'd failed to prevent me from foraging in the liquor cabinet.

The door swung open. We were on our feet in an instant.

"Phoebe, are you all right?" Max asked, tossing his drenched jacket over the chair and heading for me, arms wide. I sidestepped his embrace, almost toppling into the coffee table. Righting myself, I shoved back a lock of hair, untangled the yarn from my leg and glared. "Did you kill her?"

He stood stunned. "Kill who?"

"Edna Smith. She was run off the road tonight. Deliberately, as in murder."

Max shot a quick look at Noel. "Wasn't that an accident?"

"She doesn't think so," Noel answered. "She thinks someone ran her off the road on purpose, like maybe you or me."

Max looked aghast. "Why would we do that?"

"So I could get in the Wyndridge estate according to plan. Killing her was the contingency."

"Phoebe, get a grip. We were not responsible for that accident. I would never have someone killed. "

Then Maggie came breezing through the door enveloped in couture rainwear and some scent that grabbed me by the throat. "A man's bringing up the luggage. Thanks for helping, Maxi. Jeez, so I'm there standing in the rain and you just take off. I—"Then she caught sight of me. "Phoebe, hon, how are you doing?" She swept towards me as if to bestow kisses into my air space but I backed away, putting a chair between me and her.

"What luggage?" I asked.

"Clothes for your role. You start tomorrow, right?"

"Screw the clothes," said I.

"Mags, sit down, for god's sake," Max growled.

She glanced at him. "I got, like, maybe only a few hours to do hair, makeup and wardrobe."

"Sit down, I said."

Maggie huffed over to the couch and flopped down with a sullen stare, while I resumed my attack. I leaned forward, pointing my finger at Max. "I know you're looking for more than just Toby. Edna was scared witless. She told me that the author is sitting on a secret, a big secret, and I think you're sending me in to find it just like you did Toby."

Max's face paled. "Phoebe, I—"

"Skip it. I don't want to hear any more of your invasive tactics. I mean, evasive tactics." I spun around looking for my drink, seeing it halfway across the world on the side table beside my knitting. Turning back, I eyed my godfather. "You and Dad were up to something all those years ago, something to do with money. You think I'm going to wait patiently while you throw me crumbs. I remember the time you two took off in the boat one night when we were all supposed to be in bed. Toby and I sneaked into the kitchen and found that nautical map spread over the table under the coffee mugs, so we followed you in our dinghy."

"Bloody hell! And you two ended up clinging to a buoy after your boat capsized, and your dad and I only found you the next morning. Two little drowned rats crying your eyes out. How could I forget that? You almost bloody drowned!"

"You wouldn't tell us where you were going!"

We were shouting now.

"You were bloody kids!"

"Not anymore!" I made a dive for my drink, stumbling only once on my way to the table. I took several deep sips before wiping my mouth with the back of my hand. "I'm not a kid anymore."

"Then stop acting like one." Noel had somehow emerged at my elbow.

I glanced up at him. "What are you doing?"

"Keeping you from crashing into the furniture," he said mildly. "We don't want to lose our deposit."

"Back off. I don't need a bumper."

"You're drunk," Max said.

"And you're a liar! Toby came here to meet Wyndridge because of you, didn't he? And Dad found out and told you never to come near him again. That's what you were arguing about the night he disappeared and why you're all puckered in guilt now. You think keeping me in the dark will absolve you from guilt and grant me some kind of immunity while you risk my neck, too, right?"

He looked like I'd slapped him.

"Bingo," I said, waving my drink at him. "Nailed it, didn't I?"

He looked stricken. "I never want anything to happen to you," he said hoarsely. "Or Toby."

"Tell her, Max. She has a right to know," Noel said.

"Damn right I do. What were you, Dad, and now Toby, after, Max? What was Toby hunting down when he went AWOL? And what does Wyndridge have to do with it? Oh, wait. Let me guess: you're all after the Oak Island treasure, right? We saw the chart that night." I said it half-joking but, with a jolt, realized I'd nailed that, too. "Holy shit." Noel caught my glass seconds before I dropped it. I stood, wobbly and stunned, everything roiling. "You couldn't possibly join the legions of idiots who have sunk millions of dollars and lost lives trying to dig up the Oak Island treasure?"

Max took a deep breath, his eyes never leaving my face. "I came to Nova Scotia all those years ago on a hunch. A friend of mine had scrounged up new research on Oak Island, which indicated that it might be connected to a group of well-connected British naval officers in the sixteen hundreds."

"Sixteen eighty-seven, specifically. Lord Mordaunt, The Duke of Albemarle, Sir John Narbrough, and Sir William Phips," Noel added.

"I needed someone who knew that coastline inside and out, so I asked around, which brought me to your dad. Sheldon McCabe was up for the challenge. He knew the stories about Oak Island better than anybody and wanted in on the adventure. I was one of the financial backers of the latest dig, so I added him to my contingent. We found enough to know we were onto something, and then important new research hit publication."

"Researchers discovered that the conspirators found the remains of the Spanish galleon, the *Concepcion*, under the initial auspices of no less a personage than the then-king of England, William of Orange," Noel continued. "Only Sir William Phips, a noted royal scavenger, managed to squirrel away a significant portion of the hoard for himself. With his ships *Good Luck* and the *Boy Huzzar* in attendance, they detoured to a remote corner of what is now Nova Scotia and engineered an ingenious flood chamber to preserve the loot."

"I know all that," I snapped. "There isn't a kid in Nova Scotia who doesn't know about the Money Pit or that millions have been invested in trying to out-manoeuvre that flood shaft." Suddenly, my stomach felt distinctly unstable. "What does all that have to do with Bermuda?"

"The Money Pit's flood chamber was partly a ruse, "Noel continued, sounding more the academic and less the dogsbody by the minute" The large portion of the treasure was entrusted by Phips to his chief engineer and captain, John Wyndridge, who sailed it to Bermuda and buried it in another tidal shaft, where we believe it remains to this day."

I swung around to face them, first Noel, then Max. "Alistair Wyndridge is sitting on part of the Oak Island treasure?"

"Technically, the Bermuda treasure, since this portion never ended up inside Oak Island's Money Pit in the first place," Noel said. "John Ashley Wyndridge may have used some of the loot to finance his business dealings in the Bermudan colony and stashed the rest, or hid the whole lot. We surmise that he may have melted down the coins but kept the jewels. Either way, there is literally millions of dollars' worth in today's currency missing, the bulk of which is in precious artifacts and jewels. William of Orange appeared to have received only silver, but that galleon carried far more than that."

"Heaps of treasure were reportedly stacked on the *Concepcion* with chests of more than four million pesos, including booty unearthed from the mines of Central America, Aztec, and Mayan artifacts, jewels reportedly absconded from pirates and the like, literally a bloody fortune by any century's standards," Max said. "That's what I do, Phoebe, that's my business: I source antiquities for museums and collectors."

"By stealing?"

"Who says this belongs to Wyndridge? It was stolen in the first place!" Noel interrupted.

"That doesn't make it in the public domain. Legally, he owns it."

"Frig the law," Noel asserted. "Wyndridge has no right. His family have sat on millions for centuries while watching men lose their lives trying to unearth what isn't there!"

I shook my head, pressing my index finger between my eyes as if to push a reset button. "Is he trying to keep it for himself, trying to extract it, or what?"

"We're not sure. Can't literally get to the bottom of it. That dropkick, Frank, couldn't find anything, but he says Wyndridge seems more fixed on writing his damn book than anything else. But he has no right to hoard it!" Max said, punctuating the air with his index finger. "The treasure is stolen goods, first from the Spanish who, in turn, pillaged it from all the lands they conquered, then from William of Orange, then from Phips himself. It belongs in museums, maybe, spread among the countries as history and art. Toby went to meet him ages ago, and if he's harmed him, I'll make him pay!"

I lowered my hand, tightening my gut against another lurch. "Toby wouldn't have gone in there to steal," I said. "He'd only be interested in uncovering the mystery and the challenge of it all, but you source artefacts, Max, so you actually want all that shiny stuff, don't you? You are a treasure hunter, you and the dogsbody here—thieves."

"I want what's fair. I want that stuff uncovered. Nobody has a right to sit on that much wealth and beauty forever."

"So ironic. Dad used to say treasure hunters were the craziest, bad-assed loonies in the world. Couldn't let go of the dream of gold, would keep hunting even if it killed them." I looked up. "That's you, and maybe Toby for different reasons, and now my father, too? When did Dad pull himself away?"

"When it got real," Max replied. "At first it was just a game I was paying him well to play. Years passed where not much happened. I got on with my business and your dad carried on with the boat tours. Then Toby got wind of the Bermuda connection and your dad started bucking his involvement." He took a step towards me. "Phoebe, I made a mistake with Toby. I should never have let it go this far. I'm not making the same mistake with you. You're not going in there. I've changed my mind. You phone Wyndridge right now, say you're refusing the job."

I laughed, stepping back. "Like hell. It's too late for that." And then my stomach heaved. I spun away, heading for the bathroom, only Noel got in the way.

Chapter 8

A bruised sky loomed overhead as I waited outside the
Astwood gatehouse late the next afternoon. Yesterday had been a
nightmare and today an audition for the next. All day Maggie had
clipped and groomed me like some show poodle while I sat glued
to my tablet researching everything I could find on Wyndridge, the
Concepcion, and current Oak Island research. A combination of
hangover and heartache poisoned my mood a deep shade of foul. It
was as if I put one foot in front of the other even though I knew a
cliff lay ahead.

The new luggage stacked beside me coordinated with the
cream trench coat and linen suit. Everything pinched, jabbed, and
squeezed. I wiggled my toes in the tan leather pumps and glowered
down at my feet. Pumps, hell. Despite my family legacy, almost
because of my family legacy, I always erred on the side of honesty
but now stood dressed for deceit. Only my battered carpet bag
leaning against my ankles like a cowering puppy looked remotely
mine. I took comfort in studying the rich kilim reds and ochre in its
design. I practically clawed Maggie when she tried replacing it
with one of those designer bags.

I looked up. Noel bounded over the damp grass towards me
in black jeans and a grey t-shirt under his black leather jacket. The
damned man looked good enough to eat.

"You look very professional," he remarked, drawing closer,
hair in his eyes. "A true Susan Waverley."

"If Susan were heading for a banking job in downtown
Manhattan, maybe."

"You still look good."

Spoken like a man who hadn't quite figured out how to
compliment a woman properly. "What a relief. Except for the
headache, I'm feeling much better today, thanks for asking."

His mouth quirked. "I told you to lay off that bourbon. And I managed to launder my jeans after you up-chucked all over them, thanks for asking. Anyway, I didn't come to discuss wardrobes. I have news."

I held up my hand. "What could be worse than what I already know?"

"It's not too late to back out, Phoebe. You can turn on your sleek new heels and march right back to Nova Scotia."

"Do these shoes look made for walking? I'm going in there to find my brother and, like I've said before, that's the information I'm seeking, not treasure. Now, say what you've come for."

His expression was guarded. "It's about the driver Wyndridge's is sending, Bert."

I scanned the empty driveway. "You mean the one picking me up?"

He shoved his hands into his pockets. "Right. Wyndridge hired him after Frank pulled a cropper suddenly. He's going by Bert, but his real handle is Hector Bolt and he's done time in England for an assortment of criminal activities."

My mouth went dry. "Max mentioned him. It seems Wyndridge doesn't check his references too carefully."

"References are easily forged."

"Like I don't know that."

"My point is, be careful."

"Oh, my God!" I slapped a hand against my forehead. "I'm in danger! Why hadn't I noticed earlier?" I crossed my arms. "A bit late for that, isn't it? I suppose it hasn't occurred to you that there might be more than one treasure hunter after this loot? All of you are dangerous, no exceptions."

"Of course, we're dangerous, but I'm not the one apt to hurt your pretty little neck."

"Can't you come up with a better phrase than that?"

"Sorry. Archaic-speak belied my more expansive vocabulary. Let me simplify: Be careful. Don't try anything rash. Is that better? Just get in, get what we need, and get out. Max wants you out of there within three days, at the latest."

"Get what we need, you said. I'm going in to get what I need and to hell with what Max wants or you. I'm looking for my brother, remember?"

"That's what I meant. Avoid using your cell phone to call either Max or me. We'll contact you."

"How?"

"We'll find a way. Max will be on a yacht nearby and I'll be staying close to Wyndridge's. When I send you a signal, meet me down at the base of Wyndridge's jetty. If you run into trouble and have to contact me, I took the liberty of entering a speed-dial number on your iPhone. Let the phone ring once then hang up. I'll know you need me. The title for the contact is Yarn Maven."

"Yarn Maven. You're joking?"

"It sounded suitably innocuous. You're a knitter aren't you?" He pointed to my carpet bag.

"You have no idea, do you?"

"That's an authentic piece of antique carpet from the Ottoman empire."

I shot him a quick look. "I meant you know nothing about my knitting. You're probably imagining I make doilies or socks or something. As for the bag, Max gave it to me."

"I know. He covered a seat in his London townhouse with the same fabric after finding much of it destroyed at the bottom of a trunk at an estate sale. You'd love the work he does, you know. Many of our clients seek rare and beautiful textiles, among other objets d'art. Imagine spending your days sourcing those?"

"Gee, another job offer. It's either feast or famine these days." I sensed he had more to say but the sight of a car slipping up the drive stopped him.

"Here he comes. I'd better disappear. Take care of yourself." He turned and dashed into the shrubbery like some kind of leather-glad gazelle.

I shivered as a dark green Jaguar purred up the drive. The car whispered to a stop. A thickset uniformed man climbed out, aiming the key fob at the trunk. Tall, dark and hefty, with a brush of short dark hair streaked with grey, he reminded me of a football player melting into flabby retirement. "Morning ma'am. Susan Waverley, I presume?"

"Correct and you must be the driver from Mr. Wyndridge's."

"Just so. Bert's the name." He nodded while reaching for the two suitcases, clutching the handles with sausage fingers and striding over to toss them into the trunk. When he returned moments later for my carpet bag, I had it safely slung over my shoulder.

He doffed his cap and stretched his lips back, revealing a march of perfect teeth. The distinct scent of menthol competed with his aftershave, a war that made me sneeze. "Always nice to meet a new colleague. Care to take a seat in the car?" Cockney accent. I avoided his proffered hand and slid into the back seat, the door slamming shut while I dug around my bag for a tissue. The sounds of sea and wind instantly ceased as if we'd been vacuum-sealed. I pushed down the electric window button for breeze control.

Bert climbed into the driver's seat and power-controlled my window back up. Soon the car was slipping down the drive through the gardens and candy-colored buildings towards the South Shore Road. My Google search had identified our destination as somewhere near Stonehole Bay. Wyndridge apparently lived along the length of an otherwise uninhabited national park, something he'd probably managed through an uninterrupted and influential family presence. Old money, in other words, even if it had since drained away

I leaned back in the seat trying to relax. Mopeds, motorcycles, and the occasional car whizzed past. The ocean behind the landscape brewed deep teal under the brooding sky.

"So, how long have you been working for Mr. Wyndridge?" I asked.

"Three days. His driver took off unexpectedly." He popped a mint into his mouth, refreshing his menthol reek. "You know these young punks. Can't trust them. As soon as a better offer comes, pouf! They're gone."

"Strange how that happens," I remarked.

"Ah yes, just so. Look at that poor library lady you're replacing. Here yesterday, gone today. And Wyndridge arrives from a two-day sail only to find out that his jackass-of-all-trades has left him stranded. Staff turnover is big at his place. I just came along with my perfect curriculum minutiae packaged with a little gardening experience and a whole pile of serious chauffeuring shit, and Wyndridge snapped me up. He knew a bargain when he saw one."

"Must be fate."

He grinned. "That's what I thought."

Rounding the corner near Warwick Long Cove, I recognized the spot where Edna met her death. I couldn't look away.

"This is where the library lady died," the driver remarked. My eyes slid to his in the rearview mirror.

"How do you know that?"

He shrugged. "Small island. Everybody knows everything. Tragic, I thought, but here you are to fill her shoes. Just proves that nobody's expendable, Sue. Mind if I call you Sue?"

"Susan, please."

"How about 'Suzy'?"

"Worse."

"Right, Suzy it is."

I sank back into the seat, shivering in the air conditioning. The exterior temperature didn't warrant the enhancement. "Could you please turn the air con down?"

So he turned it up.

"You're going to love the Wyndridge digs–something else, if I do say myself," Bert said, glancing at me in the mirror. "The place has been here for over 250 years. Very nice, if you like old places. Lots of little nooks and crannies, good for rendezvousing with cute little redheads. You enjoying the ride, Suzy?"

"Go to hell, Bertie."

His doughy grin stretched wide.

The estate lay about four miles down the South Shore Road, well-hidden from the highway, as expected. I must have passed the entry twice yesterday without knowing, thinking that stretch of coast consisted of only parkland and hidden beaches. A gap between boulders marked the driveway, which plunged in switchback turns down the hill towards the shore.

The early winter twilight thickened the darkness amid the trees as the Jag nosed along the drive. Halfway down, Bert stopped the car, jumped out, and unlocked a gated barricade. Minutes later, we drove into a clearing. On a crest of a cliff bounded by low stone walls and occupied by a single freestanding garage, Bert stopped the car.

I could only stare.

Wyndridge Estate rose like a cottage-castle from the other side of a leaping span of bridge. Perched in the center of a tiny island promontory, the structure looked like an overblown cottage organism that had sprouted wings vertically and horizontally. Each section carried the typical Bermudan features of white stepped roofs, pink coral stone walls, shutters, and casement windows, everything, that is, but the single square tower rising from its midst like a transplant from another era.

"Old watchtower," Bert said. "First thing the original Wyndridge built. Gives a full view of the ocean ahead and the mainland behind. Think he had something to guard, little Suzy?"

I climbed out, too absorbed to spar. It reminded me of a blenderized sugar-pink fortress, a contradiction in every aspect.

Bert unloaded the luggage onto a buggy. "I can't drive you over. The bridge is just for people and bikes, so you just walk across and I'll bring the bags along."

But for minor repairs, the old stone bridge couldn't have changed much in centuries. Two buggy tracks grooved ridges into the cobbles with low stone walls on either side. I strode across the span with the wind whipping my hair and the crash of waves in my ears. Halfway across, I leaned over the chest-high wall. At least 50 feet below, foam boiled over rocks in a narrow channel separating the island from the mainland. Edna's death flashed into my mind before I pulled back.

"High, isn't it?" shouted Bert, the baggage buggy rattling behind him. "Treacherous for a place so lovely."

I continued without comment. Once across the channel, I followed a natural stone path curving from the bridge onto a terraced patio where a small wall hunkered against the wind. Beyond that, a tiny kitchen garden nurtured herbs spotted through with rain-battered flowers next to the house's casement windows.

The first drop of rain hit my face the exact moment I saw Alistair Wyndridge framed in the light of a doorway. In a white poet's shirt and moleskin breeches, he looked like a specter from another age, a magnificent paragon of manly beauty who just missed the mark by a few centuries. "Mr. Wyndridge, hello. I'm Susan Waverley."

"Obviously," he said with a flip of his hand. "I apologize for not being more welcoming, but I'm most distressed over Edna Smith's death. You have heard of the accident?"

"Of course. Actually, I was kind of a witness. She was showing me the Old Devonshire Church and I was following her home. I'll never get over it as long as I live. We were just driving along and then — and then she was gone." My voice hitched.

His gray eyes were searching but then he sighed, stepping back from the door. "Too many accidents is all rather unsettling. Do come in."

Wyndridge stepped aside to let me to pass. Inside, I glimpsed white stucco walls punctuated by dark wooden ceiling beams, wide-planked cedar floorboards, and a hallway stretching deep to the rest of the house. Lemon furniture polish assaulted my nostrils, waxy and pungent.

An old woman stood like a sentry beside a potted palm. Surgical stockings bound her swollen legs, and the knobby hands resting on broad hips twisted with arthritis.

Wyndridge turned to her. "May I introduce my mother, Mrs. Wyndridge, and mother, meet Ms. Waverley." And to me, "My mother will take good care of you. Consider her your main contact when I'm unavailable."

I smiled over at the woman. "Nice to meet you."

She gave me a sharp-eyed once-over. "Good day to you."

"Um, we spoke on the phone, I think."

Wyndridge held up his hand. "Mother, do take good care of her. See to it that she has what she needs. Why don't you show her to her room so she'll have a chance to freshen before dinner?"

The woman nodded. "You'll be dining at seven, son?"

"Tonight, yes. I must explain the work to Ms. Waverley and then return to my own," he said. "I expect matters to get rather hectic over the next few days and I'm eager to expedite the matter."

"I'll show her to the Bottle room, then," she said.

"Excellent. I'll look forward to speaking with you both later." And he took off down the hall. I almost tried to curtsy until I remembered I didn't know how.

I turned to the old woman, whose shrewd gaze never left my person. She had to be at least my dad's age. "I understand that Bert is bringing my baggage in."

"Well, I certainly won't be doing it, but that Bert is a useless sod if ever there was, a big sack of no-good-intent. And now you. There's just too many strangers entering our lives for my liking. Too many people gone missing or dying, like that poor Edna Smith, and no one will work for us anymore. Not that I blame them. The Wyndridges just aren't what they used to be. Well then, follow me. Bert will probably be along soon. He must be good for something."

"I doubt that."

"Mind that you tell me if he steps out of line. I'll have him out on his ear the moment we find a replacement."

I followed behind the woman's shuffling footsteps down a hall hung with painted seascapes and plenty of little mullioned windows designed to frame the real thing beyond. To be in a house where people named rooms other than "bathroom" and "kitchen" was novel enough, let alone walking corridors where every second object could be a museum piece.

"I don't believe in accidents myself," Mrs. Wyndridge muttered. "Things happen for a reason, if you ask me, not that anyone does, of course." She flashed a pointed look over her shoulder, catching me inspecting a French seventeenth century burled wood console. "Plenty of nice art and antiques in this house. I keep an inventory in my head."

"I won't steal the silverware, if that's what you're thinking." I grinned at her. "And I certainly won't be spiriting away a commode in the night."

She sniffed, turning away.

Short stairways linked different levels throughout the house as if every wing had been another generation's afterthought. I'd need to go through every room taking photos and then sketch my own navigational blueprint to find my way.

"Where does Bert stay?"

"Not in the house, I can tell you that. We give the grounds man use of a little cottage at the end of the garden. Used to be Frank's before he disappeared. That's the young man Bert's supposedly replacing." She stopped to switch on a pair of brass wall sconces where bulbs had replaced candles long ago.

"What happened to Frank?"

"I wouldn't mind knowing myself. He left suddenly with no explanation besides a note behind saying that he had a better job offer. We're very short-staffed at the moment, so keep that in mind. Come along."

Signs of age increased by the tip of the hallways, the slight skew in the doorjambs. Three stairs down, we made a left turn and ended in a long corridor where four doors opened, two per side.

"This is the bedroom wing. I'm going to put you right beside me, young lady. That way I can keep an eye on you. My son won't, you can be sure of that. He spends most of the time locked up in his study or on his yacht. Writers don't pay much attention to the real world. He needs me to make sure things go right around here."

"Is his room in this wing, too?"

"He stays in the old part, near the tower and the library, on the other side of the house. My son's a very private man. Remember that. Here, this one's yours."

The woman pushed open a door and ushered me through. Old bottles in myriad shades of blue lined the upper sills of casement windows, promising color puddles in the sunlight. A sleigh bed, its chintz spread abloom in pink roses, dominated the space between two carved side tables. Otherwise, a desk, bureau, and wingback chair were the only furnishings clustered around a Persian scatter rug.

"It's charming," I said.

"Of course it's charming. Do you think we'd go putting you in some little hole-in-the-wall? You'd be hard-pressed to find anything but a nice room in this place, anyway, even if the place is falling apart." She pointed to a door leading off to the right. "There's a private bathroom right over there—saves us from sharing. Young women like you and old ones like me spend a long time in the washrooms for different reasons."

She indicated an embroidered bell cord hung discretely near the bed. "That's not for calling servants, mind. We don't have any of those in this household these days, so don't be expecting anyone to wait on you. It's just me, Bert, the cook, and a girl who comes in to help me a couple of times a month. You'll have to make your own bed and reuse your towels until the end of the week. Nobody's going to wait on you here."

"Nobody ever has before, so why would I expect it now?"

The woman studied me from over the tops of her bifocals. "Yes, well, things aren't like they were back when the whole family came over from England on holidays. That was when my other son, George, was still alive. Then we needed full staff. Now, George is gone along with my husband and nobody comes here anymore. Now, you go do your freshening up, then knock on my door across the hall at ten to seven and I'll deliver you to the dining room. No sooner, no later, understand? Ten to seven."

"Wait. Please."

The woman turned.

"When will I get a tour of the house?"

Mrs. Wyndridge's eyes narrowed. "This is a private home not a resort. You'll be shown where you need to go and the places you're granted access to, nothing else. Consider the rest of the house off-bounds. Now, I'm going to take me a little lie-down. Remain in your room." She shuffled painfully to the door, shutting it behind her.

Remain in my room? Right. This whole place felt like somebody else's dream, perhaps some Gothic-infused preamble to a nightmare. But, all that aside, I loved the room and, strangely enough, the house. Anything with a patina of age, anything layered in history or softened by the touch of human lives, suited me fine.

Toby would appreciate this, too, the way he appreciated places that might serve as a setting for his electronic worlds. Had he stayed in this room? I scanned the space as if half-expecting some sign of his presence, something, anything, that had once been his. Crazy. Suddenly awash with loss, I sat down in the wing chair and pulled out my knitting for a dose of solace. The feel of yarn flowing across my fingers soothed me. I could almost convince myself that everything would be all right in the end; I'd find Toby, pick up all my loose ends, and we'd all live happily ever after.

Several minutes passed before, jolting alert, I found Bert standing only yards from the chair, heavy and still, his beefy hands gripping my luggage.

"Is knocking too much to ask?"

"Weren't you expecting me, Suzy?" He dropped the bags to the floor. "What do you think of Old Ironsides?"

"Keep your voice down. She's next door."

"And as deaf as a rock. Takes her hearing aid out when she naps."

I got to my feet, carefully replacing my knitting on the chair arm.

"What are you making, Suzy?"

"Nothing you'd be interested in, Bert."

He stepped closer and peered down at the piece. "My mum used to knit when she wasn't poking me with her needles. She had those metal ones, you know? Multipurpose, like. Still, she could make things without those big holes all over the place."

"These holes are deliberate." Damn, why was explaining myself to him? "Would you mind putting my bags on the bed?"

"Surely." He threw the two bags onto the bedspread. "Expensive luggage. I'm impressed a library scholar type like you can afford such niceties."

"What's it to you?" And then I caught sight of the little brass locks dangling open on my bags. I gaped in disbelief. "You pried open my bags?"

"Just took a little peek, that's all. Nothing much in it but clothes anyway," he shrugged. "Nice undies though. I took a pair as a memento, hope you don't mind. The green silk, very nice."

"What were you looking for, besides silk panties to wear with your navy serge uniform?"

He shrugged again. "Don't know, exactly. Mr. Wyndridge said that I'm to keep my eyes peeled for everything about you, Suzy. Why don't you let me see inside that tapestry bag you keep so close, as a sign of good faith and all?"

"Just get out of here before I forget what good buds we're becoming and start screaming harassment. That might get Mr Wyndridge's attention, don't you think?"

"You don't want to be doing that now, little Suzy. Harassment is so overused these days. We both got things to hide, don't we? Best that we work together rather than apart."

"Get out of my room. Now. Oh, and before you leave, give me back my underwear."

He stared at my outstretched hand. "You know, it would make it easier for you if you just resigned yourself to being nice to me. I'd accept those panties as a token of your affection and we could be that much closer to becoming friends."

"Sorry, I'm just not there yet. Guess I need more courtship. Give me back my underwear. The color's all wrong for you. Try something black and blue."

He reached into his pocket and pulled out the little clutch of lime silk. "I usually get what I want in the end," he said, dropping the bikinis on the floor. "And ends are exactly what I want. For me, it's lady's bottoms. I love nothing more than to give a good spanking on a nice bare backside. I think I'd like yours very much, little Suzy. I'll be waiting."

Slamming the door shut behind him, I stared down at the puddle of lime green silk. God help me.

Chapter 9

"Phoebe, why haven't you called?"

"Dad, I'm sorry. I've just been busy job hunting." I paced the floor, crossing and recrossing the Persian scatter rug in the bedroom, telling myself that there were worst things than lying to my father. "How are you doing?"

"Fine. Why shouldn't I be?"

"Just wondering." I braked beside the bed, inches away from where my knitting flowed textured color across the counterpane. I'd stolen an hour to knit, even working in one of the purple silk yarns I'd found in Mom's studio. The color sang with luminous magic across the piece, prompting a stir of giddy pleasure. I traced the drop-stitch undulations across the row. "Has Julie called again?"

"Not talking to her. Told Bertha to say I wasn't home. When are you coming down home again?"

"Not for a few weeks. I was only there a couple of days ago, remember?"

He exploded. "Of course I remember! Why wouldn't I remember that?"

"No problem, Dad. It's just a figure of speech, that's all. What did you do today?"

"Nothing, as usual. Read a little and Bertha came by with one of her casseroles and a bag of cookies."

"She cleaned up a little, too, though, right?"

"Right, as if I can't take care of my own business. Enough about me. I'm sick to death of myself, anyways. How are you doing?"

"I'm fine. I'm reading a novel by Alistair Wyndridge. Do you know him? He writes those high-sea romance stories set in the seventeenth and eighteenth centuries, you know, romantic versions of Horatio Hornblower."

"Toby gave me one of those books once."

I stopped, stunned. "He did?"

"Yeah, last Christmas. Said he'd like to develop one of those computer games based on the story line."

"He did?"

"Why do you keep saying that? Yes, he did, I said."

"Last Christmas?"

"Yes, last Christmas. It was called *Brethren of the Coast.*"

And Dad remembered that. That's the way it was these days: He'd do instant recall one minute and falter on the edge of oblivion the next. How long would it be before he forgot everything?

"Did you enjoy it?"

"Well enough. I got it out last night and tried to read it but couldn't concentrate. I mostly just sat and looked at the inscription like a blubbering fool."

Picturing Dad alone in the cottage staring down at the loving signature of his missing son squeezed the heart out of me. I shoved hair from my forehead while navigating around the wingchair. I could not break it to him, absolutely could not share the doctor's latest assessment of his mental lapses. He'd lost so much already–his wife, his son. To know his mind was on the way out, too...

"Phoebe, you still there?"

"I'm still here, Dad. What did the inscription say?"

"Don't remember it all now, but he made a little drawing of starfish holding a sword. Cracked me up."

I grinned. Pausing by the bed, I crooked the phone between neck and shoulder and picked up my needles. I could multi-task with the best of them. Knit and talk on the phone? No problem. I bent down to better support my emerging wild wave shawl on the bed. "I'm glad that made you laugh. Was there treasure in the story?"

"Treasure, why would there be treasure?"

"Well, high-sea adventures often involve pirates and buried treasure, don't they?" An unnerving silence followed. Did Dad catch the bait I'd dangled or was something else amiss? "Dad?"

Then I dropped a stitch. "Damn! Are you still there?"

"Yeah, but I'm thinking I should be finding my son instead of hoisted on dry dock like a useless hunk of lead."

"Dad, stop. Besides, your son's—"

"Don't say it."

My fingers froze on the needles. A pall of ache and grief filled the silence between us.

I took a deep breath. "But Dad, you know —"

The dropped stitch released, laddering down several rows.

"I know nothing and neither do you! Toby's still alive until we know otherwise. How many times do I have to tell you that?"

I swallowed hard. "Right."

"So, when are you coming home?"

"Soon, Dad." I knelt beside the bed, prayer-style, to better catch the runaway stitch with the work flattened on top of the bedspread. Armed with a cable needle, I sent the point deep within the stitches to capture the errant stitch.

"When's soon?"

"Soon, as in a couple of weeks. I have to concentrate on job hunting." If I could just slip the cable tip through the escapee stitch and anchor it until I could fix things.

"You be careful there in the city and make it sooner."

"I'm always careful."

"You are not. Hell, girl, can't I raise one sensible child? One gets himself lost somewhere, and the other does God-knows-what and thinks she can fool her old man."

The phone slipped from my neck and hit the floor. I picked it up in an instant.

"Phoebe?"

"Sorry, Dad," I said. "I'd better go. I'm going out for supper with friends and I'm not even dressed yet."

"You seeing that library guy still?"

"No, we broke up."

"Good thing. He was a stuff-shirt if I ever saw one."

I tried to laugh but couldn't. I knew he was only trying to keep me on the line. "I'll phone soon, honest."

"You'd better. Love you."

"Love you, too."

Tossing the phone on the bed, I studied my dropped stitch through a blurring of tears. No time to fix that mess now, since I was about to wade into the deep end of another.

***

At 6:50 sharp, I knocked at Mrs.Wyndridge's door, wearing a green velvet dress, the most subdued of Maggie's wardrobe choices. She had left nothing of my own clothes but a pair of jeans and sneakers. I should have paid more attention to what she was up to in my room yesterday but preoccupation ruled. Here I stood sheathed in velvet, tottering on impossibly high heels. Beneath it all, those foreign silk panties — blue, since I'd washed out the ones Bert fondled — felt as wanton as a thong in a convent.

Mrs. Wyndridge studied me as I stood unsteadily before her. "This isn't a date, remember. He wouldn't be interested in the likes of you."

I couldn't have said it better myself. "I'm sure that's true. Look, I can find my way to the dining room if you'd rather rest."

"You'd lose your way and only keep him waiting, which he wouldn't approve of at all. I'll deliver you, as I said I would. Follow me."

I obeyed, keeping pace behind the woman's labored shuffle in an effort to practice indentured servitude.

Sconces cast amber pools across walls and antiques, plunging the atmosphere into shadow and glow. I committed to memory each turn of the maze-like route, taking pictures with my phone at every clandestine opportunity until the double doors of the dining room came into view.

"Here we are. Knock first." She began shuffling down the hall in the opposite direction.

"Aren't you joining us?"

The woman snorted. "Hardly. I prefer my meals in the kitchen, as you will after tonight."

I sighed, knocking before opening the heavy wooden doors.

Positioned by the mantle of a crackling hearth stood my employer, donned in an elaborately embroidered fawn waistcoat, breeches, and silk hose, his hair flowing long over his shoulders. With one hand holding a brandy snifter and the other resting against the mantle, he awaited in what had to be a piece of brilliant staging.

How would Susan handle this one?

"Mr. Wyndridge, you do look dashing."

"Dashing? How very Regency of you but thank you, nonetheless. Do come in, Ms. Waverley."

"Susan, please."

"Susan. Do come in and try not to look so surprised, if I read your expression truly. Is it my garb you find so alarming as to cast a shadow across your countenance? May I remind you that I am a writer of historical novels and, like an actor, assume the garb and setting of my characters in a similar spirit. Tonight I shall write and thus assume the skin of my protagonist."

"Like method acting?" I stepped forward.

"Rather. I immerse my environment according to the period of my novels, in this case the late seventeenth century."

I stepped closer, fixed on the intricate silk crewel work of his jacket. It looked hand-done, all silk, and a little worn in places. With a shock, I realized it could be the real thing, and that he stood wearing a museum-quality period costume. I forced my attention back into role. "Which would be roughly when your ancestor was establishing himself on this island, correct?"

Wyndridge's smile held little warmth. "So, you have done your homework. May I offer you brandy?"

"No thanks."

The room, an area about the size of my entire apartment, glowed in candlelight, everything reflecting against polished wood and brass. Not a single electrical anything made an appearance. Against a far wall, flanked by a waterfall of blue velvet, stood a richly inlaid harpsichord. A collection of sailing artifacts hung along the single walnut-panelled wall to the right, with a particularly fine sexton holding center stage over the fireplace.

My host followed my gaze. "A lovely specimen, isn't it?"

Only a few sentences into our evening and already he'd allowed a modern contraction to slip into his speech. Not so methodical a method author, after all.

Wyndridge's spicy cologne teased my nostrils. "Am I right in saying that it is one of the original sextons created in 1757 by Captain John Campbell?"

He shot me a quick, appreciative, look. "And how would you know that?"

Because I studied the list of pieces you won at a Christie's auction and took a guess. "I'm interested in maritime sailing antiques." I sank uninvited into one of the two brocade wingback chairs beside the fire.

Wyndridge crossed one white-hosed ankle over the other while continuing to lean against the mantle. "You are, indeed, well-qualified. In fact, you may wonder why you weren't my first choice, given your academic background?"

"I realize Edna Smith had worked for you before."

"You knew her?"

"We'd met briefly only yesterday."

"Yes, well, she had worked for me, and admirably so. She agreed to again after initial resistance, insisting that I required a more erudite assistant for the nature of my collection. I convinced her otherwise, deciding that I would rather remain with a known entity. Then she met with a tragic accident. Forced back to our list, we viewed your file and, yes, you are undoubtedly well-qualified, possibly overly so, and, since I have not the time or patience to spend too long on the search, and based on your stellar qualifications, your proximity, and my need for haste, you are here."

"And I'm very happy to be. This looks like interesting work."

"I trust you will proceed quickly with little interruption. It is my intention, you see, to itemize my manuscript collection for sale."

I feigned surprise. "Sale?

"If all goes according to my desire, I will be living elsewhere within the year, after having relinquished my manuscripts and artefacts to auction and sold the house."

"You mean you're going to sell the property, too?" On the run, in other words.

"His gaze remained fixed on some distant point across the room. "With much regret, yes. Though painful, it is imperative that I move forward. A man cannot live forever in the past, though I've done better than most in that regard. But first, I must finish the final novel of my Bermuda trilogy and organize the vast collection housed in the tower library. Your task, Ms. Waverley — pardon me, Susan — is to ready that collection for auction. Ms. Smith informed me at great length what that would involve, but I wish the task completed as soon as is humanly possible, though perhaps not with all the care she recommended."

"Of course. I'll begin first thing tomorrow."

"I will also put you under certain restrictions. Pray do not be dismayed by my cautionary rules. However, a series of distressing and unaccountable accidents have occurred of late, beginning with the sudden disappearance of my grounds man, which compels me to take certain precautions."

"Such as?"

"Such as, I neither encourage nor facilitate extraneous investigations within or beyond the material I have assigned, all of which is articulated in the contract which I have provided for your signature. In addition, you must sign a confidentiality agreement forbidding you to share or use the content of the manuscripts or disclose anything you see in this house in any form without my written permission, which I assure you, I will never grant. Is this clear?"

Legality was the least of my concerns, though it held more than a passing interest. "I'd like to see the contracts in advance."

"If you wish. They will be awaiting you on your desk in the tower tomorrow morning. If you choose not to sign them, pray bid my driver to deliver you off-premises to the destination of your choice. I will be unavailable from this point on. Your tasks have been itemized for you in written form in the tower library. Do you accept the terms thus far?"

"Yes, so far."

"Excellent. On the morrow you will begin. Mrs. Wyndridge will deliver you to my tower library, where you will work for seven hours per day with a one-hour lunch period to be determined in advance. All necessary documentation will be contained in that room, and under no circumstances are you to roam the estate without my permission. I am not, however, some ogre from a Gothic romance. On your free time, you will have access to the beach, the garden, and the patios, plus the lounge areas reserved for staff."

"What lounge areas would they be?"

"The kitchen or anything unlocked, obviously," he said with asperity.

If I harboured ideas that I might be treated as a guest rather than an employee, that squelched it. "I presume I'm allowed to leave the estate on my off-hours and not be chained to my desk?"

If there was a flash of amusement in his face, it was brief. "Most certainly. You are not at a boarding school. Now, I'd like nothing more than to dally over aperitifs, but I fear time presses heavily on me tonight. You will find me very exacting, given to flourishes, and providing extraneous details only at my choosing."

"Will we have regular meetings where I update my progress?"

"Unnecessary. I will contact you upon occasion so you can apprise me of your progress, but I will be deeply ensconced in my writing and do not wish to be disturbed. Please keep a journal of your day's work, in longhand, not on computer."

"Wait." I raised my hand, traffic-cop style. "Please. I mean, presumably you have computers? You must. Don't you write your manuscripts on one? I'd much prefer to write my summary and notes by email and I can save them to disk, if needed. In the interest of time, of course."

Wyndridge slipped the empty snifter onto the mantle and straightened, hands behind his back, after which he proceeded to lift himself up and down on the balls of his leather-shoed, high-heeled feet. "I anticipated you might make such a request. Would it surprise you to learn that I write all my manuscripts in longhand and have a secretary type them into a word-processing program?"

"Well, yes and no. I mean, given what I've seen so far, no surprises at all, yet when I think of how much easier editing is on the computer—"

"All of which I've heard before in great, tedious, detail. However, I prefer to write in the dying art of longhand. Our ancestors managed communication rather admirably without technology, and in this house we do the same, except where absolutely necessary or where the staff have beseeched me otherwise."

"So, no WiFi?"

"No WiFi. I have one hard-wired connection — I am not a complete Luddite — in my security office, which we use for ordering supplies offshore and occasionally to post manuscripts to New York. Any further questions?"

How would I survive without the internet? My cell phone data bills would be astronomical even if Max covered them. "Not at the moment. Your wish is my command."

That provoked a genuine smile. "Oh, I doubt that. Now, let us dine. I will, quite rudely, I admit, leave you to enjoy dessert without my company."

He led me through yet another set of double doors to a small dining room graced by a rather long table dressed in candelabra and formal china. The overwhelming sense of being dropped bodily into some period movie intensified.

"Please, be seated."

And I was supposed to flirt with this one? Maggie had this one all wrong. On a sliding scale of sexual tension, I'd place ours 40 leagues southward, probably bordering on Antarctica.

I took the seat he drew, lowering myself down before the bleached and starched damask tablecloth, gazing at glistening crystal, gold-limned china, and silver, everything gleaming intensely. On either side of my charger, a line of cutlery stood at attention like glossy little soldiers. I may as well have saluted them since all but the obvious ones were totally foreign.

Soup arrived first, delivered by an employee I'd yet to meet, a slender, graceful woman with hair piled into a cascade of tiny braids and skin like warm coffee. Wyndridge didn't offer introductions, of course, but she flashed me a quick smile.

"Her name is Joquita," Wyndridge said once the woman had exited.

"I'm not used to such formality," I confessed.

"No doubt. I do run a formal household but that's mostly for my own pleasure. This is the manner in which my protagonist would have dined."

Joquita returned with a basket of rolls. Wyndridge watched as she scooped a thick, spicy mixture into a paper-thin china bowl. "I do hope you find the tower more atmospheric than uncomfortable," he said.

Joquita caught my eye before disappearing through the side door, presumably to the kitchen. I tasted the soup, chowder, I realized. Delicious. "That's in the oldest part of the house, isn't it?" I tried not to slurp.

"Exactly." Wyndridge sipped his soup in small, elegant gestures, something I couldn't master. "My ancestors were merchants, as you know. John Ashley built a lucrative trading empire between the colonies, and it is he who built this house. The full story will unfold in my new book."

"He was associated with Sir William Phips, right?"

Slowly he raised his gaze to me. "Why do you ask that?"

I put down my spoon. "It's a matter of public record, isn't it?"

"No, it is not."

Oh-oh.

"I did do some preliminary research before coming because I thought that might be useful in better understanding your collection."

"It will not."

"Did I say something wrong?"

Wyndridge's expression hardened. "I expected you to comprehend the nature of your position here. I do want you to organize my collection, nothing more. Is that understood?"

"Of course."

He stood up, shoving back his chair. "I require a cataloguer, not a speculator. Here, you are expected to play by my rules."

"Sorry. I'm just confused, that's all."

He flung his napkin on the chair. "I want the job completely quickly and you gone with equal haste. You'll find your first instructions on your tower desk tomorrow morning. Dine without me. I have work to do."

The cedar doors thudded behind him as he stormed out. What was up with that? I propped my elbows on the table and sighed into my hands.

"What did you say to him to get him so pissed?" a voice whispered.

I looked up at Joquita peeking through the opposite doorway. "I chanced to mention the esteemed ancestor. "

Joquita slipped into the room. "Okay, so it's like this: the guy's high-strung. Well, probably neurotic." She stirred her finger in the air near her head. "The arty-farty artiste is really quite sweet in his way but he's got boundaries. If I had a chance, I could have prepared you for His Almighty but Mrs. W likes to rule the roost and would be much happier if you got fired early. Anyway, eat your salad. Somebody may as well have the benefit of this room and all the food." Joquita scooped leafy greens onto a Wedgwood plate, whipping away the soup bowl with her other hand.

"What's your advice?"

"Say as little as possible. All the stuff going on around here is making him paranoid. We've been told not to talk to outsiders about anything concerning the estate. Here's the dressing— honey mustard, which is perfect with the avocado and rock crab."

"Looks delicious."

"My special recipe."

I took a bite, savoring the flavors and textures. "Delish."

"Good. I've got to get back to the kitchen. Enjoy."

"Joquita, thanks, but I'm going back to my room after this. No main or second or whatever comes next, but coffee to take with me would be great."

The woman laughed. "Do you want me to fix some camomile tea instead of coffee?"

"No thanks. I'll take the hard stuff. Sorry if the food's going to waste."

"Don't worry, nothing will go to waste, not with Shrek parked in the kitchen devouring everything in sight."

"Shrek was a good guy. Bert is not."

"Got that right. Sit here and enjoy your salad. I'll put on some fresh coffee." Backing through the door, her hands stacked with bowls and used cutlery, Joquita exited.

Alone, I ate quietly, attempting to Zen myself into inner calm, but playing with bunch of treasure hunters was like swimming with sharks. How could I do calm? I'd return to my lovely room, set the alarm, knit for an hour or two, and sleep. I absolutely would not panic, refused to panic.

But the storm brewing inside my gut felt exactly like panic.

Chapter 10

The floor of my room was awash in ocean, the currents
streaming past, rocking my bed violently while I clung to the
sheets. Water splashed against the sides, tossing bits of flotsam and
sea creatures onto the covers. First a glimmering fish, then a squid,
then a starfish. I risked peering over the side, gazing down, deep
down, through schools of silver fish, to the bottom of the ocean
where a merman beckoned for me to join him. A merman, red-
haired and smiling, wearing a gold coin suspended on his chest,
and a tail the color of emeralds embroidered with turquoise silk.
Toby, I'm coming. Hold on. I jumped overboard and kicked my
way downward, only seemed unable to make progress, as if
suspended in the currents. *Toby, Toby!*

Something beeped inside that oceanic dark, dragging me
back. I swam up from the bottom of a fretful and exhausted sleep,
breaking the surface knowing I was dreaming yet so wanting it to
be real. I just stared into the darkness, fumbling for a coherent
thought, tears rolling down my face. Something throbbed green.
Brain cells connected. I recognized my iPhone alarm.

It was 2:30 a.m. and I had to get up.

And Toby was still missing.

Shivering, I plunged my bare feet onto the cold floor.
Switching on the bedside lamp, I quickly pulled on my stealth gear
of couture black leather jeans and a black cashmere turtleneck,
compliments of my wardrobe mistress. After a few swigs of cold
coffee, I felt fortified enough to open the bedroom door and step
into the hall, my iPhone acting as flashlight.

The house breathed around me and, though it felt spooky
and atmospheric, I knew wind, not ghosts, rattled the windows and
blew drafty breaths into the hall. Wood creaked and the casements
thumped as gusts hit from the sea. I shivered, considered returning

to my room for an extra sweater, but nixed the idea in the interests of time.

My mission was simple: Explore, fix my bearings, take photos—a reconnaissance only. I'd use my phone camera to help commit navigational details to virtual memory and assess the layout of the house for future reference. In the morning, when I began work in the tower, I'd gain a daylight view to add to my repository. This much I thought I could do and, just maybe, I'd find something regarding Toby in the process. I resolutely would not look for anything regarding missing treasure. Not my concern.

Past the kitchen, down the little hall with its window facing a fringe of palms, take a right-hand turn by the grandfather clock, go down two stairs, and to the dining room, and onto the oldest part of the house. Once past the dining room, another set of stairs would lead down to the oldest wing. After that, I'd play it by ear.

The kitchen linked to the patio, which in turn connected to the path leading to the bridge. Tonight, the ornate wrought iron lamps gleamed across the deserted garden. I checked for signs of life. An eddy of leaves swirled over the flagstones between the low walls while a lone date palm swayed a frantic dance. Otherwise, no living thing moved.

The grandfather clock ticked away the seconds as I fumbled my way down the stairway and into another hall. Using my light by the windows was too risky, so I shoved it into my pocket until past the kitchen, where the house once again tunneled through interior corridors. Making a right-hand turn, I maneuvered by a spindly-legged Louis X1V-style table, past walls of seascapes, and a single tapestry hanging in dusty solitude along one side. Flashing the light across the threads, I realized that textile couldn't be more than 75 years old yet it was fraying from neglect and possible mildew. I moved on.

Thickening walls and lower doorjambs signified I'd arrived at the older part of the house. I stopped outside a doorway embedded with a hand-hewed cedar beam, flashing my light up and over the lintel, admiring the axe marks. At my feet, the floorboards widened, each plank grown in an age when Bermudan cedars expanded like redwoods amid aromatic forests.

Wyndridge's private quarters and the tower lay ahead. My heart thumped at the thought of penetrating his private domain. I had no right, but then, I reasoned, if this man had anything to do with Toby's disappearance, Wyndridge's rights were waived.

Once through that door, I'd have no good explanation for being there. I crossed the threshold, praying that Wyndridge didn't take to night strolling or nocturnal snack attacks. A small casement window set deep into the wall offered a square of pale illumination. I could hear waves crashing on the rocks but heard no other sounds or detected signs of movement.

I stilled, craning my ears. How could I go through with this? More important, what if I got caught?

A subtle shift in atmosphere weighed down around me as if the weight of ages had settled over my shoulders. I tried to shrug it off, fixing my attention down the hallway and the rooms I must investigate. A door lay at the end of the passageway flanked by two others, one on each side. Wyndridge's room with maybe a den? And where was the staircase to the tower?

I cringed at every creaky floorboard as I approached the first door on the left, which I fully expected to find locked but wasn't. It would be so much easier to believe I had no recourse but to scuttle back to my room and pretend I'd never left my bed. Instead, I stepped into a small study walled in book. To the right, a table and chair flanked a double casement window facing seaward. I took a deep breath and scanned the light across the bookcases, four floor-to-ceiling shelves liberally stacked with books and boxed sets of magazines.

It would take a whole evening or more to explore these. I stood riveted by indecision. Searching every book was impossible, not to mention probably useless. Then again, what better place to hide a clue than in a needle-in-a-haystack bookshelf or four? On the other hand, since I had only a couple of days to find something on Toby, wouldn't it be better to focus on a more fruitful strategy? What was I looking for, anyway?

In lieu of a better idea, I began taking pictures with my iPhone camera and was just about to focus in on shelf number two when a hand slapped over my mouth. The phone fell to the floor as an arm squeezed my waist, the reek of peppermint jabbing my nostrils.

"What's little Suzy doing slinking through the house at night without telling Bert, eh?" The hand tightened and I kicked back hard. He yelped as heel met shin. The mitt dropped from my mouth, the arm slackened, and I tumbled against a shelf of books. He blazed the flashlight right in my eyes.

"Bitch." He stood rubbing his shin with one hand, flashlight still aimed for my eyes with the other.

"Bastard."

"Why are you doing skulking through the house? Did you think I wouldn't know? I know everything."

"Take that thing out of my eyes," I said through my hand shield.

"What are you doing?" he asked, dropping the light.

"Same as you, obviously." I glanced out into the hall but nothing stirred. I picked up my phone before he could snatch it.

"He's not home."

"He isn't?"

"Think I'd be talking out loud if he were around?"

"Where'd he go?"

"Dunno. Saw him sail away on his yacht. Left after supper and said he wouldn't be back tonight. Told me to look after the ladies. It's just me, you, and the old woman. What do you mean, 'same as me'?"

"You know what I mean. You're looking for something, too." It was an act of desperation, my stab at strategy.

"Why do you think that?"

"Because you said as much earlier. Anyway, the question is, do we work together or against each other?" I was in a gambling mood.

"I'd much rather have you working against me, naked as a jaybird." He chuckled at his little joke. "I figured you weren't no real library lady, anyway. Too cute for that. Who are you working for?"

"I can't say. What about you?"

"Can't say, either. Why wouldn't I just kill you now and say it was an accident?"

"Because you don't need any more unexplained accidents going on, do you, Bertie? Wyndridge is spooked enough as it is."

"Peter Pan hired me as a bodyguard."

"Don't you just love irony? So," I said, turning back to the room with more bravado than I felt. "How about you holding that light up while I just finish photographing?"

"What are you looking for in here? Nothing but magazines and stuff. He hardly ever uses this room."

"I work on the principal that the more information, the better." That actually sounded impressive. I went back to work, trying to forget his leering presence while he cooperatively held his flashlight. Every time I bent down, I did my best to keep my bottom inaccessible.

"So, somebody hired you to come here and pretend to be a library lady?"

"How do you know I'm not a library lady?"

"Don't look the type but you don't look like much of a snoop, either. Just wondering what that really makes you."

I focused on a set of mariner encyclopedias, taking several shots in groups of five. "Think of it this way: How many actual librarians would be willing to do this kind of work? Not many."

"Right, so you're not a librarian or much of anything else, either. If you want, and ask me real nice, I might help you out for a while. It would make things easier for you, I promise you that." He thumbed over his shoulder. "Wyndridge's bedroom's at the end of the hall. The opening to the tower is right across the hall."

I stood up. "Show me."

I followed him out into the corridor, almost enjoying my doubly duplicitous role.

Bert tromped to the end of the hall and thumbed at the door. "Keeps it locked."

"Have you been inside?"

"What do you think, sweetheart? Getting into places is my specialty. What's yours?"

"Research. I'm the scholarly type. I have degrees."

"Big whoop. That's not helping you here, is it?"

"Once I'm in the tower it will."

That seemed to pacify him. "This lock's pretty uncomplicated, might even say unimaginative. I can pick it and presto! We're in."

"Pick away. Would he know it's been tampered with?"

"Not a chance. He doesn't believe in security systems. Spoils the mood or some such shit. He's got me, instead. You want in or not?'

"Absolutely. Pull a presto."

Bert donned gloves, pulled out a leather wallet of picking tools from his jacket pocket, and had the door unlocked in minutes. He pushed it open with his shoulder and stood aside for me to pass.

Inside, the eighteenth century had been preserved to the last detail. I roamed my phone light around the spacious room lined searching for a light switch.

"No lights."

"He takes this historical accuracy seriously doesn't he?"

"A pain in the ass. He only goes by candle power in this wing. Man's got a screw loose."

"Does he have a girlfriend? Not that the two are related."

"None that I've seen but he takes that boat of his out all the time, so who knows what or who he gets into there? If I were him, I would have stayed here and done the library lady."

"You're assuming the library lady would let herself be done."

Floor-to-ceiling bookcases lined one wall. Bert shone his flashlight across oil lamps and candelabras, brushing across a harpsichord, past the four-poster, heavily-canopied bed, and rested on a closed rolled-top desk. He must have concluded the desk to be the only place worth investigation since he didn't bother lighting anything else.

I took a step forward. "Is the desk locked?"

"Sure it is but I can open it for you. Here, hold this."

I held the flashlight while he deftly selected the right pick.

"Wow, you're good at that."

"I'm a professional."

The mechanism clicked with ease, and he rolled the walnut slats up to reveal a brass desk set complete with inkpot and quill. Other than a leather book, the wooden surface was empty.

When I reached for the book, he grabbed my arm. "Think like a thief instead of a scholar, or whatever the hell you are. Leather shows fingerprints real well. You need gloves."

I withdrew my hand. "I forgot to bring them."

"No thief comes into a place looking for something without gloves. What kind are you?" He stared at me.

"This is the first time, okay? Someone with my specific skill set combined with thieving is hard to find so, yeah, I'm in training. Will you help me do better?"

He pulled out a couple sets of surgical gloves. "Do I look like I a bloody babysitter? Here, use these." And he held out a pair of plastic surgical gloves.

"Why thanks, Bertie."

"In this line of work, always use gloves, and be very careful to put everything back exactly as you found it."

I nodded, snapping on the gloves and carefully opening the journal.

"Nothing much in there," he said, leaning over me.

"I need to be sure."

The initials WMT appeared on the current date but nothing else.

"Think that means anything?" Bert asked.

"It means something. We just don't know what." A chill shot down my spine. I needed to study this further. "Could you hold the pages flat for me while I take photos of every entry?"

"What's that going to tell you?"

"How do I know until I read it?"

He did as I asked, flattening the pages with surprising care while I used my phone to photograph every double-page spread that contained an entry. Not many did. The weekly two-year journal began the previous year, each page divided into seven days, with some entries more detailed than others. I didn't waste time reading, but remained focused on taking the shots. Once finished, Bert returned the diary to its spot. Conscious of the time, I quickly checked the drawers, noting stationery supplies, address books, calendars, and the usual desk plethora, but nothing striking.

"Did you check the room for a safe?" I asked.

"Natch, but the place is clean."

I began photographing the room while Bert closed the desk. "So," I asked, keeping my voice neutral, "did you kill Edna Smith?"

"I consider that an unfortunate accident. If she hadn't died, I wouldn't have gone back and finished her off or anything."

"Very big of you but why harm her in the first place?"

"Why'd you think, little Suzy? For someone trying to be a criminal, you're kind of clueless. Obviously, she knew too much. It was only a matter of time before she bleated to someone about all she saw in here. Couldn't have that, now could we?"

"No way." Seemed like I might be destined for the same category.

"Why are you doing that?" he wanted to know.

I had my response ready. "I'm getting an organizational snapshot of every room taken sequentially. It means photographing one wall completely, top to bottom, followed by the others, missing no square foot of space. It might take 20 individual shots to photograph every wall but it provides a visual reference I can use later on." I delivered that little spiel with enough self-importance to nearly impress myself and maybe him, too. Maybe now he'd actually believe I had a skill set.

"Do you know what we're looking for?"

He shrugged. "It's best not to ask too many questions in this business."

I shot him a quick look. "You really don't know?"

"As long as I get paid, that's all I care about. I work on a need-to-know basis. My employer gives me just enough info for me to get a job done. The main thing is he's real generous when things go right and not so much when things go wrong. Do you know the particulars?"

"This is a big one, I know that much."

"Stinking big."

"Does your boss have a lot of people working for him?"

"How the hell do I know? You think we've got ourselves a staff room?"

"Just wondering."

"If you're real nice, I'll put in a good word for you," he laughed. "Maybe you can get a job with him once we're through."

"Sweet. How about showing me the secret door?" I said, returning to the hall as he relocked the door.

"Behind there." He pointed his light to the tapestry in the hall.

Pulling back the fraying fabric revealed a solid-looking cedar door with a modern control panel set into the wall nearby.

"I thought Wyndridge didn't do electronics?"

"Made an exception for the tower. What does that tell you?"

"He's inconsistent," I replied.

"I'm thinking he's got something worth protecting up there."

"Do you have the key code?"

Bert grimaced. "No, and it pisses me right off. I have keys to every door in this house except there, even to your room, little Suzy. I'm the caretaker, after all, and I take very good care. I can tell you the old bag keeps her dentures in a teacup in the bathroom and wears the biggest, ugliest old-lady drawers I've ever seen. Hangs them up over the tub to dry, probably because she thinks it immodest to fly those flags on the line. Not worth adding to my collection, even if I had the room. The pretty little cook, now, she doesn't sleep here but she does do her wash sometimes. I—"

"Stop. I'm done. I don't need all the perverted details of your tiny life. Can you get me an extra set of all those keys?"

"Now, why would I do that?"

I backed away. "Obviously because we're on our way to being close friends."

"Not close enough."

"You and I are supposedly cooperating."

"Only because it suits me to play cat and mouse with a cute piece of pussy like you. Besides, I can unlock any room for you any time you want."

"You can't be with me 24 hours a day."

"Yes, I could."

The persistent smell of mint turned my stomach.

"Thank you but no thank you. We could work strategically: I could check out some areas while you're checking out others."

"So nice of you but, no. Bert goes everywhere you go, no exceptions. You want to work with me, you play by my rules, starting tomorrow when you gain access to the tower here. You'll share the code with me."

"Why would I do that?"

"Because you fancy staying alive."

"Seems an unfair balance of power."

"Get something straight, little Suzy: I've got power, you've got the will to stay alive. End of story."

I checked my phone for time: 4:32. I had to get some sleep. "That's it for tonight. I'm going back to my room."

He clutched my arm before I could move, leaning into my air space. "I said it would make it much easier if you were nice to me, Suzy. I'm just saying."

"And I am being nice to you, Bertie. I haven't kicked your shins a second time or anything, have I?"

"Don't forget about what happened to the real library lady." His fingers bit into my flesh. "You'll want us to be real close friends when the time comes."

I shoved him hard with my other arm until he released me, and then half-ran back to my room.

Chapter 11

The sun poured through the bottles lining my window, splashing blue puddles across the rug. Outside, the sea sparkled turquoise upon the waves, inviting me out to play, but I remained trapped and earthbound. Never had I been so isolated in such a glorious a hell.

I'd been reviewing the photos I'd taken on my phone the night before, studying every little detail of the house, including each entry in Alistair Wyndridge's journal. Nothing made an impact except one tiny doodle penciled in the margin of one of Wyndridge's datebook entries. Someone else might have passed it by as a random jotting, much like a few others I'd found scattered about the journal, but this was different. A merman, anatomically correct despite the diminutive size, was the exact copy of Toby's thumb tattoo and affected me like a stab in the gut.

I stared out to sea. Toby had not only been here but had been so familiar with Wyndridge that he'd doodled in the man's datebook. What did that mean? Backing away, I went to the bed, lifted the mattress, and carefully pulled out the cartoon tube from its hiding place. Spreading the stiff, crackling paper flat on the bed, I stared down at Toby's brilliant goldfish-colored merman in one corner before sweeping my gaze across to its counterbalancing mermaid on the opposite side. The treasure chest wrapped in the merman's tail took on a weighted meaning, as did the doubloon dangling on his brawny chest. Even here, Toby had hinted at treasure.

I recalled how he had insisted Mom and I embroider the treasure chest onto the tapestry after its completion. A joke, I thought, since he just bantered away until we capitulated. "What's an underwater dream scene without sunken treasure?" Toby had asked. "You think *Tide Weaver* should be some kind of image from the bottom of a kid's aquarium or something?" Mom countered, not as amused as I would have expected.

Thinking back, she'd seemed annoyed. Some kind of argument followed. I recalled the angry whispers, though I didn't pay much attention to them at the time. Toby pushing for his own way was common enough in our household, and one or the other of my parents usually capitulated. Once his charisma ,wit, and charm were activated, Toby was a hard man to refuse. I would be the one to give up, not him.

Did Mom, unhappy with Dad's focus on the Oak Island treasure, fear that her son might be getting involved? Was that embroidered treasure chest a sign that Toby had plunged deep into my father's obsession years ago?

I stared down at the drawing, willing it to speak, answer all my questions, preferably in my brother's own voice. Dad might know, whether he'd remember hardly being as significant as his refusal to tell me. I quickly refolded the tapestry and tucked it back in the center of the mattress, more angry now than I'd ever been. That settled it. I'd speak to Wyndridge now, back him into a corner, and demand he tell me why my brother doodled on his journal, and why he lied to the police.

But first, I owed to Max a call, at least.

I paced the room, trying to fix a signal. Despite the clear weather, my phone flat-lined. I was unable to get calls through to anyone. Instead, I tapped in a brief message to Max, expecting it to be delivered when I hit a good signal: BERT PREVIOUSLY EMPLOYED. He'd know what that meant. The rest I'd rather say in person.

Then I pocketed the phone in disgust, ready to track down Wyndridge, only a sudden thought ambushed me en route to the door. I stopped, balanced on the balls of my feet. Why would Wyndridge tell me anything? If he really had something to hide, and clearly he had, what incentive did he have to reveal all to the woman who'd just sneaked into his house? And if he had harmed my brother, why not me, too? No, Max was right about one thing: I needed subtlety. Two more days under this roof and, if I didn't find

118

anything, I'd decide on next steps. I turned around and readied myself for a day in the tower.

Wearing my jeans and a cashmere sweater, the only items in my new wardrobe suitable for work rather than seduction, I packed my bag for the day. I'd take my notebook, pen, and iPad. Though I imagined knitting a few rows in the tower as a possible soothing strategy, in the end, I reluctantly left my knitting behind.

I followed the scent of coffee through the halls to join Mrs. Wyndridge at a round table beside a window overlooking the garden. Joquita worked at the Aga stove at the far wall while Mrs. Wyndridge sat sipping her tea. "You are 10 minutes tardy."

"Do you have a stopwatch or something?" I asked while I pouring myself a mug from the urn. I took my seat across from her. Really, the situation was impossible.

She pointed to the wall clock. "The employees at the Wyndridge estate are always are mindful of the hour."

"You mean the only two employees left?"

She looked understandably shocked.

"I'm sorry, " I said, realizing how bratty that sounded. "I know that was rude but I'm just upset. I tried to get a call to my dad this morning, but couldn't. That always worries him and me. Anyway, I'll try to be on time from now on, though I don't see what difference it makes as long as I get the job done. Maybe if I could speak to your son, I could explain? Is he home?"

Joquita slid a plate of scrambled eggs before me, caught my eye, and made a warning grimace, her back blocking Mrs. Wyndridge. I nodded my understanding and picked up my fork.

"My son's whereabouts is no business of yours."

"I have to ask him something."

"Did he or did he not give you instructions?"

"He did, yes."

"Well, you've missed your opportunity, haven't you? Now, you will just have to wait." She sat across from me, watching as I shoved scrambled eggs around my plate. "Aren't our eggs good enough?"

I kept my eyes on the food. "The eggs are delicious, thanks. I'm just not that hungry. I don't usually sleep well my first night in a strange bed."

"Perhaps if you didn't drink coffee after supper, you'd sleep better," she remarked.

I glanced up at her, surprised. She spied on my dining habits? "Sorry if I caused too much bother."

"It was no bother," Joquita said, stopping near the sink. "I didn't mind at all."

"We don't usually drink coffee in this household, that's the point," Mrs. Wyndridge added.

Baffled, I smiled at Joquita. "Well, thanks for going to the trouble."

"Like I said, no problem."

I plucked a slab of toast chilling on the silver toast rack and gnawed away at it, wondering if son had spoken to mother after last night's dinner fracas and if I were now on even thinner ground. "Where's Bert this morning?" I asked, hoping to change the topic.

"He ate earlier," Mrs. W remarked, sipping her tea. "I'd refuse to dine with him. Quite unpleasant. Now, I'm going to deliver you to the tower room this morning and lock you in," the older woman announced, stirring her tea while glancing at the wall clock. "But I'll be back to release you at 12:00."

I dropped my toast onto the plate. "Nobody's going to lock me in anywhere."

Mrs. Wyndridge sat back in her chair, hands resting on the table. "Those are my instructions, for security reasons."

"That's not a term of my employment I would ever agree to, and your son certainly didn't mention anything about locking me in anywhere last night."

"Nevertheless, I insist."

I got to my feet. "No, I'm a bit claustrophobic. I won't do it." Based on this, maybe I could leave today, go back to Max, and forget about finding Toby, maybe leave it to somebody else? Only there was nobody else. I couldn't trust anyone.

"You have not been given free access to this house," Mrs. Wyndridge said, climbing laboriously to her feet.

Could they know about my nocturnal snooping last night? "Leave me the key or whatever, or I'm not going inside the tower."

We faced one another across the table while I sensed Joquita tense and listening. The old woman dropped her gaze first.

"I don't blame you," she said, finally, as she carried her plate to the counter. "If it were me, I wouldn't be locked up in there for anything in the world. I told him as much. I'll just leave you the key, then, and the code, though I warn you, I change it daily. Don't let Bert inside."

I stared in disbelief. I actually won that round? "I won't let Bert inside, I promise you that." If I had my way, he stay in the garden all day chained to a fence.

I watched as the older woman paused by the bay window, stopped, and just stared beyond with unfocused eyes.

"Is everything all right, Mrs. Wyndridge?" I asked.

"Just tired is all, nothing for you to worry about, Missy. Come on. It's nearly nine o'clock. Time for work."

I left my half-eaten breakfast, picked up my bag, and followed her down the stairs, almost bumping into her when she stopped suddenly to stare out a side window.

"Look at that useless piece of work," she said, pointing. Bert dug around the poinsettias lining the path, ripping out green leaves with yellowed ones, snapping off the occasional healthy flower head and tossing it to the side.

"He doesn't know a blessed thing about gardening. I won't let him take four steps near my rosebushes," Mrs. Wyndridge said.

"I think he hates plants."

She moved painfully to the window and rolled open the casement. "Hey, you there, Mr. Stone."

The man looked up. "Yes, ma'am?"

"I need you to fix the tap in my bathroom and be quick about it. It's leaking again."

Bert hesitated before getting to his feet. "Yes, ma'am. Right away, ma'am." He lumbered toward the house, hands covered in dirt.

"Well, don't be doing anything before going down to the shed and washing up first!" She called after him. "Are you daft?"

He stopped. "The kitchen sink is closer."

"I don't care how close it is. I won't be having you tracking in mud all over the house."

Bert glared briefly before loping down the path out of view. Whether by deliberation or happy coincidence, he would now be nowhere near the tower when I entered. Relief loosened the knots in my shoulders.

"That man has no more sense than God gave geese. Come with me, young woman."

She led me in the same direction I'd taken the night before, along the main corridor and into the long hall, stopping before the tower door with its impressive key code panel. "Go through there and take the staircase straight up. The library's on the top floor with nothing much along the way. That upper door's locked, too, but the older key will open that. You'll need a code for this one, however."

She reached into her pocket and passed over a brass ring clinking with two keys, one modern , one an ornate antique. "I have the other set on my key fob here." She dangled a clutch of keys on a tacky keychain fashioned like a pair of glittery flip-flops. "The code is 1923, the year my Henry was born, Henry being Alistair's father and a fine man who knew better than I how to manage his sons. I change between five codes. I'll give you the new one tomorrow. First you tap in the numbers, then use the key. Open it while I watch. The thing can be tricky sometimes."

I complied, first punching in the code, and then inserting the key. It took four attempts before something clicked and the door swung open.

"There's a light switch on the left. Best turn it on before you shut the door behind you or you'll be stuck in the dark. It locks by itself. The first window is a ways up the steps. Mind those, too. They're as narrow as the day they were built and just as steep. You can thank Edna Smith for the lamps up there. He didn't want the place wired but she insisted. She was a good woman." The emphasis implied that I wasn't, which, under the circumstances, I thought fair.

She turned to shuffle back the way she had come.

"Wait. Please."

She turned.

"When does he return?"

"Why do you need to know?"

"Because I'm working for him and have questions."

"Do as you're told and wait until he comes to you. When he's writing, this world and everybody in it ceases to exist. Lunch will be ready at twelve o'clock. Find your way back to the kitchen a few minutes before."

"Yes, of course." Suddenly I didn't want to enter that tower for anything in the world. "What's it like inside? Have you been?"

"Of course, but long ago when my legs still carried me. Henry first took me here when I arrived as a young bride so long ago. It seemed so romantic then, but now it's old and dreary, like you'd expect. Henry would never have allowed things to fall apart. He'd do what had to be done, make no mistake about it. These days we can't even keep the place clean. Is that what you wanted to hear? Get to work now. I'll be taking a lie-down. Mind that you be in the kitchen at twelve sharp for lunch or there'll be nothing else until tea."

I watched her slow progress down the hall before pushing open the door and stepping inside. An assault of musty odors trapped in shadows hit my sinuses. I braced the door ajar long enough to find the light switch which, thankfully, was only a hand span away. A single bulb dangling from a cable illuminated a low-ceiling square room with a set of stairs marching upward into the dark. I heard the lock slide into place as the door banged shut behind me.

I knew I wasn't going to like this place. Maybe a rug and a couple of paintings might elevate the stark stone interior, but the wash of white paint didn't help a thing. A small door sat tucked beneath the stairwell straight ahead. I walked over, ducked my head, and stepped under the curving stairs, uneasy to be wedged inside what felt like a pocket of shadow. Though locked, the door rattled easily in my hand as though it saw plenty of use. I guessed it must go down to a basement somewhere.

Backing away, I studied the tower landing again, recognizing similarities between this structure and the British-built military forts back in Halifax—the same regimented chunks of stone stacked one atop the other, utilizing whatever natural resources lay nearby, granite for Halifax, coral stone here. The mark of Sir John Ashley Wyndridge, the naval engineer, was in full evidence. This entrance had probably originally served for storage, with the living quarters upstairs.

The stairs. I eyed them curving up and out of sight, a structure designed to hug the outside wall, with a steep drop straight to the floor, the floor of the second landing acting as ceiling to the first. Some earlier Wyndridge had had the foresight to construct a wire-rope railing on one side for a little support en route to the first landing, after which the walls appeared to close in around the stairs.

I flung my bag midway over my back for balance and took the first step. Wouldn't constructing a tower like this indicate that someone had something to defend? But back then, I reasoned, times were hard, pirates abundant, making a tower structure more commonplace, especially as a watchtower. I doubted I'd find any clue to Toby's whereabouts up here but figured there might be plenty of interesting material for a treasure seeker.

Not that I was there to find treasure. But didn't I need to go through the motions as Wyndridge's hireling for appearance's sake? Snooping around the house after hours seemed much more promising, providing I could ditch Bert and avoid detection.

The stone steps were steep but regular with the exception of the tenth tread from the bottom, which had been cut twice as high as the rest. I was forced to hoist myself up. Two steps more and I reached the first landing. Daylight washed bleary light through a narrow glass mullioned window set deep into the stone. I leaned against the sill, catching my breath, trying to peer through the salt-scummed glass. Impossible, and the latch had rusted shut, too. Forget that. Turning, I forced myself to move. I still had a long way to go.

One hundred and fifty-five more steps followed before I arrived at the top. I sank to my haunches against a thick wooden door while fumbling for the key, which slid easily into the mechanism, allowing me to shove the door open with my shoulder. Rather than have the weighted door slam shut behind me, I propped it open with my carpet bag after removing my iPad.

I entered a gloomy stone room with a high ceiling hidden in shadows overhead. Books, boxes, and folders lined three walls, from the floor to within a few feet of the ceiling beams, with a large wooden map cabinet centering the space. A single desk had been positioned below the double casement windows on the opposite side, the only wall minus shelves and the sole source of natural light.

The space reeked of mildew as if a million microorganisms were partying among the piles. Someone, probably Edna, had begun the monumental job of cataloguing but had stopped, leaving a few shelves marching upright and orderly while most lounged in disarray. Other shelves seemed arranged by size, maybe date, and possibly color, with an entire wall of boxes and Princeton files. One look overwhelmed me. This was more storage heap than library.

Setting my iPad on the map cabinet, I tried to fix a cell signal with my phone. No luck. The walls were too thick. Repocketing the phone, I navigated around to the desk and leaned over it to study the view. One casement had been replaced and seemed relatively new, while the other retained its original blurry glass. From the tower's good "eye," I could see past the cove and straight out to sea, the vantage commanding a breathtaking view of Bermuda coastline.

I glanced down to the desk, where a fresh pad of lined paper sat in the middle of a green blotter with a list neatly written in a flourishing hand. I switched on the desk lamp and studied the pen and ink script. His instructions were clear. I was to continue classifying the shelf labeled "A" indicated by a sticky note, weed the pile to the left of the desk, which a quick glance revealed to be box of papers in various states of decay, and classify the jumble of mixed papers sitting in another box on the right. These instructions accompanied a report hand-printed and signed by Edna, which outlined her efforts to date, plus endless recommendations in point form.

Below the pad lay both my contract and confidentiality agreement, printed and described in legal terms with a Hamilton Law Firm's letterhead. I scanned the documents to check the legal terminology before setting them down with the list. I had no plans on doing anything so named and, since Wyndridge wasn't standing over me insisting, I wouldn't sign anything, either.

I had a day to pass up here before I could resume exploring in the house that night. How much of value might Wyndridge hide in this paper jungle? Clues to the supposedly buried treasure? It struck me as far too obvious. Still, it wouldn't hurt to give a sample of those boxes a spot-check while I was there. If nothing else, it would satisfy my curiosity and fill in time. Maybe I'd even make it look like I was doing organizational work before the day was done.

Back at the map cabinet, I switched on the room's only other light and pulled out each drawer, finding nautical charts and old maps, including a few old specimens dating from the seventeen hundreds. In the top drawer, a large diagram of the tower had been executed in pen and ink on parchment thick enough to survive the assault of time and humidity, since it appeared to be in excellent condition.

Pulling the drawer out fully, I scrutinized the drawing under the light of my iPad. It looked to be an old blueprint. Lifting the corner, I found several others of similar vintage, each by the same hand, signed JAW. One, which looked to be a master schematic, indicated an extensive tunnel and cave system extending below the tower, possibly linking up to that little door I'd seen below. This would interest Max and Noel, not that I planned on showing it to them any time soon. On the other hand, supposing Toby had gone down there? He would have investigated those cave warrens if he was on the hunt for something and maybe even if he wasn't, since he loved anything secretive and potentially dangerous. Using the scanning application on my iPad to commit them all into virtual memory for closer study later.

I leaned against the cabinet, fighting the tremor strumming my body. I had a bad feeling. Toby had been here; Toby had found something or knew something or did something. I just knew that without knowing how. My brother had been deeply interested in this house, this place, and the secret Wyndridge reportedly sequestered here, but I didn't understand why. Not to steal, surely. My brother wasn't a thief. He'd find all this interesting as a mystery, a kind of real-life game; but picturing him involved in a theft of this magnitude? No way. Maybe he tailed along with Max and company on a lark and maybe discovered something he shouldn't have. I shoved the hair from my eyes. Hell, what was I going to do?

A geriatric library stair sagged against the far wall. I swung it onto its wheels and into position over one shelf, more as a way to work off nervous energy than anything else. After giving the ladder a good shake, I climbed the creaking steps into the gloom. The contraption only took me about six feet up, leaving at least six more out of reach overhead. My head spun as I gazed up at boxes stacked one on top of the other, looking as though they hadn't been disturbed in years.

The first box I dropped onto the cabinet below consisted of old Bermudan newspapers, circa 1856 -1900, so fragile and yellowed that they were all but illegible. Touching them would only hasten their demise, so I set them aside. The next four boxes contained mismatched jumbles of clippings from magazines and periodicals in no particular order with no connecting theme. At least five wads wrapped in ribbons were recipes for everything from hog hock stews to biscuits written by past Wyndridge cooks. Wiping my hands in disgust, I returned the boxes to their spaces while sneezing repeatedly.

One volume of botanical drawings, circa 1600, and a leather-covered compendium of all known chemical substances, dated 1714, had been wedged between the boxes. Edna would have eventually found these and added them to the list of items worth cataloguing and, hence, selling. I set them on top of the map cabinet, reluctant to return them to that mess.

Two hours later, I stood tired, smeared with dust, and disgusted. Some of the things I encountered were already too far gone to be valuable. Though not a document expert, I did hold a passing interest in protecting the old and rotting. But the mold nailed my lungs. Wheezing, I checked my watch: eleven o'clock. Only one hour left before lunch. I doubted I could remain up here much longer, but if I had to, I might as well stay busy.

Intending to make only one final foray into the gloom, I rolled the ladder a few degrees west and began climbing, the wooden slats groaning beneath my feet. Overhead, I could just see the edge of something sticking out from the very top of the shelving. It was a box unlike all the others, a container made of wood. People might store something of value more readily in wood than cardboard, which required further investigation. Only I couldn't reach it even when balanced on the ladder's uppermost rung.

On the other hand, if I used the ruler—a nice, long, old-fashioned yardstick with metal edges I'd found on the floor—to lever the thing forward, I could pull it into my hands as long as I kept my body weight braced against the stacks. It seemed so simple. I took one more step up, as far as I could go without losing the stair's handgrip, and stretched up and out to slip the edge of the stick under the box, my left hand gripping the handrail. No luck. The box remained jammed. I grew more aggressive by propping one leg over the side of the ladder until I could apply my other foot to the edge of the shelf for leverage. The shelf lurched away from the wall, the whole thing falling backward, with me flailing my arms trying to rebalance everything.

I had time enough to imagine death by shelving and being found by Wyndridge in a hideous tangle, when the bottom end of the ladder banged into the map cabinet and catapulted me over the top. I landed on my back amid a bundle of newspapers as the shelf rained books, papers, and storage boxes down over me.

I lay in a winded heap. The light had gone out and my brain registered pain, but I couldn't tell from where. I heaved breath back into my lungs and propped myself up on my elbows. After a fit of sneezing, I tested a few body parts, finding my leg bruised, not broken. Overhead, the shelf remained propped over the cabinet, angling over my body in an ominous mass of wood. I crawled out from under the mess and managed to stand. Ouch. Damn.

What a disaster. The map cabinet lay buried under heaps of paper, with the shelf leaning against it in an unstable angle. In the thin light, I saw that the shelf's one bottom edge had collapsed with most of the weight resting on a stump of splintered wood. Leaning my shoulder into it, I managed to shove it back against the wall where it rested as if ready to pivot at the slightest nudge. As a precautionary measure, I stacked a few books in front of it for stabilization.

I wiped the hair from my eyes and moaned. Definitely a violation of Wyndridge's snooping rules. He'd probably fire me on the spot. He'd eject me soon enough if I asked about Toby, which I might risk as soon as he returned. What did I have to lose that I hadn't already lost?

I picked up a few random pieces unloosed in the deluge, including a list of weights and measures, circa 1662. Odd pieces emerged, such as notes to a servant requesting certain dishes for dinner, a recipe for pickled hog hocks, a ship's supplies list. The rest of the tower contents appeared to be nothing more than family sediment accumulated across the ages with a few interesting artifacts in between.

I rooted through the debris for the box, finding it crushed under a hefty unabridged dictionary. Carrying the pieces over to the window, I loosely reconstructed an old lap desk about two feet wide and six inches deep with a warped lid. Inside, two inkwells flanked a narrow trough that still held a single quill pen and a yellowed wad of deteriorating paper stuffed in the cavity. I gently explored under the paper and lifted the trough until I found a clump of sealing wax solidified on the edge of a single piece of paper. A note, I realized. No, a list.

Holding the deteriorating paper by the glob of sealing wax, I felt the distinctive energy of the script emerging through the blotches and blurred ink. John Ashley Wyndridge signed the page after describing the contents of a hold, mostly illegible but for the words "10 chests of igote...." The script trailed away into mildew feasts, blackened splotches, and smeared ink. I dropped the thing as if it burned my fingers—proof of treasure I wanted no part of.

I leaned against the window, fighting panic. Everything I'd discovered today was weighty with significance for the treasure seekers but not for me. I would love nothing more than to view something that rare with my own eyes, but this quest was tainted with loss, my loss. I wanted no part of any of it. I just wanted Toby back. To take or photograph any of these documents, to assist Max in any way, would only make me complicit in his theft. I was not here for that. On the other hand, perhaps something might serve as leverage. Supposing I needed a bargaining chip to find the truth or even to save my neck? I sat my iPad on the desk, replaced the carpet bag with a large book to prop open the door, and headed for the stairs, resigned to return that afternoon to tidy the mess, take pictures, and never return again.

Chapter 12

I reached the kitchen just as Mrs. Wyndridge was heading to her room, a cup of tea grasped in her fingers. "What happened to you?" She looked me up and down. "I waited until just 15 minutes past the hour but you were tardy, as usual," she said. "You look as though disaster befell you."

"Sorry." I had made some attempt to tidy myself but knew I wasn't much improved. "I had a little accident in the tower. A shelf toppled down on top of me. That place is like a train wreck. You should see it: piles moldering away, heaps of litter everywhere, and though Edna made a monumental effort to restore order, it's a huge job. And a fire hazard," I added, "Both unhealthy and unsafe," the latter phrase included just a touch of righteous indignation.

She studied me for a moment before nodding. "I keep telling him the whole lot should be carted out and dealt with somewhere else. I left you a sandwich. Tuna. We don't eat fancy these days. I'm just going to watch the telly for a while and maybe take a nap. I'll leave you to it then. Mind that you work extra time to make up for your lateness." She made for the door, her green cotton frock still wrapped by an apron.

"Is Mr. Wyndridge back yet?"

"No, he is not," she scolded. "He probably wouldn't return until tomorrow. He's writing. Now, eat your lunch."

In an instant, I was at her side, taking the cup out of her hand. "Here, let me just carry this to your room for you—your sweater too." I lifted the green cardigan from over her arm.

"I don't need your help, Missy."

"That's what my Dad keeps saying." Presumably Susan Waverley had a father, too. "But we can all use a hand once in a while."

"How old is your father?"

"Eighty-two."

"Well, I'm older than him by a few years, but have all my faculties and don't you forget it."

I thought of how Dad was losing his. It broke my heart, but I shoved those thoughts out of my mind along with the anxiety of not speaking with him this morning. He'd be so worried. Meanwhile, I helped her to her room, a spacious master suite with an uninhibited sea view, resolved to call him before I did anything more. Setting the teacup by her chair, I turned on the television at her direction.

"Is Bert around?" I asked before leaving.

"He is not. I sent him to town to fill my grocery list. He should be gone for most of the afternoon. You can thank me for that."

I smiled and shut the door, leaving her tuned into Coronation Street reruns.

Back in the kitchen, I scooped up the tuna sandwich from the plate, downed a full glass of water, and headed outside, letting the wind play with my hair. It took several attempts to fix a signal but finally I succeeded. The phone rang in my ear as I followed the path.

The garden was a series of small areas sheltered behind either low walls or hedges which, in combination, formed a long winding greenbelt following the side of house towards the oceanfront. Date palms, frangipani, and ornamental shrubbery wove into a lush green ribbon sprinkled with spots of color between the house and the cliff edge. The sea-facing front garden opened up to a swathe of lawn with marble benches and the occasional table-and-sun-umbrella combo.

I could just see the step-roofed gardener's cottage buried in bougainvillea over to the right. The phone rang unanswered in my ear. Dad didn't do answering machines, but I vaguely remembered today was a doctor's appointment to which Bertha had kindly agreed to escort him. Devouring the rest of the sandwich, I brushed the crumbs from my sweater and approached Bert's cottage. While the cat's away...

The cottage reminded me of the gatehouse at Astwood Cottages with the same white stepped roof and candy pink exterior.

A casement window had been rolled open to let in the air. I pushed back the hibiscus blocking the window and peered inside. No one home. Next, I tried the door, which opened easily in my hand. I cautiously stepped inside, ready with an excuse should Bert suddenly come roaring out of the closet. He didn't. I entered a tiny lounge with a television, a couch and a chair. Magazines and newspapers fanned across the low coffee table, positioned like displays in a hotel lobby, if hotels offered *Playboy*, *Hustler,* and the *London Times*. A single coffee mug sat on its coaster with an empty bag of chips folded neatly into quarters nearby.

The tiny kitchen continued the neatnik theme with stacks of drying dishes and a fry pan soaking in the sink. The bathroom, still faintly damp from a shower earlier that morning, revealed towels neatly hanging and a single leather shaving kit on the counter. In the bedroom, I stepped through the reek of industrial-strength men's cologne riding heavily over a note of mint, while heading for a suitcase on the bed. The suitcase, a standard hard-sided version, yawned open on the made bed, as if the owner had been searching for something in a hurry.

I stepped forward, noting the laundered boxing shorts stacked to one side on the bedcover —ugh, checked and striped patterns— with five packaged white shirts on the other. Bert must have been looking for something, too rushed to replace shirts and shorts back into the case. Clearly he stayed packed when he traveled rather than depositing his clothes in drawers or closets, which meant what? That he was prepared for a hasty retreat?

The thought of touching anything turned my stomach but I had to find out who he worked for. I slipped my hand into the case and felt around the tidy folds, not sure what I was looking for. Maybe a notebook or a letter from a boss? Everything incriminating probably resided on a laptop or cell phone, neither of which he left lying around. Yet, at the very bottom of the suitcase, flush against the side pocket, my fingers touched something hard. I tried lifting it out, but it felt as if it had been strapped to the inside. I tugged and pulled, nearly yanking the case right off the bed but ended up holding a holstered gun ,belt straps dangling over my hand.

I felt faint. A gun. I stood holding my arm outstretched as if it might bite me. I had to put it back, but had Bert packed it with the belt wrapped around the holster right to left or left to right? He'd know! He'd know I'd been in here rooting through his stuff. That was fine for him, but not for me. In my agitation, I must have nudged the case with my thigh because it slipped sideways off the bed to the floor, dumping the contents everywhere.

I stood rigid in fear. Now what? I'd never get everything back in order, and if I even tried, he'd know. Who but me would be such a klutz? Best leave it. Maybe he'd think the suitcase fell on its own accord. But what about the gun? I couldn't just leave it, too. Wouldn't that be like saying: *Here I just rifled through your belongings so just shoot me.* I made for the door, the gun wedged under my arm, straps dangling.

Outside, I jogged past a hibiscus hedge and across a patch of grass to where a moon gate opened onto the cliff and the cove below. A steep stairway carved into the natural rock plunged down. Beyond the little cove, the crash of waves on reef outlined the natural barrier between the Atlantic and the house.

All I needed to do was get midway down so I could toss the gun into the surf. More steps, oh how I hated steps! These were unnervingly treacherous despite the iron railing bracing one side. I began climbing down carefully, one hand clutching the rail, trying to keep the gun from slipping from under my arm, until it occurred to me that fastening the thing to my body with the holster belt made more sense. Perched on a step, I buckled the thing over one shoulder, leaving both hands free, and continued my descent.

Waves rolled against the cliffs below and seabirds wheeled overhead, as the wind whipped my hair and the sun bore into my eyes. Dizziness brought me to a halt halfway down. If I peered down over the stairs far enough, I could just see the edge of a jetty but not much else. Not a good place for tossing firearms. I continued down until a jingling sound disrupted my concentration. My phone alert. Lowering myself back to sitting, I plucked my phone from my pocket, and blinked at the text YARN MAVEN DOWN. Shielding my eyes with one hand, I scanned the horizon. Noel had to be watching me.

I almost leapt down the rest of the stairs, oblivious to my bruises, arriving at a wooden jetty designed as both dock and swimming platform. I peered over the edge. The water wasn't deep enough for gun disposal here, either. A small boathouse sat on one end with metal stairs descending into the water at the other. No Noel. The cliffs formed a stark vertical wall overhead . Nobody could see me from the house; nobody could see me from the water. Where the hell was he?

The boathouse sat with its wide double doors thrown open to the sea. I unlatched the side door and stepped into a relatively new peaked-roof shed. A wooden dinghy rocked in its berth with room for maybe three more. No pungent scent of motor oil or the gasoline I associated with boathouses greeted my nose. Paddles and life vests lined one wall with wetsuits, tanks, masks, regulators, and other diving accessories, on racks behind me.

I inspected the diving gear. Everything looked in good condition, if a bit dated, the tanks well-maintained, even full of oxygen, as if in wait for the next diver. Wetsuits in all sizes. Why so many suits for one, maybe two people? I stroked the sleeve of one newer green neoprene suit as if my brother's arm had just been there. He loved that color. I felt his presence so intensely at that moment, it brought me dangerously close to tears.

"My God, you're armed!"

I swung around so quickly I nearly toppled backward into the water. "Noel."

He stood on the other side of the berth, dripping in a black wetsuit, hair slicked back from his face, the imprint of a mask still visible on his cheeks. He must have entered through the sea door.

"You look almost dangerous," he remarked.

"Not as much as you. You're diving?" I asked stupidly.

"You're packing a gun?"

I glanced down at the holster. "I found it hidden in Bert's cottage and, on impulse, decided to dispose of it in case he plans to shoot someone, like me. I'm going to throw it into the sea."

He shook his head. "You'd better get a grip of those impulses of yours in case they get you killed. When Bert finds it missing, he's going to be furious."

And yet, he seemed more amused than concerned.

"Maybe I should keep it in self-defense." I patted the gun.

"Maybe you should, or you could give it to me and I'll take care of it for you."

"No thanks. What are you looking for underwater?"

He walked around the edge towards me, holding flippers in one hand, mask apparatus in the other. I couldn't see tanks. "Exploring. That's what I'm here for, same as you."

"Only you know specifics, which I don't. Do you expect to find sunken treasure in the cove?"

"You know the treasure's elsewhere."

"The only things I know, or even trust, are whatever I find out on my own. Everything and everybody are suspect."

"Now you're learning."

"Thanks for the patronizing compliment. Try answering a question for once: What are you diving for?" I turned away, shoved the hair from my eyes, and turned back to him, stabbing my finger in the air between us. "Why aren't you telling me what you know? Aren't we supposed to be on the same team?"

"You're on the legal side, remember? Because half of what I know is tied up with a planned treasure heist. Do you really want to be on my team?"

"Maybe, it means finding Toby."

"That's a bloody conundrum if I ever heard one! You can't play it both ways."

"I'm trying to find my brother. Don't you get that?"

He stepped closer until he was towering over me. "You say you don't want any part of the treasure hunt, that you're not interested in the illegalities of a heist, so accept that Max and I are protecting you from exactly that. Just find something useful and we'll take it from there. This is far too dangerous for you. You're not prepared."

I wanted to both kiss him and kick him in the groin. "Then make me prepared. Tell me exactly what you want me to find? Be specific."

"A diagram or a sketch of the Wyndridge estate would be helpful. John Ashley was a naval engineer, and it follows that he'd keep meticulous notes, blueprints, and diagrams. They've got to be somewhere."

"And how would this help to find Toby?"

"Maybe Toby went exploring on his own, playing it solo instead of working with us. Maybe he had an accident, or maybe Wyndridge found out what he was up to and did something to him.

Either way, we need full access to the property to trace his path. Did you find anything in the tower?"

"Nothing but old recipes and plenty of mold."

"Keep looking. I'm going back to the water." He swung around and padded back to the sea door to pull on his flippers. I followed behind him.

"Wait. Tell me what you expect to find out there."

He sat on the edge, pulling on his flippers, after which he pulled his mask down, shrugged on the tanks he'd hooked on the edge of the jetty, and began tightening the belt at his waist, all without speaking. In a second, he had checked his regulator, waved, and flipped backward into the water. He remained visible a few minutes longer before disappearing into the depths.

I scrambled back into the boathouse and nabbed a set of binoculars I'd seen hanging inside. Moments later, I had them focused on the cove. Minutes passed with nothing showing until I spied a bob of a head and flash of a tank at the far end of the cove.

Bastard.

Chapter 13

In seconds, I was back inside the boathouse, pawing through the wetsuits looking for one sized small to medium. The one-pieces were all too large, though I found an aged black long-sleeved jacket that fit. Peeling off my sweater and jeans, socks and shoes, I tried it on, managing to zip it up over my bra. The leggings all looked far too long and I didn't have time to try them all on. That left me no option to dive with nothing but my silk bikinis on my bottom half while trusting the jacket to stay extended over my hips. Only fish would see me, anyway.

I found a full set of double oxygen tanks and selected a regulator, choosing one with primary and secondary demand valves, a submersible pressure gauge, and low-pressure hose. I was about to break every rule ever learned about diving: Never dive alone; always use your own equipment, or at least that which had been checked by a PADI regulation diving office, and--never dive alone. That last one bore repeating, since that point among all others jangled my warning systems. In my defence, I wasn't planning a deep sea dive or a long one so, therefore, I reasoned, I'd be fine.

I tucked my socks and sneakers against the wall, shoving my phone into the toe of one shoe for safekeeping, and piling my clothes on top. Next, I took a pair of flippers in my size, tried on a face mask, and a belt weight from the shelf, tossing everything to the bottom of the boat, with the gun placed under the boat seat.

By the time I had punted out of the boathouse, the sun burned high and bright, making me visible should anyone glance out the window above. Only, I figured, with Bert off shopping for the afternoon and Mrs. Wyndridge sleeping, I had three or four undetected hours in which to discover Noel's whereabouts. Of course, I'd lost sight of him by then, but knew the direction to take: straight for the far cliffs on the other side of the cove.

On the water again brought joy, joy as if I'd returned to my element after a long, cold hiatus. The water granted me strength and confidence again. Though I hadn't oiled my rowing muscles for a few months, they woke up under the familiar activity and powered me through the rising chop. Blissfully happy for even a few seconds was more than I'd expected that day or any time soon.

The surrounding cliffs formed a near-perfect arc around the Wyndridge promontory, with only a narrow opening between the headlands leading to the sea. All around, light, translucent turquoise shone while, seaward, the ocean brewed a deep moody teal flecked with foam. Foam boils indicated reefs, of which plenty encircled the cove and hugged the coastline. Halfway across the cove, I paused, checked the house for signs of observation, and slipped the gun overboard. Looking up after watching it sink like a sluggish octopus, belts trailing behind, I saw a deep gap in the encroaching cliff—a cave, a very large cave. Pushing harder against the oars, I powered myself forward.

As I approached the cliffs, reefs broke the surface in jagged piles of coral, the sea barely covering the brilliant colonies. Low tide. My muscles struggled against the broken surf as I aimed the boat closer to the cave ahead. A channel between two reefs offered enough depth to accommodate a small boat like mine. The outgoing tide rushed between the reef ledges, funneling through the rock spars and pushing me diagonally towards the cliff. Though the sea breathed out, I wanted in. I needed to ride the next wave through the channel by keeping the boat straight and nosed forward, avoiding scraping against the reefs. I'd done it countless times before, though usually heading for a beach rather than a cave, and not with so much living coral to protect in the process.

Shoulders complaining now, I rode the bronco sea on its next forward wash until it propelled me into the cave. The roof rose thirty or more feet overhead and had to be twenty feet wide, while the walls magnified the sound of wave slapping stone. Seaweed stranded down from the ceiling festooned with barnacles and starfish. I peered ahead into the deep, narrowing throat, sure that I caught the flash of a light back there.

I used my thighs to stabilize myself and the oars to shove the boat away from the walls as the boat rode the sea deeper into the cave. Ahead, I saw the back wall looming, awash with foam, with the next big tidal exhale bound to fling me right against it. I powered the oars hard down to keep riding the surf rather than be ruled by it while scanning the area for Noel.

I saw that light, but where was he? I'd have to turn the boat around somehow or punt myself backward to exit but then I spied a large opening to my left. A secondary cave! I punted the boat inside, the oars levering me forward until the boat slid around a corner and into calmer waters. I just sat for a moment catching my breath. A pale wash of light illuminated a small area, maybe twelve feet wide and eight feet tall, rimmed with two deep, seaweed-strewn ledges.

An inflatable boat rocked from its mooring on one side. On the ledge beside it, an extra set of oxygen tanks and a black bag had been deposited. I maneuvered the dinghy to the wall opposite the *Zodiac*, hooked the rope around a rock, and leaped onto a ledge about a foot wide. Damn. I needed a lamp. Why hadn't I thought of that? I surveyed the equipment on the opposite wall. No lamp. At my feet, a ribbon of bubbles broke surface. I traced them, moving along one side as if looking for something.

Back in the dinghy, my legs braced against the rocking, I shrugged on the tanks, donned my mask, and checked the regulator. Next, I added the weight belt, removing two weights to better adjust to my body mass, and pulled on my flippers. Perching on the dinghy's side and holding the mouthpiece firmly to my face, I tipped backward into the water.

Blessed, blessed ocean. It embraced me as I twisted my body around and kicked deeper down. The cave floor rose up to meet me with coral-covered stone and enough light that I could make out parrot fish pecking away at the walls and glimpse darting purple wrasses on the cave floor. A thin beam shone like a pilot light in the darkness to my right. Noel must be wearing a mask lamp. I paddled towards him, keeping him in my sights until the light unexpectedly disappeared. I kicked faster.

The cave floor deepened. Daylight receded completely after about twenty feet. If Noel knew I was behind him, he didn't let on. His light revealed enough for me to navigate by, paddling steadily on until a black bite of darkness opening in the cliff wall ahead. A tunnel. He powered into it without hesitation, making me think he must have known of its existence.

I followed him in, pushing back my fear of dark, enclosed spaces. Soon he'd know someone followed him, since my air bubbles were about to mingle with his. I decided to announce my presence.

At first, the opening was wide enough for two to swim side by side, so I tried moving up beside him. He powered himself faster forward, leaving me behind. Now the tunnel narrowed with room for only single file. I remembered why I hated cave diving — the oppression of water and stone pressing in from all directions. Swimming blind with the light mostly blocked by Noel's body, I fought panic yet remained fixed on the pale illumination until suddenly the tunnel widened into a much larger space. Noel kicked upward and I followed.

We broke surface inside a large chamber, a kind of natural well with a steep wall of rock encircling a pool about 25 feet in diameter. Overhead, a ceiling covered in barnacles indicated it would fill with tide.

"What the hell are you doing following me?" he asked, removing his mouthpiece.

I pulled out mine. "Because I'm going to get answers one way or the other. You knew about this cave."

"I had a hunch."

"Stop lying. Toby's been here."

Noel turned full circle, using his mask light to scope out the space. A small recess jumped into view in the light.

"Wait here," he called.

"Don't tell me to wait."

But he swam to the edge and hauled himself up in one fluid movement and ducked inside the opening, his light bopping up and down before vanishing completely. That left me in total darkness. I hated this. It was blacker than black and freezing. I felt like a child locked in a closet with lurking monsters. Only, this was the sea, I reminded myself. The monsters were mine. After what felt like ages, his light flickered out of the opening and he beckoned me over.

"Take off your flippers. We'll leave them here with the tanks," he called.

In a minute, I had yanked off my flippers to clamber up beside him. Crouching on a cramped ledge with teeth rattling, I removed my tanks. Noel took them and wedged both air tanks into a barnacle-crusted opening along with the flippers. "That should hold until the tide rises."

"That won't be long. The tide's turning now."

"Let's hurry, then."

"How deep does it go?"

"Up to another cavern, " he said, pointing behind him. "There's a tide pool in the tunnel, so we know the sea comes at least that far. Come on, we'd better hurry."

I cursed myself for the lack of wetsuit leggings when we descended the tunnel. After scraping along on hands and knees for about three feet, we finally had enough room to stand up, but only long enough to slide ankle-deep into a slimy pool. The tunnel snaked around tide-smoothed rocks but luckily extended no more than 20 feet before widening into a huge chamber.

Noel gripped my arm to keep me from tumbling forward and hung on to me as he removed his mask. Swinging the light back and forth revealed a forest of stalactites and stalagmites stretching out of sight. Deep pools glimmered still and crystalline, with one large basin curving away into the darkness at my feet.

"Holly crow," I said.

"Aptly put."

Glinting pools and pink-amber stalagmites transfixed me until I caught the glimpse of something red flash in the passing light. "Wait." I caught his wrist, aiming the mask lamp on the opposite wall. We stood in silence, gazing at an arrow-like mark painted in red across the pool.

"A sign," Noel remarked.

"A bit obvious, isn't it? Almost like 'X marks the spot'?"

"Not unusual for the time period."

"Even so."

"There must be a way down here from the house. John Ashley would require easy access to his loot over the decades. I figured he'd been using it as his own little bank."

I thought of the diagrams. "Let's get back. The tide's rising. Lead the way."

I ducked back into the tunnel behind him, stumbling through the pool more carelessly now that the sea was already streaming in.

"Hurry up!" he called over his shoulder.

"I'm hurrying!"

When the water reached my hips, Noel grabbed my hand and tugged me along. I was about protest when his light went out. Fear stabbed my gut.

Noel cursed.

"Didn't you bring a spare?" I asked.

"In my boat. Come on. If we hurry, we should still be able to find our way out."

"We'd have better luck in the cavern," I called.

"Doubt that. We're going to the boat. Hold your breath!"

Ahead, the tunnel narrowed into the main pool. I tried arguing there'd be less risk of drowning back in the caverns, but Noel had already shoved me onto my hands and knees ahead of him and was pushing me into the incoming tide. Holding my breath, I kicked forward, using my arms as leverage against the water's force. My heart banged violently. I blocked out thoughts of drowning, my only thought being to reach air.

We broke into dark space in the main pool. I kicked up through the rush of water, breaking the surface before my lungs exploded. Black, black, everywhere. I reached out and caught a flipper that nudged my face. "Noel?" I called out. "This one's already flooded!"

I listened in the sloshing darkness for the sound of him breaking the surface. It took far too long.

"Phoebe?"

"Here!"

"Get the tanks!"

Everything churned in darkness. I could hear, not see, metal banging against the cave walls. Swimming toward the sound, I reached one set of floating canisters at the same time as Noel. His hand squeezed mine in the darkness. "I'll help you put it on," he said.

"What about yours?"

"I'll get it."

"Get your own tanks and take this flipper. It's not mine." He didn't answer, being too intent on fastening the tanks to my back, a tricky business in the water. I could hear metal still clanging against the cave wall. "Get the other set! We don't have time!"

"You go on ahead and I'll join you. Just push against the current."

"I'll wait."

"Don't be an ass," he called. "I'll be right behind you!"

The cave roof was no more than a foot away by then, with no time to look for flippers. I dove down, kicking awkwardly with one flipper, pushing against the streaming current, my eyes closed against darkness, sea, and panic.

Adrenalin fuelled me. I didn't think about the abyss, the surging water, or the narrow tunnel. I thought about life and how I wanted to stay a part of it. I thought about Dad sitting home in Nova Scotia and how I could not have him lose another child.

My tanks scraped against the rock while the water pushed against me, trying to force me backward. The screaming in my head could be a battle cry. Damned if I would die like this! The tide fought me hard and I fought back, grasping the sides of the tunnel at its narrowest point and pushing myself on.

Minutes felt like hours before I broke into the sea cave. Daylight at last! Up I swam until my head whacked against the dinghy, which rocked violently no more than three feet from the cave roof. Paddling backward, I flipped up the mask and searched for Noel. Nowhere. I'd go back for him, take the extra tanks in case he didn't nab his set in time.

Turning back to the boat, I was reaching up to unhook the rope when a wave slapped me hard against the rock. Briefly blinded, I spat out sea, coughing, and sputtering, and then his head popped up beside me.

"You all right?" he called.

"Fabulous," I cried, so glad to see him. "You?"

"Bloody marvellous! Get in the dinghy," he called. "I'll push, you row."

"What about the *Zodiac*?"

"I'll tie it to the back."

143

I hoisted myself up, Noel shoving me from behind, until I flopped into the dinghy like sluggish tuna. In an instant, I'd unfastened my tanks and nabbed the oars while he shoved the boat around until the prow faced seaward.

The whole thing was crazy: coming into a sea cave during rising tide in this wicked brew of surf and rock. Crazy and exhilarating. I kept the boat as level as possible while the space between ceiling and sea closed in and Noel shoved the boats toward the opening. A wave flung the boat against the cave roof when we'd almost reached the entrance, scraping my back and knocking one of the oars from my hand.

Noel held the prow, using his weight to dip us down and out under the cave roof, rescuing the oar at the same time. Once outside, I rowed with a furious energy, while he kicked alongside until were safely away from the reefs. Only then did he hoist himself into the boat, the *Zodiac* rocking on its tether behind us.

In the center of the cove, we stared at one another for a moment, knees touching, grinning inanely like two kids who'd just raided the cookie jar. And then he leaned over, framed my head in his hands, and kissed me.

I stopped rowing, caught on the crest of a wave, my insides no steadier than the boat. His lips were cool and salty, his fingers tangling in my hair. Then he pulled away and I recovered long enough to start working the oars.

"What did you do that for?"

"I've been wanting to since the day we met." He scraped his hair back from his face, arms braced on his legs, a smile on his lips.

"Who should keep their impulses in check now? Besides, your timing's crap." I kept my gaze focused on the boathouse far ahead.

"I'm opportunist and you're good," he called over the waves. "Full of surprises. I would never have expected you to follow me in."

"You don't know me."

"I'm learning."

"I'm not here to be seduced. I came to find my brother."

"You won't give up, will you?"

"Never."

"One of the many things I admire about you." He leaned forward. "I'll find Toby, like I promised, but help me, too. I need those cave diagrams, Phoebe. They have to exist and you have to find them."

So that was it. I rowed harder, biting down on a string of curses. They had to think me stupid as well as gullible: Just go into the estate and find your brother. Oh, and while you're at it, how about helping us steal a fortune? Did he think kissing me would make me fall for him, turn me into putty? I'd return to the tower all right, but it wouldn't be for Noel and Max.

I'd do it for Toby.

I acted as though rowing took all my concentration. He didn't offer to take over and I proved he didn't need to.

"You know how to handle those oars, my lady. I'll leave you to it, then."

He was leaving? "Where are you going?"

"Back the way I came," he said, untying the *Zodiac*. "I'll be in touch. Oh, and before I forget, I love your mermaid. She's a corker." With a salute, he tipped backwards into the water and swam towards the inflatable.

Hell. I uttered every expletive I knew, adding a few cobbled on the spot. I'd forgotten I was practically naked under the wetsuit jacket. He must have got quite an eyeful when he pushed my rear into the boat. Despite the dim light, the little tat on my upper rear thigh must have made an impact.

Drenched and bone-weary and now burning in a mix of emotions, I rowed against the tide all the way to the boathouse. By the time I had the boat secured inside, the sea had risen to the edge of the jetty. The air blew chill and the sun disappeared behind a scud of clouds. It had to be close to four o'clock.

I stood shivering, wondering if my legs would even carry me up those stairs. And what about explaining my appearance to Mrs. Wyndridge this time? Say I'd gone diving in my undies? On a seriously extended lunch break?

I sank to the floor to pull on my sneakers and socks when I realized my clothes were gone. I'd piled them on top of my shoes. Standing up, I looked around, thinking maybe they'd been knocked over in my haste to get seaborne, but no, they had totally disappeared. Panic hit. Who would have taken my stuff and why? I sat back down to put on my sneakers, determined to get upstairs as soon as possible.

Shaking my left shoe with my palm outstretched, I waited for the weight of my phone to land. It didn't. I shook both shoes again and again before clambering to my feet scanning the shed. I checked every shelf, between, under, and inside every compartment in case I'd shoved it someplace without thinking. But my clothes and phone were gone.

Gone!

My clothes weren't nearly as important as the phone. Oh, my god, someone took my phone! Not Wyndridge, since he wasn't home, and not his mother, obviously. That left only one possibility. I pulled a strand of seaweed from my hair and swallowed hard, pulled on my sneakers, and readied myself to climb those damn stairs all the way to the top.

Chapter 14

Dad was at the end of that phone, along with Nancy, Max, *everyone who mattered,* plus all my personal information, including email, notes, and photographs. A survival pack for modern civilization lay stored in that little device. Open the apps and expose my life: how much I weighed, my grocery list, a favorite stitch pattern, what movies I watched or books I read, all my photos of everyone I loved and lost, my addresses and emails. My limb had been amputated and I had to get it back.

I arrived at the top of the stairs totally spent. I could only perch on a marble seat and stare blankly into the nearest hibiscus for a few minutes. Bert took my phone and I took his gun. Did that make us even? No way, no damn way. Only my goose-puckered flesh prompted me to stand and stumble into the house.

I slipped inside the kitchen door, my legs trembling, teeth chattering, readying for a sprint to my room when Joquita appeared. "Good lord, woman, what happened to you?"

"Joquita, oh, hi." I gave a little wave, wiped the hair from my eyes, and lowered myself onto a wooden chair.

"You look like you were hit by a ferry boat. Stop dripping on the floor." She untied a dishcloth from her waist and threw it at me.

"Oh, sorry," I stood, wiping down my legs with the cloth. "May as well have. I thought I'd go for a swim, only I forgot my suit," I indicated my abbreviated dive wear with a shrug. "So I borrowed a wetsuit top and went anyway. Only I ran into a bit of trouble." It sounded like the lie it was. All I could do was wrap my arms around myself and keep from shivering.

Joquita stared. Hard.

"What time is it?" I asked.

She glanced at her watch. "Nearly four-thirty. I'm just getting supper ready. Mrs. W isn't feeling well and may not join us and the mister is still away, so it might just be you and Bert for supper tonight. We'll make it early, say six o'clock, in the kitchen."

"Is Bert around?"

She rolled her eyes. "Somewhere. I haven't seen him for the last hour, thank heavens. You'd better clean up in case the missus arouses. See you later." And she strolled back into the kitchen, her demeanor three degrees cooler than at breakfast. At the door she paused. "Oh, I almost forgot. A lady called here about an hour ago. Said she was your aunt and wants you to call her back." She fished a recipe card from her apron pocket and held it out.

I snatched it eagerly. Flipping the card over, I silently read "Aunt Margaret. Call Astwood Cottages" with the number. "Do you have a phone I can use? My cell isn't working."

Her eyes narrowed. "Having all kinds of problems today, aren't you? There's a phone in the hall." She indicated the direction with a jerk of her head.

In an instant, I was in the long front corridor. I located the Georgian map-press serving as a phone table and leaned against the paneling while I dialed. Soon the ornate phone buzzed in my ear. Maggie picked up immediately. "Hello?"

"Aunt Margaret. Susan here. I understand you called?"

"Susan, how delightful to hear from you! How are you, darling?" Maggie had assumed a mangled upper-crust New England- meets-the-deep-south accent. "How is your position progressing? Are y'all enjoying the new wardrobe I gifted you? I do miss you so."

"Yes, I do miss you so, too, so much, in fact, that I can't begin to say. I'd love to see you again soon. How about right after supper, say 7:30? We can discuss my wardrobe malfunctions then."

"Perfect! I'll pick you up. Be on the other side of the footbridge at 7:30."

"Wonderful."

"Perfect."

I dropped the receiver back in its cradle. Just this once, I really did want to see her. Needed to, in fact. No sign of Bert yet. I dialed my dad next, only the phone rang and rang. Damn. Maybe Bertha had lured him over to her place for supper.

Taking a deep breath, I proceeded down the hall, itching with anxiety, praying for minimum interference en route to the bedroom. First, change, then go into disaster management. I had just reached the bedroom wing, unzipping my neoprene jacket along the way, when out stepped Bert. Up went the zipper.

"Well, well. Don't ruin the view, Suzy, or should I say Phoebe? Let Bert take a better peak at those two beauties of yours."

"Go to hell, Bert, or should I say Hector? And give me back my damn phone."

He stepped toward me, rolling a mint in his mouth, hands clenched at his sides. "Give me my gun first, bitch. Where'd you hide it?"

"Some place safe. Let me pass."

He shoved me back against the wall, one hand cupping a breast. "First, get my gun and then we have business to attend, in that order."

"I threw it in the sea." Try as I may, I couldn't keep my teeth from chattering.

"What the hell did you do that for?" His hand tightened on my breast.

"So you wouldn't shoot me with it?"

"Girlie, surely you don't think shooting is the only way I could kill you? I can think of maybe twenty others, most right here, all made to look accidental. And you were even dumb-assed enough to rummage through my stuff, too. Shit, if I didn't know better, I'd think you had a death wish." Now both hands began squeezing my breasts.

I kicked out at him, tried shoving him away. "I need my phone!"

"I have needs, too, Phoebe. Feel one pressing against you now? "He was back on me in seconds, his full body pinning me to the wall.

"No! I'll scream. Joquita will hear me. She'll call the police!"

He stepped back an inch, still keeping me pinned. "You do that and I'll kill you here and now."

"And ruin your chances of getting rich?"

He seemed to consider that. "Yeah, best to have my cake and eat you, too. Here's what's going to happen, little Phoebe: You're going to keep Bert informed from now on in because you'll be working for me." He dropped his hands.

I tugged the jacket taut over my hips. "You mean, I'm to keep Hector informed. I know all about you, too."

"My reputation exceeds me. I suppose Noel told you."

I hesitated. How well did Hector know Noel? "Of course. He said you two were such great buds."

"Yeah, brothers-in-arms, you might say."

"Charming. So, where does stealing my phone fit in?"

He plucked my cell from his pocket, holding it from my reach. "After I saw you two in the boat and realized you were looking elsewhere without telling me. Poor choice, sweetie, 'cause that puts you on the losing team. No way he's going to nab a heist this big."

Did the "he" mean Noel or Max? Maybe he didn't know about Max, since he hadn't mentioned him. Could it be that the godfather played that far in the background? "Is this a heist?"

He shrugged. "Call it what you want. Point is, I'm going to get it and he's not, which puts you in a very bad spot." He loomed down over me now, one hand now fingering the zip of my suit, the other holding my phone behind his back. "If you play nice, I'll give you back your phone. I might even forgive you tossing my gun and maybe offer you a job myself when this is over."

"Define 'play nice'." Buying time seemed my immediate option. Besides, he made no reference to my assignation with Maggie, which gave me a brief lilt of hope.

"I want access into the tower. Now."

"And, in return, all I get is my phone back and maybe improve my job prospects?"

"No, sweetheart." His hand moved to my throat where he squeezed gently. "In return, you get to stay alive and daddy doesn't have some nasty accident back in Nova Scotia."

I felt the blood drain from my face. "You hurt my father and, my god, I swear I'll kill you."

Bert smiled his overbright grin. "Yeah, yeah. And aren't you in just the best position to be making threats? The little ex-gallery worker pretending to be a fancified library lady who doesn't know her ass from a hole in the ground? I'm just quivering in my boots. Oh, yes, I've found all kinds of things about Phoebe McCabe, thanks to your phone. Handy little things, aren't they? I even spoke to Daddy."

"What?" I went rigid, hating the squeak in my voice. "What did you say to him?"

"Just that I was your new boyfriend and was phoning to make myself acquainted. Said you and I were going for a date tonight. He sounded all upset, kept asking to speak to you and asking why you hadn't called. I said you were too busy."

Damn him all to hell. I was trembling now, tears spilling down my face, helpless and afraid. "Let me call him now. Please. He'll be worried. He has a bad heart."

"Aw, bad hearts can be so tricky, can't they? Better not mess things up then, hey, little Phoebe. Wouldn't want him to die from shock now, would we?" His hand moved from my throat to my cheek, stroking it as if calming a terrified animal. "First the tower. Then, if you're good, you can have the phone back. And, like I said, if you're really good, I mean, really, really, good, Hector will keep you alive." The hand slipped from my cheek to my breast, pinching it hard. "Understood?"

"Understood."

He stepped away. "Now, get changed. We'll go to the tower now."

"No," I said, between chattering teeth, almost doubling over. "Please, I mean not now. Look at me, I'm freezing. I have to change, and then, if we don't appear for supper at six, Joquita will know something's up. Why not meet me outside the tower tonight at 9:30 after Joquita leaves? That makes more sense, doesn't it? And what's a couple more hours? I'll be there, I promise. I just need a chance to catch my breath, get something to eat."

And then I started crying, as in full heart-felt bawl, nothing feigned. I felt so weak and idiotic, so helpless and vulnerable. My tears were damn real.

He grabbed my wrist, twisting viciously, eyes hard. "Stop blubbering. I hate blubbering women. Go make yourself all pretty again. We'll make like normal over supper and meet at the tower at 9:30 but don't mess with me, Suzy-Phoebe. If you try, I'll have the

151

old codger back home done in and have it filmed for your pleasure, just for starts. I've got friends who'd love nothing better than pick up a few grand for an easy kill. Get it?"

"Got it."

He grinned. "You be a good girl now and make Hector happy." Then he swung me around, patting me on the bottom before giving me a push towards my room. I heard his footsteps lumbering down the hall as I flung open the door and stepped in.

And stopped dead. The place had been ransacked. Clothes lay strewn across the floor, the contents of the drawers tipped out on the floor. In two strides, I was at the bed, gazing down in anguish. My carpet bag had been upended, my knitting ripped from the needles and tossed into a tangled mass.

Chapter 15

As if the threads holding me together had unraveled, I could not stop crying. Like my beautiful knitting, which now lay like a pile of tangled entrails, I had been ripped off my supports. All I could do was wail, bent over like some plush toy with the stuffing kicked out of me. He's threatening Dad! He knows where we live, who I am, everything about me! He ruined my knitting!

And then I smartened up. Call it a bolt from above, or maybe just a sudden catapult back to my senses, but I knew absolutely all would be lost if I floundered. I could not afford to lose anything more.

I straightened, took deep, steadying breaths, and tried to pull myself together. First, I assessed the damage with my head, not my emotions. All my papers had been rifled through, but my notes contained mostly generic information on Oak Island, which wouldn't have offered Hector anything new. He had also tipped over the mattress but missed Toby's drawing between the mattress cover and the box spring, not like that would have told him much. In fact, the bully boy would have learned nothing from his search.

My clothes had been tossed over the room, with one green silk bra slung over the lampshade for added effect. The pink version with matching panties were gone, no doubt taken as a trophy. So, I reasoned, Bertie-Hector had probably ripped my knitting out of spite because he hadn't found anything worth taking. He'd still think me here to find the treasure.

And my iPad was still safe in the tower. All was not lost. I took another deep breath. I would survive this. I would pick up my stitches and go on.

I stripped down and climbed into the shower. This late in the day, all I got was a cold, fitful trickle that sluiced me clean but did nothing to warm me up. I shivered just as hard getting out as I did getting in. Wrapping myself in a towel, I administered to my cuts and bruises with a makeshift first-aid kit found in the cupboard under the sink while struggling to pull myself together.

That bastard threatened my father! And Hector's employer would kill anyone who knows the truth about the treasure, no matter what Hector says. I'm as good as dead! A surge of panic threatened to swallow my newfound calm but I shoved it way back. Hector the hatchet man would kill anybody who got in his way, of that I was sure, so my usefulness would probably expire right after he had those diagrams, *if* he got those diagrams, unless of course, I offered special benefits. The thought of me giving Hector special benefits turned my stomach.

I stared at myself in the bathroom mirror. Hector thought me an inexperienced, weak little ninny in way over her head; and in some respects, he was right. The other respects might shock him, might shock me. Something was happening at my core, something I couldn't define.

I tore through Maggie's wardrobe offerings looking for something suitable. Did those leather pants and a vintage Yves Saint Laurent silk gypsy blouse qualify? Did I care? Nothing remained but dresses and gowns, anyway, so on went the luxury wear. I scraped my hair into a ponytail, applied a bit of the makeup Maggie had provided and surveyed the result. God, I looked like a trespasser at a costume ball. I cursed Maggie's sense of irony for packing this nod to pirate couture, while tucking the voluminous blouse into the pants. Though skintight, they offered just enough pocket space to shove in the room and tower keys.

I spent a few moments mourning my ruined wrap, lifting it by the wing like a wounded bird. Somewhere deep in those ravaged stitches, I glimpsed a thread of hope. If I could unravel back to the few remaining inches, I could begin again, perhaps even making the next version more beauteous than the first. But not now. I tucked the tangled mess lovingly into my bag, tossed my old companion over my shoulder, and left the room.

On my way to the kitchen, I knocked on Mrs. Wyndridge's door.

"Who is it?"

"Susan."

"Come in."

I entered, expecting to find her still propped in her chair watching reruns, but instead, she lay on the bed with an afghan pulled up to her chin, her pallor alarming.

"Are you all right?" I noticed a pot of tea and a half-full teacup on her side table along with a plate of nibbled sandwiches.

"Just tired, that's all. When you're old, weariness hits out of the blue." Then her sharp eyes roamed up and down my person. "What in heaven's name are you wearing?" She pointed a finger at my overflowing silk blouse and leather pants.

I tried a nonchalant shrug. "I thought the blouse sort of goes with the house."

She smiled grimly. "More like you thought you'd impress my son, isn't that so? Well, you're wasting your time there, my girl. Mind my words, he won't be attracted to the likes of you. All young people do is think of mating. Best focus on your job, instead. How are things going in the tower?" Her tone sounded more sad than cutting.

"Fine," I lied. "I did a lot of rearranging up there and plan to go back up after supper to work some more."

She nodded. "Good, you must make up for all your tardiness. Now, let me rest."

"Can I get you anything?"

"Joquita will bring me my supper a little later."

I exited, closing the door softly behind me.

Supper was a dreary affair. Joquita said little while serving Hector and me generous helpings of grilled vegetables and baked chicken, casting sharp glances at us both. I ate in silence, trying to deflect Hector's occasional leer, while he shoveled food into his mouth and chewed noisily. The man nearly put me off my fodder. Everything tasted the same to me, anyway.

"Mrs. Wyndridge isn't looking well at all," I commented. "Do you think we should call Mr. Wyndridge?"

"She wouldn't appreciate anything like that and neither would he unless it was an emergency," Joquita responded. "She has off days like this once in a while and just needs to rest.

Besides, I wouldn't know how to contact him even if I thought it a good idea."

Joquita slipped a bowl of ice cream in front of us after clearing the plates. "But the weather might send him back. Report says we're getting the tail end of that storm that hit Jamaica. Mrs. Wyndridge says you must bring in the lawn furniture and latch the shutters, Mr. Stone. That means the tables and umbrellas around back, plus anything that might fly around has to be secured. We usually bring in the flower pots, too."

Hector stopped chewing, considering the request. I could almost read his thoughts: Should I bother doing that grunt work when I have other fish to fry? He weighed on the side of caution. "Sure thing. I'll get right on it. How long are you staying around for tonight, Joey?"

"Don't call me anything but Joquita, Mr. Stone." Joquita slapped a dishtowel against her apron before draping it over a rack by the sink. "As soon as I make the missus her supper and clean up a bit, I'm out of here. If the weather's bad, I won't be coming in tomorrow, either, so I'll just prepare a few meals in advance. Expect cold food tomorrow. Salads. In the meantime, Mrs. W asked me to show you what needs to be done, Mr. Stone. As soon as you're finished, I'll do that. My boyfriend's picking me up at 9:00 and I have lots to do in between, if you don't mind."

"As soon as I've devoured this delectable feast, we'll just tally-ho and all that," Hector said, obviously enjoying the night's prospects, presumably the episodes that included me.

"Is the storm supposed to be bad?" I asked. It was a stupid question, as all island dwellers know.

"They're all bad this time of year, plus the electricity usually cuts out. High winds and rain is what they're saying, the usual stuff." She turned her back on us and began chopping vegetables.

I glanced at Hector and caught him glancing back. He beamed. "Worried about big waves, Susan?"

"I can't knit much in the dark, can I?"

He grinned.

"There are lots of flashlights and batteries in the drawer there." Joquita pointed to a cabinet next to the door. "Now, excuse me while I take some supper to Mrs. W. I'll be right back."

The moment she exited, Hector leaned over and squeezed my knee. "You look a right dish in that getup, little Phoebe. I like a tight ass encased in leather. Did you dress up just for me?"

I fixed him with a look. "Sure thing, Hector. I dressed just for you."

He smirked. "I'll enjoy it when you undress just for me after we finished our little business. All part of your new working conditions."

Joquita entered the kitchen seconds after Hector had snatched back his hand. "Mrs. W isn't looking great but she ate a little."

"I'll check on her later on," I said.

Joquita nodded and went back to food preparation.

I dawdled over the ice cream until Joquita led Hector out to the garden. The moment they disappeared, I dashed to the drawer and wrapped the two flashlights and three packages of batteries into a dishcloth, which I tucked under my arm.

Hiding places were bountiful, but I needed someplace Hector wouldn't likely look. My room was definitely out. In the end, I settled for the dining room where I'd met Alistair Wyndridge. There, I tucked the bundle inside the harpsichord, wincing when the strings twanged a complaint. That done, I had exactly 15 minutes left to get across the bridge to meet Maggie.

***

Night glommed onto the shadows as I dashed over the bridge to the parking area. Though Hector and Joquita were nowhere in sight, the green shutters at the front of the house had all been levered down. I could only hope the other tasks would keep him occupied while thinking me cowering in my room waiting for the clock to chime 9:30.

I couldn't see Maggie at first, but the moment I headed up the drive, a car engine roared into life as headlights blazed. I ran towards the car, climbing breathless into the back seat.

"Hello, Susan, darling. Driver, take us to the Henry the Eighth Pub."

I was in a cab heading for a pub? I turned to Maggie, shrouded in darkness next to me, her perfume so strong, it socked me in the temples. "I thought we'd go someplace a little more private."

"Noisy is best, sweetheart, if we girls are going to share."

We girls. Share. Crud. I clasped my hands together and stared out into the night.

The Henry the Eighth Pub & Restaurant embodied every element of an old English pub except location and authenticity. As Maggie paid the driver, I plowed into the crowd, a waiter steering me past through the mock Tudor decor to an empty booth. He slipped a couple of menus in the waiting spots as music launched from somewhere—an Irish singing group designed to work the crowd into a hand-clapping, beer-swilling mood.

Damn. I needed a phone. I leapt to my feet, ready to seek one out, when

Maggie arrived in her pink cashmere twinset and Bermuda shorts.

"Where you going?"

"I need to borrow your cell."

"Please."

"Please."

"Who are you calling?"

"Dad. I'll explain everything in a sec." I plucked her Blackberry out of her hands and pushed through the throng, searching out an eddy of calm. The closest I came was the bathroom, where I dialed Dad's number with my back against the stall door.

He picked up immediately and I almost yelped in relief.
"Dad!"

"Phoebe? Is that you? What the hell's going on? I've been worrying myself to knots!"

"Dad, I'm so sorry. If you received a call today from someone saying he's my boyfriend, it's a lie."

"He didn't sound your type. You go for those overeducated, stuck-up sorts. This one had an English accent, but not the kind you like. What's going on? And don't try hiding anything."

I couldn't lie to him anymore, I just couldn't. There had been too many lies for too long and the time to solder our family together with the truth was running out. "Dad, I'm tracking down Toby and I need you to stay calm."

Maggie scowled at me as I approached the booth minutes later. Two deep blue colored drinks with drunken-looking parrots perched on their rims sat on the table. "You look like shit. Guess my grooming tips didn't take. So, like, I get the ponytail thing but those sneakers kill the look. That's Yves Saint Laurent. Show some respect. Here, I ordered you a martini. You look like you could use it." She shoved the drink towards me.

"I'll share my opinions about your wardrobe choices some other time." I clutched her pink-nailed hand as it reached for the martini glass and tugged her forwards. "Listen, Maggie. Hector knows I'm not Susan Waverley. He thinks I work for Max and is blackmailing me to help him find the treasure. He's threatening Dad, not to mention me."

Maggie, froze. "Shit."

"Exactly. So, I need to contact Max. Can he can send somebody to the cottage to watch Dad unobtrusively? Hector stole my cell phone. He knows everything about me, everything."

Maggie twisted her hand around and gripped mine instead, giving it a hard squeeze. "How'd he get your phone?"

"Let's just say I left it by the wharf when I went for a dive earlier today."

"You went diving?"

"With Noel. He can fill you in with the details later."

"You went diving with Noel? Did you find anything?"

I pulled my hand away. "Just let me speak to Max. Noel said I wasn't to try calling anyone in the usual fashion but, since my phone's dead, I can't anyways."

She snatched her phone from the table and typed a quick message. "I'll contact him for you, but it's Noel you need to speak to, not Max."

"I want to speak to Max."

"It doesn't work that way. He's on the boat on the other side of the cove. So, I text a number, which contacts another number, and so on about five times until Max gets the message. Then, he texts me back with an address that I go to, usually a phone booth or something, and wait for his call." Catching my look of exasperation, she added, "Look, cells are open season in this business. Anybody can listen in, and ditto with landlines. We don't take chances."

I shook my head, grappling yet again with my godfather's business. "It's so cloak and dagger."

A waiter appeared at the table. "May I take your orders?"

Maggie beamed at him. "I'll have a Caesar salad with the dressing on the side, no bread. What about you, Susan, dear?"

"Nothing for me, thanks, Auntie Margaret." I smiled brightly.

The moment the guy slipped away, Maggie leaned forward. "I haven't spoken to Noel today. He's not responding to our agreed signal."

I leaned forward, too, pitching my whisper above the rising noise. "I don't care about your HR issues, Mags. Focus on the problem here, okay? I need help."

"Yeah, I get it but this is the issue. You need to speak to Noel, not Max. Obviously you can't go back to the house now."

"I have to go back. I have no choice."

"That's nuts. You need to get in touch with Noel first. He's the one handling Hector. He's a mean bastard unless he's kept in line."

I stared at her. "What do you mean by *handling Hector*?"

She sipped her martini. "Everybody knows everybody in this business, I mean. Noel knows how to handle that one. He's dangerous."

"Tell me about it. Who's he working for, anyway?"

She shrugged. "We're trying to figure that out since Hector doesn't work on his own. He's too small a fish for that."

"I think he's graduated to shark status." I sunk back in my seat, thinking ahead to my night locked in the tower with Hector. "How do I contact Noel now that my cell phone's caput?"

"I'll keep trying." Maggie continued amid sips. In memory of last night's bourbon, I left mine untouched. "But look, hon, it's just got way too dangerous with that brute on the loose. You've got to see that. Max wants you out now. Your three days are almost up."

"I don't care what Max wants. I still haven't found what I came for."

Maggie paused mid-sip. "Toby?"

"Of course Toby. I still don't know what happened to him."

"And maybe you never will. Risking your own neck won't help."

"I'm not stopping until I have answers."

"Look, I didn't want to say anything so soon, but we have plans for you. You need a job and we have an opening."

I was almost too stunned to speak. "Am I hearing right? I'm here with my neck on the line and you're offering me a job? That's the second I've had today."

"Think of it as long-range planning."

"More like poor timing. Besides, if Max wants to offer me a job, I'd rather he do it himself. No offense."

Maggie sipped the dregs of her aperitif and moved on to mine. "The dish ran away with the spoon."

"What's that supposed to mean?"

"Means don't be a snot. Max isn't the only one with a brain, though he thinks he is. I'm trying to help you here."

"The only help I need right now is protection for Dad and a way to get out of tonight alive. Do you have something for that?"

Maggie leaned towards me lowering her voice. "Yeah. I'll get to work on the first and you can take my gun." She patted her bag knowingly.

My eyes widened. "I don't know how to use a gun."

"It's easy, like a camera. Just point and shoot."

"I'm not taking a gun."

"You can hide it easily enough in that sack you drag everywhere. Take it."

"No. I just tossed Hector's into the cove today. If I wanted a gun, I could have kept his."

"Don't be an idiot."

I leaned forward again. "I'll use brains over bullets any day. Hector thinks I'm stupid, so I'll use that to my advantage."

Maggie nodded. "That works for me, only brains can't stop a killer at 20 feet the way a gun can. Look, once I get hold of Noel, he'll take care of Hector."

"But what about Max?"

"What about him? Noel's the man on the ground."

I checked my watch: 8:15. Maggie's salad arrived, and after the perfunctory thank yous and no thanks to the waiter, I began again. "How can I contact Noel? How do you contact him?"

"Same way as for Max."

"What good is that convoluted business in emergencies?"

"That's what guns are for and keep your voice down," she hissed, picking up her fork.

I watched her pluck the choicest leaves from her salad while the minutes clicked by. "I have to go," I said, finally.

"I'm still eating."

That did it. I got to my feet. "And I'm still breathing— so far. I plan to keep it that way."

"Wait!"

She didn't stop haranguing me even while we waited for the cab outside the restaurant. When we finally parted company, me heading in one cab, she in another, she gave me such a fierce hug, I practically had to wrestle myself free.

"You need the gun, sister," she hissed in my ear.

"No, I don't," and I shoved her off and scrambled into the cab.

Chapter 16

Hector ambushed me halfway between the bridge and the house.

"Where have you been, Phoebe?" He twisted my arm behind my back and steered me up the path.

"Let go. I went to meet my associate. If I didn't, she would have been suspicious, wouldn't she?"

"What did you tell Mags?" He yanked my wrist so hard, tears sprang to my eyes.

So he knew. Of course, he knew. "Not that I'm planning to jump ship, if that's what you're thinking. Let me go!"

He released me, sending me stumbling into the pontisettas, my carpet bag all that saved me from cracking my shins on a marble bench. "When I set a time, I expect you to be there, not when you feel like it. You're 10 bloody minutes late."

I stood there rubbing my wrist. "Big deal. You sound like Mrs. Wyndridge minus the profanities. Look, I'm trying to keep my current employer from suspecting anything."

"Wouldn't want old Maxie to get twitchy, is that it?"

"Yeah." So he did know about Max.

He laughed. "You do that, little Phoebe, but just remember what it takes to be on the winning team."

"Pleasing you?"

"Got it."

"And ruining my knitting, what was that about?"

"Consider it a warning and be glad that holey mess wasn't you. Now let's just proceed to the tower and get the job done."

I nodded, hoisting my carpet bag more securely on my shoulder and making for the kitchen door. His paw landed on my butt the moment I turned.

"Stop it!" I swatted his hand away.

"Ah, Phoebe, I'm issuing a touch of male appreciation. Don't you like male appreciation? I bet Noel appreciated you a whole pile this afternoon dressed the way you were , or weren't, I should say. Didn't he? Besides," he added, leaning closer, "I'm just getting a little taste of what I'll be enjoying later."

I sprinted up the path.

"What are you going to do about it, anyway?" he hissed after me. "Charge me for sexual harassment. Haha. Hey, do you know there's an 'ass' in harassment. Bloody brilliant!"

The house felt too quiet. Though Joquita had left the kitchen light on, something heavy and dark had descended on the atmosphere. My own fear, probably. I scanned the neatly stacked dishes, the notes left on the fridge and counter, and commented absently. "Funny, very funny. Let me check on Mrs. Wyndridge first, okay?"

"Not okay. The old bag is sleeping soundly. I drugged her tea."

"What?" I turned to face him. "You can't do that! She's on other medication and the drugs might conflict and make her sicker!"

He mimed a violin, his arm sliding a bow across imaginary strings. "You're breaking my heart, little Phoebe. If you want to succeed in this business, it doesn't pay to be too soft-hearted. Now, move."

Anxiety flooded every nerve as I walked through the corridors. As if I climbed a moving stairway up a steep precipice with no way off, I strode through the too-quiet house towards the tower, unable to figure out how to avoid calamity. Clutching my carpet bag more closely to my chest, I realized how desperately I wanted to survive.

When we reached the darkened corridors of the old wing, Hector flicked on his flashlight and jangled a set of keys before my eyes.

"Those are Mrs. Wyndridges," I said.

"Very observant. I just borrowed them from her seeing as she won't be needing them for a while."

I swallowed. "Did you hurt her?"

"I drugged her, I said." He shoved me aside and inserted the key. "Now enter the code, slow-like, so I can watch." He beamed the light on the key panel.

"Fine, but you're not going to find much up there."

"Is that why you were sent in pretending to be a librarian?"

I sighed, realizing I had no choice but to reveal the code under his piggy eyes. I tapped in the numbers and the door swung open, Hector singing a merry little tune under his breath.

As soon as the door slammed behind us, the darkness swallowed us whole. "The light's burned out. You'll have to use the flashlight," I lied.

He flashed his light around the stone walls, muttering. "I didn't expect him to have electricity in here except for the lock. I'm almost impressed."

I pointed to the stairs. "There's no elevator, obviously. I counted one hundred and ninety-six steps."

That launched a string of invectives and, while he studied the bottom landing to the sound of his own voice, I bolted for the steps as fast as my bruised legs could carry me. He heaved after me seconds later.

"Wait! Slow down, damn it!" he panted.

I hoisted myself over the weird irregular step, calling back, "What's the matter, Heck? Not keeping up with your gym dates?" Several times I paused, bent over, catching my breath while listening to him gasping below. He had a light, I didn't, and I was too aware of the wire rope forming a thin barrier between me and the drop below.

Once I reached the top, I plunged into the room, still propped open by my book jamb. Fumbling towards the window, I made for the desk lamp that had toppled over earlier. I found it in seconds and soon had it righted and the bulb tightened, sighing relief as it bloomed light. I placed it on top of the desk and dashed back to wedge my carpet bag behind the door, careful not to dislodge my makeshift doorstopper in the process. Retrieving my iPad on the way back, in seconds I was at the map cabinet carefully placing the key letters I'd found back onto the debris pile, leaving them with what I hoped was a just-fallen look.

When Hector arrived panting minutes later , I was standing by the cabinet studying an aged parchment under the light of my iPad. "Not going to go all cardiac on me, are you, Heck? I'm not much good at CPR," I said without looking up.

He didn't have the breath to do more than growl at first. I thought he might really have a heart attack but that was only wistful thinking. He stepped into the room. "What the hell happened here?"

"I was rooting around on the ladder when the shelf toppled over."

"Shit. Is this what you academics call methodical? You're a bloody disaster."

"Who said I'm methodical? Can you help set things to rights here?"

"What do you take me for, a house boy?"

"No, I take you for a thug. Do you want to find what Wyndridge has been hiding or not?"

"Got your smart mouth back, I see. I prefer you servile but what does it matter since you'll look the same naked, either way."

I watched him maneuvering over the mounds to stand opposite me with the map cabinet between us. He glanced at the broken shelf behind me and then down at the tumble at his feet.

"You made a right mess, all right. Shit, couldn't have done better myself."

"Thank you." I pointed down at the pile. "I went through some of that stuff earlier and found some letters but haven't had the chance to go through all of them yet."

He bent over and picked up one I had deposited, holding it under his flashlight before letting it fall again. I'd hoped he'd study it more closely, but instead he began pawing through the pile like a foraging bear.

"Be careful. Those are old and fragile. Hey, look, here's something you might be interested in. I read aloud from one of the pages I'd left on the cabinet. "*The B*oy Huzzar sailed... "

"Sailed where?" he asked, standing up.

He tried to snatch it from my fingers but I held it away. "Careful. It's delicate, almost completely illegible. I can't make out what the rest of it says, see?" I passed it towards him. "Take care. That's it. You hold it for me and I'll take a photo."

"Why the hell would I do that?"

"So we can magnify it later to scrutinize more carefully."

166

"You know anything about old writing?"

"Cursive script? Sure I do. Do you know anything about the *Boy Huzzar*?"

"Never heard of it."

He did as I asked while trying to squint down at the faded script. I held my tablet up and took the shot.

"I got a proper camera in me pocket. Here, you hold it now and I'll take a picture." Which I did, watching him snap away with a tiny but powerful spy-worthy tool. If I had doubts about what he was after, they ended there. He recognized the name Boy Huzzar.

"Can you read anything else it says?" he asked.

"Not in this light. Maybe later. Anyway, where there's one, there may be others," I remarked, pointing to the pile. "Should we divide up the work? I'll start looking in that pile and you take the map cabinet?"

"Not bloody likely. I'll start looking right here and you do the map cabinet."

I wiped my forehead against the back of my silk sleeve, which was filthy already. "Suit yourself."

Hector snorted. "I intend to, little Phoebe, and don't try giving me orders, see? If you want to start working for me, prove yourself useful."

"I will. Two of us can sort through this stuff independently faster than in tandem, don't you think? "

He nodded, lowering himself to his knees with a grunt. "That works as long as you don't try anything stupid. Time's running out and I'm losing patience." Soon, he was rooting around for more letters, his heavy breathing filling the space.

I began pulling out drawers, careful not to knock against the broken shelf leaning tipsily against the wall behind me. When I had the diagrams in full view, I also pulled out a wad of nautical maps to slide over the top for shielding purposes. I began taking shots of each diagram with the tablet camera, trying to get in every quadrant clearly with one eye fixed on Bert. The iPad registered a red low-battery alert. Like I needed that right then.

"Why'd he give you that thing for a camera?" Hector asked, catching sight of lining up a shot.

"Why not? It works."

"If you'd worked for me, you'd use real tools."

I looked over at him. "I thought you work for somebody else?"

He smirked. "Used to. Not anymore. Hector's going solo as of today. What have you found, anyway?" he asked while photographing something on his side, a letter, possibly.

"Just some old maps."

"What kind of maps?" He huffed to his feet to take a look.

I slipped the nautical maps across the diagrams and pointed to a seventeenth century map of Jamaica. He peered over, studying the parchment with his flashlight.

"What good's that?"

"Aren't we looking for something buried or sunken like a shipwreck?"

"Is that what Noel told you he's doing, looking for shipwrecks?"

Noel, why Noel? "Maybe." My breath caught as his stubby fingers flicked through the sheaf, the diagrams flashing past without interest.

I took a deep breath. "What are you looking for?"

"Said I don't know."

"Find anything interesting in that pile?"

"Maybe. Found a couple of letters from a certain captain to the king of England," he chuckled, knowing damn well the significance of those. He was finding all the stuff a true treasure hunter craved, original tertiary documents. I doubted I'd ever see them, but why would I want to? I wasn't there for treasure.

"What kind of shape are they in?" I asked.

"Not bad considering the dates are between 1687 and 1688."

"What do they say?"

"How the hell do I know?" he growled. "All kids of curlicues and stuff. Those dudes wrote like a bunch of faggots."

That made me hate him even more.

I finished photographing the diagrams, paying specific attention to one showing the tower above a mass of arterial lines leading to the sea. Notes in tiny script labeled various tunnels and chambers; a main access point clearly noted running from the base of the tower to the underground system. My blood pounded in my ears. It was exactly what everyone wanted and the very thing I couldn't let anyone see. It had to go with me. While the lug was preoccupied with the letters, I folded the parchment into quarters, breaking every conservationist's rule plus a few of my own, and slipped it under my blouse.

The windows thumped fitfully in the wind. The single banker's lamp cast nothing but a greenish glow into the shadows punctuated by Hector's flashlight and my iPad's ambient light. My companion breathed heavily, oblivious to either time or tide. He was studying something beside the failing flashlight he had propped on the edge of the cabinet. I picked my way over to stand by the leaning shelf.

"Looks like your flashlight's giving out," I said. "Don't you have spare batteries?"

"Eh? Yeah, sure. Damn torch. Should have brought a better one." He plucked the flashlight off the counter, giving it a slap with his fist before heaving to his feet to dig around his jacket pocket. He climbed over the pile to lean towards the desk lamp, angling for light. I watched as he opened the battery compartment, counting the seconds until he stood up again and headed back towards his spot. When he reached midway between the desk and the cabinet, I gave the broken shelf a furious sideways shove, sending the cracked wood hurling down right on top of him. He fell to his knees with a curse.

I estimated mere seconds before he'd be on his feet, time enough to leap over the shelf and mounds of books, and yank the desk lamp cord from the socket while holding my iPad ahead for light. Hector was still groaning in the dark when I grabbed my carpet bag and kicked the book from the door. The door clanged behind me as I hurled downstairs, the adrenalin pounding in my ears, aiming my pad light towards the stairwell's well of darkness. I fixed on keeping away from the edge; I fixed on the rhythm of the steps; I fixed on what I would do once I got to the bottom. I fixed on everything except that one wonky step. When I jettisoned into the darkness, I flung my carpet bag ahead of me like an offering to the gods.

Chapter 17

Impossible to know how long I lay at the bottom of the stairs. Probably only seconds. When I came to, darkness suffocated me. I couldn't breathe.

"Goddam bitch. I'll kill you for this!"

I shoved myself upwards, pushing air into my lungs, energy into my legs, staggering upright. My carpet bag lay directly below me and probably cushioned my fall, but my right knee had hit hard.

He was coming! I bent down, grabbed my bag by the strap, and stumbled just far enough to the left to slam into the wall. I stood stunned in agony as my knee stabbed vicious pain all the way up my spine while Hector huffed downwards like a fury in the dark. I couldn't move, couldn't see. *Couldn't think!*

A brute cry preceded a thump-thump of a mass tumbling downstairs. Turning around, I stood shivering, my back pressed against the wall, as a large shape landed only inches away. I held my breath, listening. Nothing. I fumbled for the wall switch behind me and blazed light into the space.

Hector lay face-down on the stone floor, an immobile mass of flesh. I prodded him with my foot, wanting him dead. He lay with one arm bent beneath him at an unnatural angle, the other flung out where he tried to buffer his fall. Crouching, I felt for a pulse, finding it strong. Damn brute should be dead, not just knocked senseless! I should finish him off.

I picked up my cracked iPad lying a foot away and considered whacking him over the head with it but slid the damaged tablet into my bag instead. Maybe he'd be badly enough concussed to stay put? I fumbled in his pockets for Mrs. Wyndridge's keys, plus his wallet and my phone, dropping everything into my bag.

Getting unsteadily to my feet, I resolved to come back with a rope to bind his feet and hands. Then I caught sight of my poet's shirt, splattered with blood, thinking, bizarrely, how pissed Maggie would be. I identified the metallic taste rolling around my mouth as blood but couldn't figure out where it was coming from. No time to think. Had to move, had to go, but felt so damn dizzy. I opened the door, flicked off the light, and exited the tower, the door slamming shut behind me.

Outside in the hall, I stood trembling and disoriented, my body fracked. It was so dark and I needed a light. Did I even have a light? I fumbled inside my bag until I grasped my iPhone, clutching the thing as if it were a lifeline. I brought it to eye level. When pressed, it emitted a feeble red battery alert and nothing more. Damn it! I flung it back into the satchel in disgust. Which way to my room? The world tilted, my legs buckled, and down I went, the shock of knee hitting floor so brutal, I yelped.

Dragging myself up again, I stumbled forward, cursing every stab of pain. I must have twisted something and bruised something else. Dizzy and knocking into furniture, I made my laborious way to the bedroom wing, lugging my carpet bag behind me.

Wind rattled the shutters and howled beyond the walls, mournful and threatening all at once. Somehow, I made it through the house in a blur of pain, noting that there were lights on that shouldn't be, including the one in my bedroom. I leaned against the wall in the corridor staring at my half-opened door. I knew I'd shut it before meeting Maggie. Hobbling forward, I lurched in. Lamplight pooled on the walls, silhouetting the dark figure of a man rifling through my bureau drawers.

"Noel?"

He swung around. "Phoebe! What the hell happened? I've been looking all over for you!"

That didn't make sense but neither did anything else right then. He was before me in an instant, his concerned gaze taking in my wounded person. He looked damn good right then.

"Whoa, girl, you look a mess." I swatted his hand away when he tried to touch my face. His hands dropped to his side. "You need bandaging. You're bleeding. What happened?"

I looked down at my blood-splattered, once-snowy silk shirt. "I fell," but for a moment I couldn't recall when or where.

"Mags said you were in trouble, something about Hector stealing your phone? I came immediately. The kitchen door was unlocked so I walked right in, searched the house far enough to find Mrs. Wyndridge sleeping next door, and your room deserted. What do you mean, you fell? You look like you were hit by a truck."

"In my drawers?" I touched my mouth where something small and bulbous had fastened to my bottom lip.

He lifted his hands in a kind of shrug. "You cut your lip. Let me fix you up. Where's Hector?"

I pushed past him, heading for the bed, struggling to remember the sequence of events. "Bottom of the tower stairs. He tripped." I eased myself to sitting on the bed and tried pulling up my pant leg, but skinny leather pants don't do scrunch. "I had a crash bag and he didn't."

"Crash bag?"

I pointed to the carpet bag on the floor where I'd dropped it. "Yarn saved me. Always said it would." I rolled my tongue inside my mouth and winced. Puffy and sore.

He knelt beside me. "You're hurt and confused," he said, his voice as mellow and soothing as a narcotic. Maybe I could slip away to another world inside a voice like that.

"Stop trying to talk. I'll clean you up."

"Is Mrs. Wyndridge all right?"

"She's sleeping next door."

"Hector drugged her."

"Bastard."

"Tie him up," I mumbled. Mumble was all I could do.

He checked his watch. "Leave Hector to me. First, I'm going to ice that lip and bandage you up. Let me look at that leg."

He passed over a bottle of water pulled from a leather pack worn slung across one shoulder. I took it and drank deeply, dribbling lots down my shirt in the process, while he bolted into the bathroom. I stared down at my ruined blouse, watching the blood dilute to pale. What color was that? Pink? Light red? The sound of Noel in the bathroom prodded my stunned brain cells. I had forgotten something critical but the details wouldn't come just then. Fainting seemed a galling possibility.

He called out. "I found bandages." A moment later, he was trying to ease me to standing. "Come into the bathroom where the light's better."

He overruled my protests and picked me up in his arms, a sensation I found half-pleasant, thinking that must be what it feels like to be carried away by your knight, only mine was a crook. He deposited me gently on the toilet seat, which ruined the effect. There I sat enthroned while he knelt before me like some knave of first aid, dabbing my lip and bandaging my forehead.

"How gallant," I said. He looked so damned sexy in the overhead light, something that penetrated my foggy senses despite pain and dizziness. In any state, he got to me, but, I reminded my battered self sternly, I could not afford to be got. Or had.

"That's me, Sir Dogsbody. Now, let me look at that leg. Take off your pants."

I would have laughed if I could. "Hell, no," said I.

He looked amused. "I'm not trying to seduce you but I've got to see that leg."

"I can't imagine pulling these things down. I'll never get them back up. Don't have anything else."

"Is it your right leg?"

I nodded.

And he pulled out a knife from his shoulder pack and sliced the bottom half of my leather jeans clean off, revealing an ugly blue-black bruise the color of a storm at sea puffing as mightily as my lip. He glanced up at me. "My God, woman, you're lucky you didn't break this or worse. As it is, I think it's just sprained. I'm going to bandage it. Here, hold on while I get ice. Take this for now."

I took the wet washcloth he proffered and sat with it pressed against my mouth, feeling as though I was about to be swallowed alive by fog. I could not, would not, faint. I leaned over, head between my knees and waited. Noel disappeared for a few moments, maybe years, returning with a mug of cold coffee, two baggies of ice, and a couple of Advil. "I found the cold coffee still in the pot and the pills in that rug thing you carry around. Take two."

"Went through my stuff, again," I muttered as I swallowed coffee and painkillers and waited for the world to refocus. "Did you find what you wanted?" I asked after a bit.

"You know I didn't." He was just finishing bandaging my leg in a layer of flex bandage, while I sat wincing with the ice pressed to my lip when the next question came. "Where'd you hide them?"

"Hide what?"

"Don't play with me, Phoebe. The diagrams."

My left leg shot out and caught him in the thigh.

"What was that for?"

"Reflex. Always happens when I smell a rat."

He jumped to his feet while I got unsteadily to mine, hanging on to the sink for support. My brain toggled images of the diagram folded inside my blouse. I could feel the parchment where it had slipped under my arm to hang in a sling of ruined silk. It was all I could do not to glance down.

"I need those diagrams, Phoebe."

I threw the ice bag into sink. "That's what you're here for, isn't it? The diagrams? Did you think I'd stick them in the drawers for you to find?"

"But you did find them?"

My eyes met his. "I didn't say that."

"You're a terrible liar. Where are they? And, thank you for coming through for me."

"Nothing I do is for you."

He shot me a wry smile, turned, and strode back into the bedroom. I leaned against the door frame long enough to see him shake the contents of my carpet bag onto the bed in a mass of tangled yarn before I slammed the bathroom door, and secured the feeble hook into the catch. I pulled the folded parchment from my blouse seconds later, finding it just as damaged as expected, splotched in blood and bleeding ink. No time to study it.

The door rattled dangerously. "Let me in!"

"I have to use the bathroom!"

"I'll find the bloody thing!"

I desperately scanned the tiny area for a hiding place before turning the taps on full and letting the rushing water mask the sound of me lifting the toilet back cover. Everybody in every drug heist movie I ever saw hid things in toilets, making it a bad idea but the only one I had. Under the bath mat hardly made a good alternative. I emptied the ice from one baggie into the sink, wiped it dry, and refolded the parchment into eights before squeezing it into the bag and wedging it by one corner on the edge of the tank. When I flushed seconds later, the plastic would touch water but hopefully the document would stay dry.

When Noel kicked the door in moments later, I had just finished washing my hands. I turned to him. "You didn't need to break the door down. I only took a few minutes."

"Where is it?"

"Where's what?" I leaned against the sink, struck by the dangerous glitter in his eyes.

"Don't waste my time, Phoebe. You found the diagrams. You know I'm going to see this through."

"And you know I'm not going to help you."

"Even when you know that finding the treasure connects to Toby?"

"Don't use that on me. Finding Toby and stealing the treasure are not synonymous. Start telling the truth for once."

"You don't know the half of it. Toby's not quite the noble one you take him for. He came here looking for it, too. What you don't know is that he found a copy of the diagram, information that he texted to Max days before he disappeared. Max hasn't told you everything."

Like that surprised me. "What else?"

"Toby has been working off and on with Max for the past five years. Max sent Toby here to infiltrate the Wyndridge estate, which he did very successfully. He found something, Phoebe, something important. He alluded to charts and diagrams, but wouldn't give specifics. Instead, he returned home to tell your dad and presumably hide a clue relating to the treasure."

Dad was in on this, too. I knew it. I shook my head. I'd been so stunned and clueless.

"Toby planned one more trip back here before joining you at your father's birthday party for the big reveal. He told Max to meet him there, only Toby never returned. Are you going to help me or not?"

"No. You can just go to hell with the rest of them. Get out of here and leave me alone."

"Phoebe," his voice dropped, "treasure hunters never stop until the treasure is found, you know that. Toby didn't stop and neither did Max. You can be damn sure I won't."

"Even if it kills you?"

"That's the risk you take when the stakes are high."

Toby would have said something stupid like that. I swallowed hard. "Toby wouldn't steal anything. He might track it down— God knows he loved nothing better than solving a good mystery — but he'd never steal."

"He had the information that leads right to it. He was working with us, Phoebe. He did dive that cave we were in today and followed the signs to the shaft. I was just checking to see how good an escape it might make if I have to exit in a hurry. What I need is this," he indicate the diagram, "so I can access the caves from here."

"Toby wouldn't steal. He wouldn't run off without seeing Dad. Something happened to him."

"I can't give you answers yet."

I snorted. "Oh, please."

"We were friends. We shared a lot on our dive trips. He told me all about you, even the story about why you got that mermaid tattoo."

Toby told him that? I held my breath, staring at him, transfixed in pained disbelief. "Are you...?"

"No, of course not, but we were friends, I said. He told me how much he loved you and appreciated your support for encouraging him to be himself, no matter what. The merpeople tats were—"

"Stop!" That did it. *Toby, Toby. You can't be dead! How can so much life and energy just end?* I fixed on a single floor tile while it blurred with tears like I was staring down at the bottom of a bitter sea.

"I'm sorry, Phoebe." He stepped towards me.

"Don't touch me," I said without looking up. "You can just go to hell." Salt rolled down my cheeks, searing everything it touched.

"First, the treasure, then maybe hell, preferably in that order. I'm going down there with or without a diagram."

"Do you know how to get there from the here?"

"Toby said there's a hidden door right outside the base of the tower."

I squeezed my eyes shut. It was true, then. *Toby, why? Dad needs you; I need you.* The sound of the toilet tank cover being lifted jarred me from my pain. I watched Noel remove the baggie but made no move to stop him.

"There was only one place you could hide anything in here," he commented as he unfolded the parchment. "And you bled all over this."

"Good."

"But I can still make out enough to confirm my theory: another tidal shaft built right into the natural stone and probably rigged to flood with the tide as in Oak Island."

"A trap just like the Money Pit."

"It may be a trap but it's a simplistic one. The Wyndridges used this one as a bank, so you can be sure they enabled an easier withdrawal than the Money Pit."

"Why keep the loot bewied for two centuries? That's crazy!"

He turned to me then, lean face tense, eyes sparking fiercely. "Because the Wyndridges were a family of collectors. They couldn't bear to destroy precious jewels like Queen Isabella's pectoral cross or Aztec ceremonial gold. They melted down the coins but kept the main pieces intact."

"How do you know that?" I cried.

"Toby."

"You lie. Toby would never do that. I knew him better."

"Believe what you will. I have to go. This shaft isn't an exact duplicate of the Money Pit. This one was constructed to be a kind of bank where the Wyndridges could facilitate easy withdrawals. I'm confident I can work out the specifics."

"Did Toby tell you that, too?"

He glanced at his watch. "The tide will be fully turned within the hour. I've got to go."

"What about Max?"

"He's waiting on the boat offshore."

"You go out that door and I'll call the police."

He strode from the bathroom, me hobbling behind him. "Right. Knock yourself out trying. The landlines have been cut and your cell phone is drained. Oh, and your iPad is smashed, too. I'd say you're incommunicado." He pointed at my devices tangled amid the yarn pile on the bed. "Wait until morning and then make a run for the shore, but until then, stay here and, for god's sake, keep the gun close in case Wyndridge returns."

"What gun?"

He plucked a pearl-handled pistol from the yarn nest and slid open the chamber. "How many do you have?"

I stared. "Maggie."

"She's loaded it for you. Do you even know how to use this thing?"

"No."

"Listen up."

I tried taking in the details of which mechanism did what and when but befuddlement ruled. All I could think of was death and betrayal on multiple fronts. How could I be so blind-sided? Why at my age couldn't I at least be smart? Why did Toby get into this mess and why did I track him into the vortex? Question upon question screamed inside my head.

"I'm going now." He replaced the gun on the bed and in two strides, was beside me, looking down like he wanted to kiss me but couldn't find a suitable place .His hands hovered over my arms, barely touching my skin though, I swear, I could feel the heat. "Phoebe, I want you to know that I—"

"Get out."

He stepped away, taking a deep breath. "Right. I'll find a way to come back for you. Be careful in here in the meantime. If we're alone in this house now, we won't be for long, and you could be in danger still. Use the gun if you have to." Then he swung around and reached the door in three long strides.

CHAPTER 18

I hobbled forward as the key turned in the lock. Damned man thought he could lock me in! Even if I had to drag myself out, bone by bone, I was leaving that night. I'd tell the police, unravel the whole ugly story, and the hell with the consequences. Toby was gone absolutely, maybe I'd known all along, but my fury over what he had done burned holes in my heart. He had been involved in this plot—and Dad, too, not to mention Max and Noel— each one of those stupid men risked their lives for this idiot quest.

Back at the bed, I gazed down at the tangled mess, my grief and anger writhing. The gun glinted menacingly from atop the mass of blue fiber. The yarn below it tangled around the disparate objects like fibrous seaweed, slipping around the iPhone, snagging my charger, and catching among all my stuff.

After a quick inventory, I realized Noel had claimed Mrs. Wyndridge's chatelaine of keys but appeared to have left everything else. How kind. I'd just take my belongings and go: my unraveled knitting, dead cell phone, smashed iPad, a bottle of pain killers, plus Toby's drawing, and cram them back into my carpet bag amidst the jumbled artifacts from my ruined life. That left the gun. I buried it deep within my bag, only adding to its mounting weight.

But before leaving, I had to retrieve Toby's drawing tube from deep in the boxspring hiding place, something I could have done with ease a few hours ago but that now seemed monumental. I dumped the carpet bag by the door. Then, with my bum leg stretched stiff in front of me like Long John Silver on crack, I lowered myself to the floor, my back against the bed. Using my operable leg levered against the wing chair which, in turn, pressed against the wall, I applied all the pressure I could. I shoved and shoved until sweat beaded my forehead and I cried out in pain. After several agonizing moments, the mattress budged, slipping far enough off the frame for me to reach in and pluck the tube from the hole. I remained on the floor in recovery mode, panting for several minutes with the back of my head against the frame and the tube resting on my lap.

Toby, Toby, why? My brother was gone and now I knew the fault was at least partly his. His reason for coming here involved this damn treasure. I'd never hear his voice again, never see his face, or find out why, why, he had risked his life for *this*. And to think he participated in this monstrous act with Dad only infuriated me more. Who would I rail against, my demented father or my missing brother? In the end, only I'd been left out of the loop. Maybe they'd thought that, as a former law student, I wouldn't approve, and they'd have been right but not because of the law.

I thought I'd break in two, as if grief and fury ripped a jagged line right through my core. Nothing left but mementos, memories, and this twisting, bitter rage threatening to tear me apart. I wanted to slap my brother, yell at him, and hug him all at once, only I'd never be able to do any of that ever again.

Slowly, I pulled the rolled cartoon from the tube and spread it out across my thighs, wanting to see something in Toby's hand. Maybe my elevated emotions, my sense of total desperation combined with caffeine and pain killers, left me strangely focused, but the crinkling paper struck me as too thick and that fact now meaningful. We had painted the original on a sheet of white poster paper bought at an artist's supply store. Though thicker than the regular stuff, this felt unnaturally so, double, maybe triple. And then it hit me. *This* was what Toby had hidden and Max sought. *This!*

I held the paper up to the light. The outline of a third sheet silhouetted a shadowy square. Three sheets of paper, not two! All I had to do was peel away the two sheets that had been glued along the edges to reveal the secret third sandwiched between. It took a few fumbling moments, a little impatient tearing on one corner, but finally I had pulled out the secret sheet, holding it up in triumph.

A drawing so totally Toby, my heart swelled in my throat. It could have been a fanciful, stylized, felt-tipped mock-up of one

180

of his computer games or maybe a board game like some underwater snakes-and-ladders-merged-with-Monopoly-does-Atlantis. Sinuous snake-like forms undulated in a submerged world peopled by upside down mermen, skull and crossbones, and starfish wearing tricornered hats, arms brandishing swords. The largest snake, a very ominous thickly drawn creature, twisted like a mutant intestine, dominating center page and curving downward before straightening into an exploding head, swirling skulls, and exclamation points. Oh my god! Not a snake, but a tunnel!

I leaned over absorbing every detail, slipping into Toby's imagination, thinking in my brother's symbolic, whimsical style. The snake's tail in the upper right-hand corner represented the cave entrance; the little house above it, the tower, and the reptile's tortured body twisting below was, clear to me now, the treasure tunnel. And it ended in destruction, no doubt about it, all those crossbones and signs of alarm, but how?

I swallowed hard, not grasping every nuance, not getting what this portrayed or why Toby had hidden it, but understanding the warnings clearly. I could almost feel my brother then, as if he'd dropped down around me enveloping me in a sense of imminent danger confirming my own. STAY AWAY! And, whatever it was, Noel was walking right into it.

I hoisted myself to standing, rolled the sheets back up, and inserted them back into the tube. Let it not be said that I was a total idiot. Bad enough I came here against my instincts, but now I had to leave fueled by intellect and raw self-preservation alone. I would contact the authorities so a team could descend into the caves and save Noel. And, yes, he'd be arrested and, maybe Max, too, and, no, that would never bring my brother home, but would Noel listen to me if I tracked him down with a drawing of exploding snakes and parrying starfish? No. I'd take that seriously but nobody else would. I had to think of me, of Dad. I had to get the hell out of there. I jotted a quick note to leave on Mrs. Wyndridge's night table: HAVE GONE FOR THE POLICE. SUSAN

My leg had stiffened now, making bending it impossible, even if it weren't for the bandage. Hobble was all I could do and that not very well, considering I had to simultaneously drag a textile albatross on the floor behind me. Nevertheless, I made it to the door, where I bent down to insert the tube into the bag without falling over. I felt in my leather pants for my room key, which I had fortuitously stuck deep into the pocket. Ha! In went the key, I flung open the door, relieved to find the hall lights burning.

I made to hop my way out, hauling the bag, only its weight anchored to the floor, nearly knocking me off-balance. Hell and damnation! I would not leave that bag behind. Hopping back, I bent over with the bad leg stretched off to the side and reluctantly pulled out the iPad. That would just have to stay.

Propping the wounded tablet against the hall table, I tried again, this time managing two feet before sagging against the table in exhaustion. Then I realized it was far too bright. Only my room light had been on an hour ago. Now a bar of light beamed from under Mrs. Wyndridge's door and the table lamp opposite her room glowed. In fact, it seemed as though every lamp along the way shone brightly. Noel wouldn't have turned those on. And then, as if the house caught my thoughts, everything went out all at once.

Afraid to breathe, I strained to listen. Except for the wind beating against the shutters, everything was silent. Didn't Joquita say the power often went out in high winds? Taking a deep breath, I shuffled towards Mrs. Wyndridge's room, planning to check on her and deposit the note. Fumbling along the wall and navigating by memory, I pushed her door open and hopped forward, letting momentum propel me until my thighs hit the bed.

"Mrs. Wyndridge, are you awake?" I felt the bedspread, sweeping my hands back and forth searching for her sleeping form. "Mrs. Wyndridge? Wake up!" The bed felt strangely flat. The wind shook the shutters, blocking out subtler sounds. Could I hear breathing? "Mrs. Wyndridge?" I sensed another presence in the room.

"Stop where you stand, or by God, I will slice you asunder!"

***

I swung around, lost my balance, and tipped backward against the bed, arms flailing. "Wyndridge?"

Light flared, shooting the haggard face of Alistair Wyndridge into focus as he stepped out from behind the door, a lantern in one hand, a sword in the other.

"Thank God!" I said. "I'd given up—"

"Silence!" His face sealed in a mask of fury, his usually perfect garb was shredded and soaking wet. He looked like he'd been in a shipwreck three centuries ago.

"But I've been waiting—"

"Do not speak! I've had enough of your lies! Did you think I would permit you to harm my mother as well as steal me blind?" He bore down on me, sword glinting silver.

I pressed my back against the bed with no place to go, staring at the sword with a sickening sense he knew how to wield it. "I would never hurt your mother,"

"Indeed not, for I have transported her to safety, the better to deal with your gang unencumbered. Ms. Waverley, or whoever the hell you are — a detestable little thief, by any definition. Get to your feet!"

"Let me explain."

"I am disinterested in your lies, madam! Do not deny that you conspire with my enemies, murderers and cutthroats all. Get to your feet!"

"I-I can't get up without help."

He held the lantern over my head, swiftly assessing my condition. "Met some measure of your just rewards, I see." Satisfied that I was suitably helpless, he sheathed his sword and hoisted me to standing by practically wrenching one arm from its socket.

"Take it easy!"

He yanked me up until my face leveled with his: "You, ma'am, are not worthy of my consideration. I will not hear your lies," he said between his teeth. "How many times need I say it? Now move!"

He shoved me towards the door. I couldn't balance in time and hurled forward into the hall, crashing into a table. The lamp shattered on the floor as I gripped the wood to steady myself. He was on me in seconds, grabbing my arm and dragging me down the corridor.

"Wait!" I cried. "My bag. Back there." I let my full weight drop towards the floor. "In the bag. Can't leave it. Bert."

He released me like a sack of potatoes. I fell in a heap as he marched back down the way we'd come. "Where?" he called over his shoulder.

I lay on the floor, squeezing back the pain. "By. my. door."

He returned in seconds, the bag slung over one shoulder, and hauled me upright again. After that, I stopped trying to speak. It was enough just to keep from crying as he dragged me stumbling through the house. I had no idea where we were heading. Everything sunk into agony blurred by twisting hallways and leaping shadows, surreal images stabbing me with sharp edges and glinting surfaces. Shadows jumped out at me then slunk back into darkness after the lantern swept past. Nothing slowed him down. The man's fury burned into the air around us and I was in too much pain to fight. Besides, all I could think was guilty, guilty, guilty. I was here under false pretenses. My family had conspired to steal from him.

I squeezed my eyes closed, gritting my teeth. I was close to fainting by the time he finally jerked to a halt. We had arrived. Somewhere. I hung limp, all my weight borne on the arm he gripped while he fumbled for a key. The latch caught and he kicked the door open, pitching me forward into a room. The momentum propelled me across the floor until I banged into a piece of furniture, a bedpost, I realized. I clung to the carved wood, realizing we were in his bedroom. What was he going to do to me here? I thought of the gun in my bag. Maybe I could get to it somehow but what then — distract him, reach in and what, *shoot*? Hell, the man had every right to be angry, even unhinged, and I *had* entered his house under a ruse. I couldn't shoot him, even if I figured out how to work the damn gun.

He strode over to the bookcase lining one wall. A latch or a lever clicked and the bookcase slid back, revealing a secret room. Just like the movies, I thought, resting my forehead on the wood. Would I ever wake up from this nightmare?

"You did not discover this on your little night ambles through my property, did you? No, you did not! And that brute, Hector, could not detect my house's secrets no matter how many times he clumsily searched, being far too bovine for that. You, on the other hand, just could have but, fortuitously, did not."

I lifted my head. "You knew?"

"I knew!" He wrested my grip from the bedpost and shoved me into the secret room, forcing me down into a chair. There I slumped, watching him hook the lantern on one wall and lighting others from a long taper — two more lanterns, a candelabra and four wall sconces, including a cluster of pillar candles inside the craw of a huge, empty fireplace. Gradually, a large, cluttered space came into view dominated by heavy dark wooden tables flush against the walls, display cases everywhere, and two seventeenth century carved chairs angled companionably with a small table between. A grandfather clock standing at attention in the far corner tick-tocked away. No windows. Wyndridge unbuckled his sword belt, letting scabbard and belt thump to the floor along with my bag, now forgotten. The door creaked shut behind us in a wall of books.

"But how?" In retrospect, that probably wasn't the line I should have taken just then.

He swung towards me. "From the moment you entered the house, I knew you were part of the plot to steal from me!"

The fact that theft wasn't my intent hardly mattered now. Wasn't I guilty by association, guilt embedded in my very DNA? Since my brother and father had been involved, my true motivation seemed too weak a point to mention. "Why didn't you stop us?"

Placing hands on hips, he took a deep breath as if struggling for composure. His eyes swept the ceiling, fixing on the cedar beams for a count of seconds. When he refocused on me, he seemed slightly calmer. "Because I was awaiting my trap to spring, and spring it did. I was on my ship until a few hours ago watching my plan unfold."

"Watching?"

He held up his hand to silence me and shot me a tense, triumphant smile before turning and moving about the room. I watched him shuffling papers before he took a brief swig of some deep ruby liquid from a decanter and goblet.

The details of the room began distracting me in an impressionistic blur of candlelit antique tapestries on stone walls, heavy dark wood tables, and carved cabinets everywhere. Along with the furniture, I took in lots of sparkling and gleaming objects inside glass interiors. A small oval case at my right elbow held a huge mounted necklace encrusted with pearls and gems. I leaned towards it, slack-jawed as the clock chimed once.

"Yes, indeed, Ms. Waverley, do look." Wyndridge appeared beside me. "By all means, retrieve it from its perch. Try it on, do, for wearing a piece of history will be the only reward you will ever gain for your efforts in this matter, regardless of what you were promised."

I shook my head, only half-listening. I couldn't believe the glory in my line of vision.

"Oh, now, do not be timorous. You have come all this way, after all." He leaned over, flicked the latch and lifted the gleaming rope of pearls from its stand to drop over my head. I caught the lower length in both hands, struck by the cool, smooth weight of pearls the size of gooseberries, lifting the lower end into the light to better see its dangling gold cross. Rubies, emeralds, and sapphires sparked brilliantly in the light, each piercing me in some unexpected way. I had never seen anything so gorgeous. The piece hung heavy and lustrous, the gold cool against my skin as I let it drop to my chest.

"It's gorgeous!" I said, totally gem-struck. "Is it a pectoral cross, fifteenth century Spanish, maybe?"

"Indeed. I believe this piece was once worn by Queen Isabella herself. I would pose the worth to be millions in today's market, should it ever see the light of day, which sadly, it will not. Ask yourself, beauteous as it is, is it worth dying for?"

My eyes met his. "That's a question I usually ask."

But he wasn't listening. "Feast your eyes on the rest, Ms. Waverley—" He spread his arms to encompass the room.

"My name is Phoebe." Why that mattered to me then, I'll never know.

"Phoebe? Not Phoebe! The irony that you should be named after an object of light when, in truth, you are an agent of corruption, is more than I can bear. You introduced yourself as

Susan Waverley, the late Susan Waverley, I understand, and so you shall remain."

I didn't try to protest further. That he'd keep calling me after a deceased person seemed all that I deserved.

Arms still spread, he stepped back. "Precious artifacts from pirate hoards, the famed treasure my ancestor, Sir John Ashley Wyndridge, did abscond at the request of Sir William Phips, who would never return to claim his prize, lie herein. Mounted in every case, an artifact of great worth. Yes, a fortune lies encompassed here, a fortune gleaned across many centuries and civilizations, a fortune drenched in the blood of the conquered and the misfortune of multitudes— the shipwrecked, the plundered, the murdered! It has become the quest of many to wrest it from me at any expense, regardless of the wash of bloodshed and mishap that ensues. Death and beauty are my legacy. For, by the blood of my ancestors, I am Ward of the Tides."

Ward of the Tides, from one of his novels? Were fact and fiction mingled in his brain? I leaned forward. "I'm sorry for—"

"Silence!" He lifted one hand, raking his hair with the other, which only served to drag wet strands from his queue. His anxiety had begun to rise again as he began pacing the room, gaze fixed downwards. "Apologies hold no merit under the circumstances. You came to steal, madam. You sought out dear Ms. Smith and drove her to her death."

"I did not!"

"Do not deny it! You were even in the company of that brute when you entered my bedroom and pawed through my personal effects. I have you on film!"

"Film?"

He waved his hand. "Digital whatever it is called. I know not the name. Suffice to say that I saw you with my own eyes."

"By camera?"

"Of course by camera and on film!" He ripped the ribbon from his queue, letting his hair fall across his shoulders in damp straggles while flinging the sodden silk to the floor. "You thought me a Luddite, did you not, for I convinced you of such easily enough; but in truth I have ensured that this entire estate is wired, as they say. At the urging of a dear friend of mine, I —" He stopped suddenly, pressing his hand to his lips, "I—warded my— my *home* against trespassers and thieves. Here."

He snatched papers from the sideboard and flung them at me. A series of black-and-white photos rained over me, most sliding to the floor. I picked one up, then another, all still shots of me searching Wyndridge's desk and one of me foraging through his map cabinet with Hector looking on. Guilty.

"The others tell a similar tale, "he remarked. "I have hidden cameras all over the house and, in testament to your arrogant stupidity, you believed me when I stated I did not use technology." He gave a grim little laugh. "That should have been your first inkling that I was dissembling. Technology is a tool I could not afford to ignore, given my circumstances."

A sudden jolt of vertigo sent my head reeling. "I—"

"Silence!" he shouted. "One after the other, a stream of brutes and criminals have dogged this bounty for decades, nay centuries, with this being only the latest insufferable attempt on the treasure. Only," and he stared straight ahead, fixing at some point on the far wall and took a deep breath. "Only, it will end here, now. It must."

I looked up as he strode towards me, one index finger stabbing the air. "You thought me a fool you could play, but it is you and yours who are the fools, not I. You have befallen my trap, not I yours."

I tried to straighten in my chair. "Then call the police," I said.

"Too late for that by far! And yet, if I do not make this stop, more will die here and beyond. This is my legacy, and I must man up to the task." He shot a quick look at the clock. "The bell has chimed once. I must begin preparations but I will return. Pray, do not expend your energy trying to escape, for I will secure this room so you cannot leave. My ancestor's design is brilliant in all respects." Picking up his sword, he made for the wall.

"Wait, what are you going to do?"

With his back to me, he flicked something and bookcase-cum-door began sliding jerkily open. "Set the stage for the ultimate finale, the grand denouement, of course, whilst simultaneously writing the epilogue."

What the hell? I heaved myself from the chair to hobble towards him, but a wall of books slid shut before I even made it partway.

Chapter 19

A rusty lever was clearly visible in the opening between two embossed books, yet no amount of twisting or lifting or pulling activated the mechanism. He had locked me in. Not the first time that night a man had thought to keep me caged. Fine. I'd take his advice and wouldn't waste energy trying to break out, since I didn't have much left. I turned, hobbled over to where my bag lay dumped on the floor and hefted it up to the chair, cursing my leg as I went. I needed painkillers. Badly.

I set Toby's tube on the chair before fumbling around inside for my phone and pills. My hand encountered the gun. That damn gun! I pulled it out, glared at it, and finally shoved it under the needlepoint cushion for safekeeping. Back inside my bag, my fingers tangled in yarn as I dug around for phone and Advil bottle. I pulled out first one and then the other, staring in exasperation at my now dead cell phone. Even the red line had gone. I threw the phone on top of the bag in disgust and hopped around the room, blocking out the come-hither gleam of precious objects glinting from the cabinets.

At first, I was only looking for a power source, thinking maybe he had this room wired, too, but I could see nothing as obvious as a plug outlet. I doubted Wyndridge could bear having electronics in this sanctum, anyway. Probably surveillance cameras focused on the exterior of the room only. So, forget the phone. Besides, the walls were so thick and windowless, I doubted I could fix a signal even with a charged cell phone. No, this secret retreat of Alistair Wyndridge remained thoroughly ensconced in the seventeenth century and me along with it.

I slipped a candle holder from the table to study the contents of the display cases next, taking in what looked to be an Aztec ceremonial mask keeping company with other ancient artifacts, all incredibly rare and valuable. If Max, Toby, and Dad understood even a fraction of its worth, I could almost understand their compulsion. Almost. Max claimed he'd see it go to museums, if possible, though he hadn't ruled out private collectors' higher bids.

Who knew who really owned this cache under international law — Spain or the ancient civilizations she plundered? Wyndridge's lawyers would claim three centuries of possession holding sway for the family, but the other nations would argue their ownership, too. Either way, sorting out rights in court would result in a battle royal and could tie up this loot for years, if not decades.

That didn't excuse my family's involvement or "Uncle Max" for leading them into it. Wrong thinking. No one leads anyone into anything. Each person makes his or her own choices, including me.

I swallowed hard, moving on to a case of jeweled earrings and gem-encrusted bracelets, all probably the same vintage as the pectoral cross. Another case held religious objects and still another, gold buckles. I leaned against the buckle case, pushing back a headache building behind my temples. God, the worth of this treasure must surpass anything except King Tutankhamen's tomb. Since most treasure is found encrusted in barnacles on some sea bottom or picked away in underground tombs, I couldn't imagine what a cache of pristine artifacts might fetch. Since no doubloons or pieces of eight were included, I surmised the family must have melted down coins to finance their dealings across the centuries.

Leaving the display cases, I hobbled towards the sideboard, one of those sixteenth century carved monstrosities where Wyndridge kept a decanter of red liquor with a silver tray and two matching goblets. Why two, I wondered? Two chairs, two goblets. Did he regularly entertain a guest in this little museum-cum-treasure nest? I tried picturing his mother sitting in one of those chairs sipping wine but couldn't do it. A tea set, maybe, but not liquor.

I poured a small amount of the deep crimson liquid into one of the goblets and downed two pills. Being no connoisseur of fine liqueurs, I couldn't identify the stuff but liked the taste enough to pour myself another. With the goblet in one hand, I shuffled along the waist-high sideboard, investigating the papers spread across its surface. The first pile consisted of more security stills of either me or Hector each about some nefarious-looking task, including rifling drawers or prowling rooms we had no right to be in. Most had been taken with a night-vision camera, testifying to Wyndridge's sophisticated equipment, wherever he had it stashed. Several revealed me in the tower digging through the map cabinet.

I held one photo up to candlelight. By the angle of the shot, I figured the camera must have been positioned somewhere on the shelf that crashed, which explained why no evidence of me ambushing Hector lurked in the pile. Said camera must have already toppled with the shelf. Like that would prove my innocence. Wyndridge had at least seven clear shots of me folding his diagrams and stuffing them in my shirt, enough evidence to look me away for a long time.

I let the photos slide back to the surface and studied the room again. Wyndridge must have a bank of monitoring equipment somewhere, including printers and possibly WiFi, though walls this thick required a router per room, and hiding a router wouldn't be easy. Hard-wiring made a better choice. Cameras, on the other hand, were used by the police for covert operations with many small enough to fit into a peephole. Who knew what Wyndridge had seen?

I turned back to the sideboard to focus on a large diagram anchored flat by four paperweights, one per corner. I set down the goblet and stared. It was a duplicate of the one I found in the tower, yet somehow different. The paper seemed older, for one thing, the ink legible yet faded. It almost looked as if this were an original and the tower version a copy.

I leaned over, studying the drawing in the flickering candlelight, my mouth gone dry. The tunnel, the cave, the tidal shaft, I followed the trail with my finger down from the tower all the way to an opening at the cliff face marked "Entrance to Cavern 1", which I recognized as the sea cave Noel and I had penetrated. Though the opening had been rendered much smaller here, the shape was unmistakable, as was the tunnel and pool that followed. Had we gone further, we would have been led along a convoluted tangled of corridors and tunnels, caves and pools, all conveniently marked by periodic red arrows such as the one I'd seen on the cave wall, until we reached a large space labeled "Cavern 2 :Amber Lagoon". The Amber Lagoon linked, in turn, with an even larger natural cavern labeled "Cavern 3" shaped like a bowl. Lengthy entries had been penned in tiny script all over this area, with the words FLOOD CHAMBER in block letters accompanied by an arrow pointing into what looked to be a hole in the cavern floor.

A small boxed drawing of what looked to be a floodgate or some kind of mechanism had been inked in a careful hand on one side, an addition I knew hadn't been on the tower version. This mechanism appeared to be bit of engineering designed to be lifted or closed to allow in more water, a floodgate. Should the gate be lifted, water would rush through the tunnel along with the tide, rendering the shaft inescapable. But even more startling were the wavy lines running counter to one another with notations indicating "Tidal Pull" and "Extreme Current" and the ominous "Tidal Spout" accompanied by a tiny set of skull and crossbones spewing from the center of the hole like a geyser or an undersea volcano.

Hobbling back to the chair, I pulled Toby's sketch from the tube and hopped back to spread the drawing next to the diagram. I anchored the corners with goblets, a decanter, and my hand, as I stared hard. Toby had sketched a version of the flood chamber, his whimsical diagrams belying the horror should a diver penetrate the treasure pool. Divers like Noel. It all played out like a rolling video game: Diver enters a hole in a cave floor expecting to find treasure at the bottom, only to be sucked down by a combination of tidal pull and diabolical engineering and later spit out again by a furious force. That last part boggled me. Did it imply an explosion? And then, in a touch of poetic justice, my split lip reopened, and a drop of blood splattered on the diagram. I dabbed my lip with my once-white sleeve as the clock struck two.

Noel could be heading for death that very moment.

I made my way back to the chair, fished out the gun, and lowered myself down to wait, a full goblet of liquor at my elbow. When Wyndridge entered a few minutes later, he found me sitting

with my bum leg propped on a display case and a gun pointed at
his chest.

***

He paid me no notice at first, so intent was he in lowering a
leather satchel carefully to the floor before making certain the door
closed properly behind him. When he lifted his head and saw me,
his expression was almost comical.

"A gun?" he asked, agape.

"Yes, a gun. You know, I've been almost on your side from
the moment I entered this house, under false pretenses, I admit, but
still not intent on thieving or causing you harm once I got my
answers."

"How dare you!"

"Shut up." I waved the gun at him.

"I have no time for this."

"Too bad. Sit down. We're going to have a back-and-forth
dialogue, as in conversation. If anyone yells 'silence!', it will be
me, though 'shut up' works just fine in my books. Now, I'll ask the
questions, you'll answer them, got that?"

He hesitated, gaze swinging to the clock and back to the
gun. "I doubt you even know how to use a firearm."

"Oh, please. Modern guns are like cameras: You just point
and shoot. Sit down, I said." I nodded towards the second chair.

He did as I asked, keeping one eye on the gun. "You drank
my port," he said in an irritated and accusatory tone.

"Was that port? I like it. Okay, so as I was saying, I had
been feeling sorry for you, guilty even, thinking poor Wyndridge,
boohoo, everyone's intent on stealing your plundered fortune,
including, apparently, my family. Everyone's breaking into your
house, harming your staff — though that would be Hector doing
the harming, by the way, in case you hadn't figured that out — and
I was sucked in by it right up until I realized that your family are
the real murderers and the thieves here. It's all in how you look at
it. First John Ashley partakes in a devious plot to plunder from the

plunderers and steals the Spanish loot and designs an ingenious flood chamber in Nova Scotia."

"I beseech you to hear me out, for I—"

"Shut up and speak like you know what century you're in. Where was I? Oh, yeah: How many treasure seekers did that kill—4 or 5, last count? And then self-same ancestor slips away to Bermuda and constructs an equally deadly device to further kill anyone trying to unearth said treasure here. So, more people die, either directly or in the treasure's galaxy, such as Edna Smith. Then you, Alistair Wyndridge," I leveled the gun at him, using both hands. "Damn, but these things are heavy. So, you planted a bogus diagram in the tower to lead seekers down into the caves to meet their end. Nasty and murderous, any way you look at it. That's when I'd had enough."

He leapt to his feet, one finger stabbing the air. "All the documents in the tower are either fraudulent or copies! Do you think me fool enough to leave something potentially dangerous or valuable available to prying idiots? I care not who found or acted upon what. And you, Madam, are as conniving as the rest, insinuating yourself into my home, poisoning my mother, and rifling through my private belongings! Did you think I would just stand by? No, for I deliberately led you here once I realized the devious intent that was afoot and, furthermore, anything that befalls you and your kind is all that you deserve. Any person descending those tunnels has no right to be there, and thus, if they die, 'tis by their own greed!"

"Don't talk about greed to me. Look at this stuff! Your family have set up their own private art museum, paving the walls with precious artifacts for their own damn pleasure while others die trying to find it! For centuries!"

"It is our legacy!"

"Bullshit! Sit back down!"

Wyndridge collapsed back into the chair, burying his face in his hands, as I hoisted myself to standing and hobbled over to hold the gun inches from his head.

"Tell me what you did to my brother," I said in a small, tight voice.

He glanced up. "Noel is your brother? My god, but Max Baker has made this a family affair."

"Not Noel, Toby, Tobias McCabe, my brother. He came here and you lied about it to the police. That's why I'm really here, to find Toby. What happened to him?" My voice caught in my throat. I swallowed hard. I didn't need my bravado sinking into in a swamp of grief.

Wyndridge's face registered shock. "It cannot be." I stepped back as he rose to his feet, his eyes studying my face like a hungry man, oblivious to the gun. "Can this be true? Yes, there are similarities about the eye and chin and the hair color, certainly, but I hadn't seen it earlier. Toby mentioned a younger sister but I—"

"But you didn't expect her to track him here, is that it? What did you do to him?"

"Nothing! I would never harm Tobias, for I loved him!"

"Loved him?" I asked, almost losing my balance.

"Love him! Toby is—was—my partner."

Chapter 20

"Toby, dear Toby, my friend, my lover, my dear merman. We have been involved for a year, a relationship that would have continued forever, had I my way, until this! We were true mates." Wyndridge sank back into the chair, staring straight ahead. "I loved him, *love* him, oh how I *love* him, and now he's gone, gone, I know not where."

"You *love* him?" I stood wavering, unsteady on my feet, trembling equally inside and out.

Wyndridge looked up with moist eyes. "You knew of his predilection, I presume? Toby claimed that his sister had always been his lifeline."

And he mine, now severed. "Of course I knew he was gay, if that's what you mean; I just didn't know about you. Why didn't I know about you? Surely he'd share something that important? You'd be like my brother-in-law or something."

"He planned to disclose all and to you first. It was his intent to reveal our relationship at your father's birthday gala, to make his declaration and to simultaneously prevent the move on the treasure. I was to join him at the cottage a day later."

I shook my head, not getting it but trying so hard to grapple with the shock. Of course Toby wasn't a crook. Of course he'd be on the side of the good guy. "My father's had trouble enough accepting Toby's homosexuality, let alone meeting his partner under his own roof. He'd storm into a rage every time Toby alluded to it, as if yelling at him would somehow make him less gay. Toby said Dad would have a heart attack just from blustering at him, and you say he was going to introduce you?"

"Your father reacted much as did mine when I disclosed the truth over a decade ago. I vowed from that point forth to hide my predilection rather than suffer ridicule by the public and my family, both. My father even vowed to disinherit me should I reveal my true nature broadly. Therefore, I assumed this garb," he indicated his costume with a flick of his hand, "by way of camouflage. Prior centuries granted men more freedom of expression by way of clothing, did they not? One could aspire to be both manly and gay, like Toby, like me. Behind this I chose to hide. I left England for Bermuda and have lived here as a recluse ever since, both writing and living in an earlier time. I assumed a life of solitude with none but my mother and a host of imaginary characters chattering in my head, thinking this would always be the way, until Toby. Toby changed my world, my life."

I could see it all now, Toby and Alistair. My brother would be so drawn to this flamboyant and deeply passionate man, revel in his creativity, ache for his plunge into solitude, plus the measures he had taken to survive. "And yet, you were planning to carry on the death and destruction?"

Alistair sobbed into his hands.

I limped over to his chair, touching his shoulder both to steady myself and him. "Alistair, it seems as though we both love him, which should make us allies, don't you think? I could use an ally right now and maybe you, too. How exactly did he plan to stop the move on the treasure?"

He wrestled down his emotions and took a deep breath. "We had contrived a plan. I would donate the treasure to four major museums in four countries, an act designed to coincide with the publication of my final novel in the Bermudan trilogy, *Ward of the Tides*, which tells the true story of John Ashley Wyndridge. The writs are drawn up and ready to mail, along with communications through other media destined for the appropriate authorities."

I shook my head. "You would really give up the treasure?"

"I would, truly, for how else can I be free? Toby convinced me of such and finally I saw the wisdom. He had concocted a

198

brilliant plan designed to protect the treasure until it officially passed into safekeeping, the gist of which primarily involved technology, of which I had no previous comprehension. After the treasure was safe and my novel released to the world, I would sell the house and accompany him to a tropical island where we would design our own home and live a new life together. It was to be my ultimate happily ever after, a fitting denouement to this appalling legacy of grief and greed. And now it is ruined! I cannot go on without him!"

I stared down at him, gun hanging forgotten in my hand. "Then what happened?"

"I know not what and that is the God's truth! One day he left to fly home and that is the last I heard of him. I was to wait for his call and then take the next flight to Halifax. No word since, absolutely nothing! I have been frantic and twisting with anxiety ever since. I thought perhaps he had abandoned me, but no, no, Tobias would never do so, not with all we had awaiting in our future and everything between us. I hid nothing from him. We were partners, our fates explicably entwined."

His sobbing intensified until he spoke between gasping heaves. "I love him and he is gone!"

Not knowing how to console him, I refilled his glass and set it on the table. "I love him, too. Alistair, we have to stay strong, both of us. Let's try to save the grieving until later."

He glanced from the glass to my face. "This treasure is accursed, I am accursed! Someone must have deduced our intent, though not from me, for I have disclosed this room to no one, nor has anyone in my family for centuries, the secret having gone from lip to ear only within my immediate circle and then but to a chosen few."

"Who in your immediate circle, what chosen few?"

"My mother is the only one remaining, and she has long thought the treasure cursed and beseeched me to be rid of it. My brother is deceased, which leaves me to struggle with whom to pass on the burden now that the male bloodline dwindles."

"Oh, right, the male bloodline dwindles but no females are worthy, is that it?"

"No, that is not it! I have no female relatives but untrustworthy second cousins — flighty socialites more interested in partying in London than assuming a burden like mine. My brother died childless; his wife divorced him before he could sire children."

"How do you know your mother didn't tell somebody?"

"If possible, she is more reclusive than I. Besides which, she knows nothing of Toby's plan, only that I have the details of the treasure's location sealed in a London safe with instructions for it to be opened only upon my death."

I slid the gun on top of the table. "Well, something went wrong, didn't it? Somewhere between Toby leaving you to fly back home, something or someone intervened, but who?"

"Could Tobias have disclosed our plan before the appointed time? Did he entrust the secret to someone he believed trustworthy? "

"He wouldn't be so foolish." I certainly hoped that were true.

"He planned to demand that Max cease his search, intended to record the discussion secretly on some device, and then threaten to release it to the media should the Baker clan not comply. He had no intention of revealing the treasure's true location. That would be foolhardy. My merman thought of every contingency. He was a brilliant strategist!"

"Gamers are master strategists," I remarked sadly, reaching for my goblet and taking a big gulp. "Only sometimes even they miss the endgame."

"Surely, as his sister, you would know whom he would tell?"

Wiping my mouth on my sleeve, I set the glass down. "Maybe he didn't tell anyone. I mean, the treasure's still here, isn't it? Aren't they looking in the wrong place, thinking the treasure's stashed in that tidal shaft in the cave? But I'm betting one of the bastards crawling through your house right now knows something — Max, Hector, or Noel. Those are the ones who can give us the answers."

"Yes," Alistair nodded. "I stake my bets on Noel as most likely, for he masterminded this whole plot."

"What?"

"Toby assured me that Noel exerts power behind Max's throne. He visited the pair of them at Baker's London office numerous times, always returning with tales of Noel's ambitions. He envisioned Baker & Associates as a major player in the ancient artifacts and antiquities market, serving primarily wealthy clients willing to place exorbitant bids on stolen goods."

"The black market?"

"Exactly, the black market. Before Noel became involved, Max was naught but a middling antiquities dealer, flipping through Christie's catalogues and attending auctions, successful enough, albeit small-time. Then matters took a more deadly turn."

"But Max treats Noel like a dog."

"Dog and master have been known to play out a complex relationship, much like father and son."

"Alpha dog in sheep's clothing, you mean?"

Alistair smiled grimly. "Indeed."

"I didn't trust that man from first."

"And yet you are attracted to him."

I shot him a sharp glance. "What do you mean by that?"

"One of the multitudinous benefits of watching this drama unfold through secret cameras is that a wealth of context emerges. I observed from my laptop and upon the many monitors Toby installed, a myriad of subtle details regarding the players in this nefarious game. One such insight I gleaned as Noel descended on a battered Hector sprawled on the bottom of the tower steps not but a couple of hours ago. He was fiercely furious that Hector threatened you but equally incensed by the fact that Hector had disobeyed his orders."

"Hector works for Max?"

"Hector works for Noel. I remain unsure as to where Max fits in any of this."

Which explained why Noel was unconcerned when I stole Hector's gun. "Only, now Hector went solo! Damn it!" I slapped the table, dribbling port in the process. "Oh, sorry. Crud, I have been so blindsided! Noel warned me to be careful of Hector but implied he worked for someone else. Even Max said as much. What else did you see?"

"I ceased my observations after Noel forced Hector to his feet and down into the caves."

"Hector's still mobile? When I left him he was unconscious, and I'd hoped he broken a few important parts."

"I suspect a broken arm and possible leg, but he was still able to stand at Noel's prodding."

"I should have smashed my iPad over his head. So both of them are in the caves now?"

"I presume so, since I sealed the door to the house at that point and then proceeded to turned off the power to the house and thus to the cameras. Their only way out now is through the sea tunnel which, in high seas, is most treacherous, if not impassable. They are trapped down there. What is your relationship to Noel?" He added suddenly.

I turned away to study the clock. "Nothing. It's getting late. We should do something."

"He seemed rather too solicitous of your well-being considering the circumstances. Did he not take time from his machinations to attend to your wounds? Are you not romantically involved?"

I turned back to face him. "If you're concerned that my loyalties are divided, don't be. I accompanied Noel on a dive to the outer cave entrance. Oh, and he kissed me. Is that what you saw? I didn't ask for that, though I admit I didn't fight too hard, either. Blame hormones for drowning defenseless brain cells — an old story. Biology can be such a bitch. Anyway, we are not an item. Wait, if you saw the kiss, you must have external security cameras, too."

"Several are installed about the property, compliments of your brother, who urged me to heighten all my defenses. He installed everything himself. So masterful is Toby at all he undertakes. He taught me so much and beseeched me to be rigorous in reviewing all those saved security files, though I admit much remains to scrutinize."

"You don't buy into brevity, do you?" I hobbled back to the chair and collapsed. "So, Toby's plan has fallen apart for some unknown reason; the enemy is crawling around under our feet looking for treasure that's not even there; and Noel is the true ringleader, though presumably Max is involved somewhere, too. What were you planning to do about all this when you dragged me in here?"

Wyndridge sighed. "I have staged a secondary trap, albeit a clumsy one next to Toby's machinations, but the best I could do on

202

my own. I vowed to end this tonight once and for all. Everyone associated with this treasure suffers death or calamity. At one time, we successfully limited the mayhem by keeping the treasure locked away here, but that will work no more. Once those damnable researchers published *The Money Trap: The Greatest Web of Intrigue,* all was lost and 'twill be only a matter of time before the treasure's true location is disclosed. So I lured you and the others to my estate and devised an abrupt but calamitous end."

"Could we just cut the verbiage in the interests of time? What calamitous end?" I leaned forward. "What are you talking about?"

He jumped to his feet, dabbed his tears with a handkerchief pulled from his waistcoat, and began pacing circles around the room. "I should never have believed my life could be any different from what it has always been. All this," he waved at the photos still spread on the floor, "is just a feeble attempt to stop the inevitable. Nothing is worth the price my lineage pays to keep this monstrous secret. Yet, my dear merman would not allow me to remain shackled for the rest of my life. He intended to liberate me, set me free in heart and mind, so that I, too, could claim happiness. He would not betray me!" He swung back to me, pausing to fix me with his gaze, his face wrought with pain. "He would not, correct?"

"I knew my brother better than anyone. He wouldn't betray you. It's not in him. He was," I took a deep breath, "he *is* a kind and good person as well as being a brilliant one. What calamitous end? Are you planning for Noel to die trying to dive for the treasure, is that it?"

"Do you care?" he asked sharply.

"I care if someone else gets killed, yes, and so should you. The treasure has enough blood spilled over it. Noel took the diagram I found in the tower and is using it to locate what he believes is the treasure shaft. Is his death by drowning the calamitous end?"

"No, for I could not guarantee that end. Besides which that floodgate fell into disrepair centuries ago, though the cave, and that pool in particular, has natural perils enough. Furthermore, just to clarify, that bogus diagram you discovered was the design of a previous Wyndridge four generations ago. Everything in the tower is a red herring, so to speak." His face ragged with pain, he pointed to the satchel by the bookcase. "No, my concept is more definitive."

"Definitive how? A one-phrase answer, please."

"I planned an explosion."

I looked from him to the satchel. "You're kidding me. Blow up the caves?"

"No, the house — everything, treasure and all."

I held up my hand. "Wait, wait. You can't be serious. How would that help? You say there's a plan in place to donate the treasure to museums? Then, follow through on that. Forget explosives. We need answers and justice, not big kabooms. We need to find out what happened to Toby, and the only ones who know the answers are likely crawling below our feet. Let's bring *them* down, not the house."

Alistair regarded me in silence for a moment. "You truly are Toby's sister," he said finally. "The same resolution, the same focus."

"Is that a yes?" I pulled myself up, retrieved the gun, and stuffed it back into my bag. "Okay, let's think." I took a slurp of port and slumped back into the chair for a moment's rest, bad leg stuck out before me in some male bus lounger pose. "We've got to get our proverbial ducks in a row and come up with a plan."

Chapter 21

"For that, we shall need a steady mind and hand, thus must forgo the port." Alistair whisked away my goblet. About to turn away, something caught his eye and left him staring down at the sideboard.

"I never even liked alcohol until I came to Bermuda, and here I am turning into an overnight guzzler," I remarked to his back.

But Alistair wasn't listening. "What is this?" He slid away my makeshift paperweights and lifted Toby's drawing up to eyelevel. "My God, I thought I would never see this again!"

"You know it?"

"Know it? Toby sketched this in this very room! What a night that was, so full of dreams and plans! Where did you find it?"

"Hidden in Toby's old room back home."

Alistair stepped towards me. "But why, why would he hide it? Why would he even take it with him?"

"I don't know. It looks like a sketch for a game based on a treasure hunt in the caves but I can't figure out its significance."

"It is a sketch for a game, for, in truth, he fully planned to continue creating his technological fiction even after we had launched our new life together. Yet, why hide it?"

"I don't know, " I repeated. In fact, the whole thing made me a little sick, as if a snake twisted itself in my gut, tying the world and me in knots. I knew my brother, understood him, didn't I? So why didn't anything he supposedly did make sense? I reached inside my bag and fished out my pills, taking two with the last inch of water in Noel's bottle. "Okay, back to the ducks," I said after a moment.

"Ducks? Oh, yes, ducks." He strode back to sit across from me, rolling up the drawing as he went. "How do you propose to align aforementioned ducks?"

"You switched off the power? Let's switch it back on and see what they're up to down there on your monitors. Where is the best viewing?"

"We must traverse to a secret location just off the kitchen. Can you manage that?"

"Sure."

He strode about the room, dousing the candles, leaving a single lantern burning, which he held in the crook of a finger. "Toby insisted I have the main monitoring depot here inside the house, whereas I used my laptop via satellite on the yacht. We shall proceed to the kitchen."

"Does anyone else know about it?"

"No. It was installed during one of my mother's forays to England, and nobody but Toby and I were involved in its design or implementation. He insisted we even keep it from Frank, my previous driver." After refastening his scabbard, Alistair offered me his hand. "Let us proceed."

I realized he carried his satchel as well as my carpet bag. "What are you doing with that?"

"It contains both tools and my laptop."

"And explosives?"

"And dynamite."

"Why do you need dynamite if you're not going to blow up the house?"

"A precaution only."

"Alistair, there is nothing remotely practical about using dynamite as a defense unless you still plan to blow something up."

"That is no longer my intention."

"Relieved to hear it."

"Nevertheless, I think it wisest to carry it on my person. Toby once explained the underlying principles behind standard gaming strategy: Bring all the tools in case it may prove useful some unforeseen way."

I nodded. "Okay, point made, but dynamite hardly seems the most practical weapon. But then, to my view, neither does the sword. Now, a gun is another story."

206

I took his arm and heaved myself to my feet, clinging to him while he hefted both bags over his shoulders. He was strong, lithe, dashing, creative, and tortured, the perfect romantic hero. How could Toby not have fallen for him, even hoped to rescue him? "So," I said, "Just to be clear: we're going out after a pack of thieves with a sword, a gun, and a pack of dynamite."

"Indeed, not to mention my far more detailed knowledge of this property."

"Right." I watched him twist the lever so that the bookcase slid open. "Not run by electricity, I presume?"

"Powered by ingenuity," he said. "This is the same mechanical design John Ashley engineered three centuries ago and has required naught but a touch of oil to keep it in working order ever since."

The door slid into position behind us, leaving what appeared to be a seamless library wall as we made our way across the bedroom. In the hall, the darkness hung heavy, the sky obscured by shutters with nothing but the lamp gilding the gloom. Wind rattled the slats less ferociously now. That the storm might be abating did nothing to ease my nerves. Treacherous currents flowed through the hallways that night, eddying up against the walls, eager to suck the unwary down. I could feel what I couldn't see. The mermaid was in way over her head again.

"We must be quick about it," Alistair said. "Who knows what mischief those brigands are about."

A man burdened by baggage, a sword strapped to his waist, and a wounded woman hanging onto his arm does not make easy progress down narrow corridors. Once my bag brushed against a vase, flinging it to the floor in shards.

"Damn," Alistair muttered, picking up his pace."1710 Meissen."

"May it rest in pieces."

"How very amusing."

We had just reached the junction between the new extension and the old when he lurched to a halt. Damp, fresh air blew down the hall. "Someone has entered the house," he whispered. "The front door must be secured lest it blows open in the least wind. Come."

"Who would enter the front door? Why not a side door?" I asked.

"Hush!" he cautioned.

He tugged me down the stairs into the kitchen, where we could still hear the door banging in the wind.

"Aren't you going to shut that?" I asked while furiously hopping beside him trying to keep up.

"No."

By the time we crossed the floor, he was half-dragging me into a narrow space where coats hung from a brace of hooks. I would never have taken it for more than what it looked like: a kitchen corner near the far wall where boots, coats, and gloves were deposited before the wearer exited to the garden.

He dropped one of the bags to better reach behind the umbrella stand, and soon the wall shimmied open wide enough to allow a person to squeeze through. He pushed me inside first and followed after.

"You have more hidey-holes than a Jacobean manor." I dropped onto a stool, gazing around an area no bigger than a closet, where a monitor had been installed on every inch of wall space with a keyboard, a compact printer, and assorted remotes, cluttering a single long shelf on one side. Alistair set the lantern on the shelf, before sitting down on the other stool with his long legs crammed between the narrow walls.

He sighed, rubbing his temples. "First, the central power controls." In an instant, he had flicked a couple of switches, turning on the power and closing the secret door simultaneously. He began pointing a remote control at each monitor. "There are but five controls, each manipulating five cameras."

"Toby didn't rig a universal remote?"

"That was his ultimate intention but it did not arrive from America in time. This is the captain's seat of all Toby's surveillance efforts. It disquieted me at first, but I soon appreciated the power behind the twinkling lights and of knowing what and who prowls one's domain. Watching him design and install the system was, well, thrilling."

"Technology can be such a turn-on."

I watched as the monitors lit up, one by one, counting fifteen all together. At first, I couldn't tell which camera focused on what except for the obvious scenes: the hall in the old wing, the den, the upper library room, the kitchen, the boathouse, Alistair's room, his mother's, and mine — not the bathroom, thankfully. Almost every scene appeared illuminated by infrared, and a few showed lights burning, but nothing or no one moved in a single frame. I leaned forward, quickly scanning them again. "This can't be," I said. "There are at least two people, maybe three, in this house, yet everything seems empty. Look," I pointed to the tower's bottom landing where I had fallen hours before. The door leading to the caves yawned open.

Alistair rubbed his temples. "That is not as it should be. I secured that door."

"Can you remotely move the cameras?"

"I have never been able to manage such."

I recognized the pool where Noel and I had surfaced from the cove what seemed like eons ago. It foamed and boiled like a witch's cauldron, leaving the camera lens filmed in salt. "Which monitor features the bogus money shaft?"

He pointed to one on my left. By craning my neck, I could see a black-and-white scene of a large dark space dominated by what looked to be a tipsy tripod with a floodlight attached. The tripod appeared to have all but fallen over, leaning at a 90 degree angle braced by a pile of equipment which might be pulleys and ropes. The light still blazed, but upward towards the cave ceiling rather than down at the bubbling hole midcenter. I guessed that someone had rigged the tripod to lower a pulley system into the shaft, but something or someone had knocked it askew.

"The floodlight's not your style, I presume?"

"Indeed, not."

"So someone's in there or down there or both."

"So it seems." His calm unsettled me. It was as if all energy had expended itself and he was subsiding into his own denouement. "They may already be gone."

"Gone where?"

"Into the pool, the shaft, the sea."

"That shaft?" I pointed.

"Just so. All signs point to that pool by my ancestor's design, but there is no escape from there, nor treasure to find. One can exit only by the sea cave entrance, which, as you can see, is now impassable, or the door from the tower."

"Which is hanging open as we speak."

"It is, but it appears as though someone has attempted to dive the treasure pool this night. The sea has its own wards, does it not? The endless cycle of the tide, the force of storms that batters against the fluid edge of time?"

"What are you talking about? Alistair, don't go all weird on me. Hand me the camera remote." I held out my hand.

He passed me a device without a word, watching as I pressed various buttons, trying to bring the camera to life, to no avail. The thing stayed resolutely fixed on the same location.

I turned to him in frustration. "Maybe Toby's down there," I said, pushing all the buttons once again. "We've got to go down and find out."

"No. I have traversed every inch of that cave, but he is nowhere to be found. He is gone, they are gone. The curse continues."

I shoved the hair from my eyes and hitched myself to standing. "Listen, Alistair, whoever is down there knows what happened to Toby, remember? And maybe they need help. Where's your fire?"

"Despite all I've said and done, I pity the fool that tries to dive that shaft. My ancestor used it as a decoy with which to lead on the unwary. Only the outer lip is manmade; Nature has designed her own blowhole to erupt in certain weather conditions, which this time of year is often enough. Tonight, the spout has been most active. Anyone who goes down will certainly not survive."

As if on cue, the camera caught a blast of water bursting from the hole, spewing at least eight feet into the air in a horrific force, spraying water across the cave and hurling the tripod and the lamp into the boil. For a moment the cave whirled in sea, surreally illuminated by a waterproof lamp bouncing around in the foam before even that went dark. The infrared camera kept rolling as the renegade spout retained its vertical deluge for seconds more before a powerful force sucked it back down in a gulp of foam. I watched transfixed, Toby's sketch exploding in my head. "My God."

"Precisely."

In my shock, I had unknowingly pressed two buttons simultaneously, and the camera jerked alive. One eye on the screen, I maneuvered the up and down buttons until the camera could sweep the perimeter of the cave. Besides a flotsam of beached equipment, somebody's jacket bunched in a sodden heap, a sneaker, and an oxygen tank, in its extreme right position the camera finally landed on a set of legs jutting into view with the upper half caught in the blind side.

"Damn! Someone's hurt!" As we watched, one leg lifted before falling back limply. Those legs were long but not thin, wearing what looked like jeans and crocodile boots. "It's Max and he's hurt! Get up. We've got to help him."

"Certainly not," he said from that faraway numb place he now inhabited. "The area is fraught with danger. That man entered knowing the risks. He has no one to blame but himself."

I tossed down the remote. "Don't say that! Don't you dare say that! He's my godfather and I am not, I repeat, *not* going to lose another family member! We're a team, remember? Get up and help me or I'm going without you!" I tugged on his arm, trying to force him to stand, which he did but only just to try pushing me back to sitting. At that moment, with the two of us braced in a will-wrestle, the power went out. Again.

"What just happened?" I whispered.

"I believe someone just cut the main power line."

Chapter 22

"How to you know it wasn't just the storm?" I asked.
"Listen."
We stood clutching one another, senses keening. Not more than a foot away, on the other side of the wall came the unmistakable sound of scraping, as if someone were sliding a heavy object across the floor. The wall rattled briefly and then stilled. Pattering footsteps retreated.

I threw myself against the wall, rattling the lever as if I could make it slide open by will alone. "Let us out! Who are you? Come back! Don't you dare leave us here! If you hurt Max, so help me I'll kill you!" I banged, knocked, and shook the wall until Alistair stilled me with a hand on my shoulder.

"He is gone."

"Who? Who locked us in? Not Max! God, I have to get to Max! He's hurt. And Noel's down there trying to dive that shaft! Open up!" I cried, resuming my assault.

Alistair grabbed me by the shoulders and twisted me around to face him. "Calm yourself!" He shook me gently.

I breathed deeply, pushing down my panic with every exhale. "Okay," I said, holding up my hands. "Good now, thanks." I stood still, bracing myself on the shelf as Alistair lit the lantern.

"The door is not operated by electricity, for Toby duplicated John Ashley's mechanism. We need only break the — "He stopped abruptly, staring in horror at his feet.

"What?" I looked down at my crumpled bag.

"My satchel! I must have left it outside when we entered."

"Oh, hell, Alistair. Are you saying whoever locked us in is now running around with a bag of dynamite?"

"That appears to be the case."

I bent down and hoisted my bag up to drop it onto the chair. "Well, I've still got a gun and you a sword. Let's move to the offensive." I felt around for the gun, touching its cool surface with trembling fingers. Good, still there. "How do we get out of here?"

"We need only break the lever and push against whatever has been shoved before it to break free. Or, so I hope." With that, he lifted one booted foot and began kicking at the brass lever.

I joined in by shoving a shoulder in time with his kick. After several minutes of battering, the latch remained intact. "How does this thing work?" I asked.

"The door is operated by a lever-and-pulley system but my guess is that the brass lock, which slid into the housing when I closed the door, is now jammed by whatever barricades said door."

I dove back into my bag and pulled out the gun, clutching the grip with both hands, aiming for the lever.

"Surely you do not think you can blast it apart?"

"Watch me." But first I had to figure out how to unlock the safety catch, which required slightly more dexterity than I expected. When finally I figured it out and pulled the trigger, the shot reverberated through my arms and knocked me backward into Alistair's arms. Pushing me back to standing, he held the lantern over the hole in the door, revealing how badly I missed. I shattered the wood in parts but not much else.

"Guess I need practice."

"Stand back." Alistair drew his sword.

"Surely you don't plan to impale it?"

"Perhaps I can slice the wood until we can get a hand through."

"Let me try to shoot it again."

"Then aim for the indentation below the latch, and this time, do try to shoot to kill."

"Very funny." I braced my legs, tensed my arms with the gun in both hands, aimed the barrel straight for the defined spot, and fired. The blast exploded the wood and pinged against something metallic to send a flurry of sparks into the air.

"Step away," Alistair ordered. Bracing himself against the shelf, he lifted both feet together and hurled his boots at the damaged latch. The door splintered as bits of metal and wood shards dropped to the floor. With both of us shoving at the damaged door, we managed to push the chair positioned on the outside away from the opening and send it clattering to the floor.

Once free, we scanned the empty room. "I don't suppose you have a secure phone line anywhere or even a cell? We need to call the police."

"I detest cell phones, and though Toby did insist I have one, I left it on the yacht."

"A cell phone is no good unless you keep it with you."

"How revolting! On the other hand, we might have sent an email before the power eclipsed."

I sighed heavily. No time for any of that. My only thought was to help Max and Noel but not by relying on a single lantern to light our way through the caves. I beckoned Alistair to take me into the drawing room, where I had stuffed the batteries and flashlights, my hopping gait hardly stealthy. If the enemy was hanging around, we couldn't help but announce our arrival. Luckily, nobody was.

"Whatever possessed you not to take these torches with you?" Alistair whispered as we plundered my stash from the harpsichord accompanied by a ping of random chords. He set the lantern on top of a table and doused the flame.

"I forgot." I handed him a flashlight and a handful of batteries, taking one for myself and tossing the rest of in my bag slung over his shoulder. "I had things on my mind."

The front door no longer banged in the wind, a worrying point as we proceeded down the corridors towards the old wing. Alistair's flashlight picked up wet footprints tracking ahead of us. I still gripped the gun in one hand and, though the thing felt unbearably heavy, I couldn't let it go. He kept his sword drawn, too, holding it out in front of us ready to spear the first interloper who dared cross our path.

"What do you think they're going to do with the dynamite?"

"Hush." He urged me towards the outer tower door, which stood propped open with a chair. Nobody in sight. We stepped through into the tower base where I flashed my light across the bottom steps, wincing at the sight of dried blood, either mine or Hector's, it didn't matter. My beam hit a black duffle bag positioned against the wall as if in readiness for a speedy exit. Alistair rifled through it, pulling out a coil of wet rope, a spotlight, and a watch, casting me a questioning gaze.

I shrugged back my answer.

Straightening, he looped my arm in his and led me tentatively to the threshold of the cavern stairs, where we stood gazing down the curving rough-hewn steps to where a light shone somewhere far below.

"It is most steep," Alistair stated the obvious.

The logistics of a lame woman climbing down those slabs of stone hit me hard. Could I do this? Did I have the strength, or even the courage, since who knew what lay in wait down there?

The same thing must have occurred to Alistair. "I shall proceed first," he whispered, releasing my arm and dropping my bag. "If the way is safe, I shall return."

"No, wait! I'll go with you!" But he dashed down the stairs and out of sight without another word. The damn man was going to play hero armed with nothing but a sword! How could I follow him? The stairs may as well have been a straight drop to hell for all my stiff leg could manage. Struck numb by indecision, I stood wavering. I couldn't do this and yet, I had to. Maybe I didn't have to topple head-first down those steps to make progress. I would butt-shuffle.

Not for the first time did I thank Maggie's leather pants as I hoisted my way downward over rough stone, arms back behind levering me up and down. I focused on speed and stealth, relieved to discover my passage surprisingly quiet. No scraping or thumping. Reluctantly, I left my carpet bag behind on the landing, confident that no one else would find the contents valuable. The gun stayed with me, caught in my back waistband, the safety catch secured.

When I approached the bottom landing where the light beamed, I stilled, listening. Detecting no movement, I proceeded cautiously, rounding the corner and making my way down the remaining two steps like a bad-assed spider until I reached the stone floor. Two duffle bags sat heaped one on top of the other against the wall, where a modern lantern hung on an iron hook overhead. A set of double oxygen tanks and a pair of flippers had been tossed mid-floor, still wet. I scanned around looking for a safe place to hide, but with only the tunnel ahead and the stairs at my back, I had no choice but to move forward.

Hitching myself up, braced against one wall, I hopped to the tunnel entrance, and balked. The shaft dropped like a stone ramp into the darkness. The occasional lantern only revealed the steepness of the pitch. I visualized Toby's diagram, knowing this would be a long slant deep into the earth, followed by caves and pools, and who knew what else, maybe monsters of the human kind. Hector, for sure, and now some unknown person. Maybe they were armed, certainly they were dangerous.

A coward at heart, I never pushed too far outside of my comfort zone but here I was dangling by the neck. Might as well sever the rope. I stretched my arm on either side until my fingers touched the tunnel walls, a flashlight gripped in one hand, hopped into position, and readied myself. I thought of Toby, my dad, Max, and now Alistair — where was Alistair?— took comfort in the gun, and pitched forward.

My hopping leg fought furiously to keep me upright as I hurled on a downward trajectory, more than once landing my full weight on the wounded side, and yelping in pain. Sweat broke on my forehead, I panted with effort, and whammed into a turn before lunging around and pitching downward again. The flashlight fell with a clang, leaving me in the dark for part of the way only to dash into light from a lantern around the next corner. And just when I thought it would never end, the bottom arrived abruptly, dumping me up to my thighs into an icy pool. A wild arm dance followed until I regained my balance, catching images of a large well-lit stalagmite-forested cavern. I grabbed a stalagmite and hoisted myself up to the cave floor, wincing as salt water seeped through my bandages.

Ahead, a black figure bent over a bag, unaware of my presence—not Alistair, not Noel or Max but some shapely female encased in a black leather cat suit. I tottered forward, dumbstruck. "Maggie?" I slipped one hand behind me and tugged my shirt down over the pistol. "Where's Noel? We've got to get to Max. He's hurt! Did Noel try diving the shaft?"

She swung around. "Oh, shit. How'd you get here?"

216

"What's going on?"

"What's it look like? I'm helping the guys." She straightened and stepped towards me, looking uncharacteristically competent and menacing in her leather cat suit with the thigh-high boots. All she needed was a whip. "You look like hell. I told Max not to bring you into this, but once again, he didn't listen. Look at you, the poor little mermaid with half your tail scraped off. And you ruined that blouse."

"You're not answering my questions."

"Because you ask too damn many of them. No, Noel didn't dive the hole, and, yes, Max is a bit shook up but fine."

"He didn't look fine. I was afraid they tried to dive the shaft, but the whole thing is just another decoy. That's what I want to tell them. There is no treasure." My gaze shifted from Maggie to the equipment piled behind her. Was that Alistair's satchel?

"Yeah. Thanks for the dynamite," she said, catching my gaze. "Noel's found a use for it."

"Like what?"

"It will work into our plan nicely." She studied me for a few seconds. "It's not too late, you know. You can still join us and get rich beyond your wildest dreams."

"Gee, thanks for the chance to be a criminal on the run all my life. I'll pass. Besides, there's no treasure, I said."

"Oh, give it up."

"What?"

"I said, stop pretending there's no treasure. You never could lie."

"You locked us in the control room, didn't you?" I took one hop back, latching on to the nearest stalagmite.

"Yeah, I did, and that's where you should have stayed . It's safer. Do you still have the gun I gave you?"

"Lost it. Sorry."

"How could you lose a gun?"

"Because I didn't want it in the first place."

"Incompetent little snot. You never could go the distance, though I'm shocked you got this far. I suppose you blabbed everything to Wyndridge?"

"I told him everything."

"Which explains why he's running around acting like Errol Flynn. And here I thought I could make something out of you."

"Guess I'm just cut from another cloth."

"Some ratty old rug, you mean. Why couldn't you do what you were told instead of trying to mess things up? And getting all cozy with Wyndridge is a waste of time. He's gay."

"And I couldn't possibly relate to a man unless sex was in the picture. Where is he?"

"Have no idea. Scrambled into the tunnels after Hector, but Noel decided he had better things to do than chase after the two of them. With luck, they'll both stay lost forever or do each other in. Now, Noel, there's a real man. He's got guts and vision. You should have nabbed him while you had the chance. He likes you."

"And I actually thought I might save him from walking into a trap."

"He's been one step ahead of you all along. Sucks, doesn't it?"

"But the treasure is gone." I tried for a more compelling tone. "The Wyndridge family disposed of it all. I keep telling you that but you're not listening."

"You're talking a pile of shit so just stop it."

Why did she seem so damned unconcerned? I tried again. "If you all leave the house tonight, Alistair just might not press charges. It's worth a try, isn't it? I mean, why end up in jail trying to steal something that doesn't even exist?"

She laughed and paused to adjust her chignon, tucking an escaped lock back under her chic beret. "Oh, Phoebe, I don't know whether you think I'm stupid or you're just denser than I thought. We've already got the treasure and we *are* leaving tonight, as in 38 minutes. We have a rendezvous with a boat in the cove, followed by an express pickup by helicopter at sea so, like, I don't have time to stand around and chat, you know? "

I shook my head. "Max planned all that?"

"Max didn't plan shit. He doesn't have the guts."

"Mags, what's happening? Is Max still lying in Cavern 3 or not?"

"It's all under control. Don't you worry." She stood smiling only inches away from me now, and I knew absolutely that I should worry with every inch of my being. "You know, hon, you

218

should have been nicer to me when you had the chance. I never wanted anything to happen to you."

"Is something going to happen to me now?" Surely she wouldn't hurt me, and yet, what did I know about the people in my life?

"It's just getting messy, that's all. After tonight, we'll probably never see you again. That's sad."

"Then let me say goodbye to Max. He looked hurt when I saw him in the monitor a while ago. I want to make sure he's all right."

She glanced over her shoulder towards a large opening on the far side of the cave. "It's rough going here. You won't make it by yourself. I'll help you but you've got to hurry, okay?"

"Okay." I reached up and knocked off a long, skinny stalagmite.

Maggie lifted her perfectly groomed eyebrows at me.

"Serves as a cane," I explained.

"Right, so take my arm and let's go." She positioned me on her left, the side opposite her holstered pistol.

"I see you carry a spare," I pointed to the gun.

"Always come prepared."

I hopped beside her across a slippery surface where shallow pools reflected the stationed spotlights, using my new cane as leverage when needed and her arm the rest of the time.

"Does Hector work for Max?"

"He worked for Noel, but Heck's just as big a no-good piece of shit and tried going solo. And, yeah, he killed your library friend 'cause he gets off on killing people. Max would never put him on the payroll, but Noel had to. We were running out of hired hands in the end." Maggie spoke with so much nonchalance, she could have been referring to inconvenient weather.

"We?" I hesitated by a narrow ledge of stone edging the lagoon.

"Me and Noel. Hurry, will you?" She tugged me forward , forcing me to hop-jump more quickly. Realization jarred my skull with every hop: Hector worked for Noel; Noel didn't work for Max; Max was out of the picture. What were they going to do with him, us? Hell. Damn.

"Maggie," I said, suddenly holding her back. "You shafted Max?"

"Yeah, okay? He thinks too small and never lets me in on the game. There, satisfied? Here we are, on the brink of one of the biggest finds this decade has ever seen, bigger than even the Cheapside Hoard, and Maxie gets all hesitant, like, "Oh, we can't do this or that,"' she mimicked his accent. "Like hell we can't. I'll adorn myself like Schliemann's wife. Remember those photos of her wearing the golden headdress?"

"The golden diadem presumably held in Russia?" I nearly slipped into a pool until she yanked me back. "Yes, sure, I remember it: solid gold, a priceless ancient artifact."

"Right on. I always wanted to be Sophia Schliemann at that moment. I'd even have designed a silk robe to get the look. I so get that photo."

"Wow," I said, forcing enthusiasm. "How will you pose for your cache?"

"I was thinking one of those velvet boleros that Penelope Cruz wore in a Vogue shoot a couple of years ago—black lace, sexy lace-up boots, the Spanish thing, you know? I'd get Noel to dress as a dashing bullfighter. Can't you just picture it?"

"Sure, only there'd be more bull than bullfighter under the circumstances, wouldn't it?"

She gave me a little shove. "Very funny."

"What about Toby," I said suddenly, desperately.

"No can tell."

We had arrived at the entrance of the next cavern. I stood staring into a large still body of water the size of an Olympic pool rimmed by a forest of stalactites and stalagmites rising like stone branches, top and bottom. Two high-powered lamps had been fastened onto a couple of stalactites rising from the depths, casting the cavern into an eerie amber glow.

"What do you mean, 'no can tell?' Tell me!"

"Shut up. This is the Amber Lagoon. Watch yourself here," Maggie said. "We had a boat to ferry us when we were carrying stuff across, but Noel's using that elsewhere now."

"What stuff? Thought you said you didn't go diving?"

"I didn't say that. We didn't dive for the treasure, but Noel still needed his props."

220

"Props? What aren't I getting?"

"Stop the third degree already. Keep moving and watch your step. We broke a path through here."

We began to weave single file through the stone forest, me clutching anything I could hold onto to keep from slipping into that dark expanse.

"Where's Toby? Did you kill him?"

"No, we didn't kill him. The less you know the better. Now, move!"

Finally, we almost reached Cavern 3. Maggie shoved me up to the natural threshold and held me fast. "Watch it. There's a piss-hole of a chasm at your feet that I nearly fell into earlier. Noel's fixed a board on the left to make it easier to cross. See?" She aimed her flashlight straight down the crevice, revealing a deep, stony gouge with water at the bottom. I nodded, remembering Toby's drawing. We shuffled across the planks, one behind the other, me holding the wall for support, focused towards the pale light ahead. When we reached the threshold to the next cave, I stood trying to take it all in, the infamous Cavern 3.

Just as the diagrams indicated, it was larger than all the rest, and sunken like a wide, deep bowl, with three tunnels veering off in different directions. A sea hole bubbled in the center illuminated by a single spotlight propped on the floor by the broken tripod. A mess of objects and equipment lay beached around the perimeter, including Max, splayed face-up against one wall.

I gasped, so focused on him that I didn't feel Maggie release my arm or anticipate her shoving me forward into the bowl. I trip-stumbled downward at full hurl until I caught myself on the tripod and stood steadying myself, anchored by my cane. Maggie now pointed the gun at me.

Chapter 23

"But why?" I asked, turning to the woman I thought I knew..

"Because I'm not spending my life as somebody's assistant or somebody's not quite anything important. Did you see how he treats me? Like he treats Noel, like always the servant and never the partner. I'm so done with it."

I pulled the gun out of my waistband and tried to hold it steady.

"You don't seriously intend to shoot that, do you?" Maggie said, pausing three yards away from me.

"If I have to." I glanced at Max, still and deathly pale against the far wall. "What happened?"

She checked her watch and then me, as if not quite sure which concerned her more. "I don't have time for this."

"What happened?" I shouted.

"Max wasn't supposed to follow Noel in here. He was supposed to wait on the boat while Noel dived the hole, though there wasn't going to be any diving. This is all for Max's benefit, like a set, see? Max was supposed to wait on the boat while we took off with our ride. Noel sent him pics of the shaft and said he found something but to meet him in the cove, only the stupid ass followed him in, worried about *you!*"

I glanced quickly at Max, who was trying to lift himself on his elbows. A livid gash dribbled blood from his forehead and his face bleached pale. Drenched to the bone and quaking, he could barely hold himself up. "Get—away, Phoeb'!" He fell back down with a moan.

"Max!" I wanted to go to him but couldn't take my gun off Maggie. "Why not leave him? Why cheat him, why hurt him?"

"Oh, please. I didn't hurt him, Hector did. And why would I leave empty-handed? I'm grabbing a piece of the action. You could have gone in with us and shared the stash, but you can't even figure out what you want to be when you grow up. I'm just so done. Put down the gun. You know you don't have the guts to shoot it. Besides, that spout's going to blow soon and you'd better be away from that hole when it does."

"No," I said gripping the gun with both hands while bracing myself against the tripod for balance. "You're going to tell me about Toby or we'll both get thrown in the wash!"

"Setup," Max mumbled. "Go."

"Do as he says, Phoebe," Maggie said. "You don't want poor Uncle Max to be defenseless when the spout blows again."

The gun was shaking so badly, I thought I'd drop it. "The dish runs away with the spoon? This is preposterous!"

"It's not like that. Noel and I aren't lovers, we're partners. I'm done with lovers. Now, get away from that hole before you get hurt."

And then Alistair sprang into the cavern, his sword held high, spun around, and caught sight of us. "Phoebe!"

"Hold steady, Errol," Maggie warned him. "I won't hesitate to shoot you."

Alistair scanned the scene, shifting from one of us to the other. "Phoebe, move to the safety of the wall."

"Max is hurt," I told him, fixed on Maggie. "I'm not letting her leave."

"Like you're going to stop me. I've got a gun, too, only I know how to use it."

"Hector is raging around in the tunnels armed," Alistair said, inching closer to me. "I gave him chase to lead him astray but he may yet find his way back. Where is Noel?"

"Good question. Maggie?" I tried lifting the gun higher.

"Look, I'd love to stay here and chat, but the bridge is going to blow any minute and I'd like to be on the other side before it does. I'm not the diving kind. So you two stay here and take care of Maxie while I make a run for it."

"What kind of man leaves his father to die?" Alistair demanded, sweeping in behind me to lay a steadying hand on my back.

"Father?" I said, turning to him. Another sucker punch. "What do you mean *father*?"

"I believed you knew. Noel is Max's son."

"I didn't know. Again." Oh, hell, I felt like cursing like a banshee, raging my fury against all these damn secrets! "Is that true, Maggie?" But when I turned back, she had ducked back towards the lagoon and disappeared.

"Come," Alistair said. "Let her go. We must leave here before the spout blows again. I know a secret route."

"I can't leave him," I said, running to Max. "I'm so mad right now I want to shake him until his teeth drop out, but I won't just leave him to die. After Dad, he's all I have left." A shock to realize the truth. Where did these emotions come from?

"We will move him to a safer location," he insisted.

I caught his eye. "But, Alistair, what was so damn important about Noel being his son that Max couldn't tell me?"

"Because I told him not to," came a voice at our backs.

Noel had entered from the lagoon wearing a wetsuit and carrying two duffle bags, which he dropped at his feet.

"Bastard!" I spat at him. "Lies, everything about you is a lie!"

"Not everything. My feelings for you are the truest thing about me. Hear me out, Phoebe." He took one step into the bowl.

"Nothing you say can ever justify what you are doing to me, to Alistair, and your own father! Your *father!*"

"Biology alone does not a parent make. I have my reasons for doing what I do."

"I didn't know she was pregnant," Max came a weak voice from the floor.

"Would it have made a difference? You knocked her up and then went on your merry way, Pops. She was foolish enough to believe a handsome white bludger like you might actually return and pluck the Abo girl and her half-breed kid away to a better life. It never happened in her lifetime, did it?"

"Stop," Max moaned.

"There's no stopping me now. Now, I'm taking something for myself."

Max lurched to his elbows and rasped, "I love you! I gave you everything," before slumping back.

224

"Save it, Max. Mags and I are starting our own enterprise, sourcing the rare and precious all over the world, financed by the biggest find this century has ever seen. Thanks for that, Wyndridge. And, yeah, *father*, I learned the business from you. For that you have my thanks."

"What are you referring to? What find? There is nothing here!" Wyndridge said, waving his sword at the surrounding cave.

Noel flashed his smile. "Right you are, mate. Nothing here. Nice trick, by the way, but we've had the inside track all along. Must bid our adieus now." He checked his watch. "Our ride will be here soon." His eyes found mine. "Phoebe, come. You'll learn everything you need to about Toby if you come, I promise."

"You're crazy if you think I'd go anywhere with you. And what about Toby? You know about Toby? Why you won't tell me?"

His face, sharp-angled at the best of times, now seemed sliced in pain and exhaustion. "Come and I promise I'll tell you everything."

"Tell me now!"

"It has to be this way. I have no choice."

"Do you actually think I would go anywhere with you after this? You're despicable!"

"Sadly, I'm afraid your opinion of me is about to get worse, but I can't linger any longer to explain."

"You will go nowhere!" Alistair called out, falling into the classic en guard position, dancing his way towards Noel with his sword extended.

Noel glanced at him with disbelief and pulled a pistol from his belt. "Back off, mate. I don't want to hurt you."

And then Hector stumbled into the cavern from one of the tunnels, a raging bull, head down, bloody and holding a gun aimed at Noel. "You're not going anywhere, kid." He stood wavering, one arm hanging limp at his side. "You bloody cheated me, damn you, and you," he swerved the gun in my direction, "bloody tried to kill me! You're all dead!"

"Shoot me, I shoot you," Noel warned. "Again, only this time I'll finish it, believe it."

Alistair slipped to the perimeter to approach Noel from behind while I swung my gun towards Hector. Noel's gun went off the same time as mine, only my bullet went pinging against the cave, or maybe it didn't since, at that moment, the blowhole erupted like a pressure cooker gone mad, knocking everyone off their feet, flinging the spotlight into the boil and the cave into a dark, frothing maelstrom.

I grappled for a handhold, thinking only of Max helpless against the far wall. My hands slid away from everything, and everything slid away from me. The swirling mass of darkness and water disoriented me until I couldn't tell up from down. Grunts and cries perforated the roaring water. Somebody called for help, maybe me.

I heard cries and shouts and somebody calling my name. I felt the water sucking me backward headfirst toward the hole. Scrabbling for a handhold, blind and dizzy in the darkness, acting in some kind of mindless survival mode, I somehow turned myself around. My flailing hand found another's but the fingers weren't friendly. They grabbed mine viciously, intent to haul me with him into the hole, the combined weight a sure thing. Hector.

And damn it if the bastard didn't have enough strength left in him to pull us both away, him dragging me up towards the lip of the bowl, his good arm hooked around my neck. I fought to get my bearings. A prick of light. The lagoon ahead. I couldn't breathe, and then he jerked backwards as somebody kicked him hard. The arm dropped away from my neck.

"Oh, no you don't. You're done, mate."

I sat slumped in the threshold between the two caves, dazed, as Noel shoved Hector into the chasm. I heard the man cry out then go silent. I thought to myself, I should push Noel in, too. So easy, as he stood there staring down into the crevice, maybe two seconds too long. But I couldn't do it, didn't want to do it. Only when he crouched before me seconds later, did I notice black oozing from his shoulder.

"You're shot," I said weakly.

"Thanks for that. Practice your aim, will you? Now I have to try diving out of here with a bad wing." He touched my face. "You'll be all right, no worries there. Father's safe with Wyndridge. Dear old Dad called the cops just before Mags tossed his phone into the lagoon, so help will come. Sorry I can't hang by until they arrive. Can't miss my ride."

My teeth chattered like machine-gun fire. "Don't do this, Noel. Don't."

"It's already done."

Yet he still held me while I gagged up water, stroking my face with unbearable gentleness. "What about your precious treasure?" I asked, once I caught my breath.

"Safe. It's been safely hidden down here for months. Tonight we take it away. I see you're wearing a memento." He pulled the pectoral cross from my shredded blouse and held it for a moment before letting it drop. I'd forgotten about it. "You'll understand soon enough." He got to his feet. "Goodbye, Phoebe. I wish circumstances had been different, I really do."

I gazed up at him, this black figure faintly backlit yet consumed by shadows. I barely had energy left to move. "I'll find you," my voice rasped.

He managed a smile. "Good. I'll be waiting." He turned to leave.

"Tell me about Toby!"

"I can't," he said with regret.

"Why?"

"Because it's not my story to tell." And with that, he left.

Leaning against the cave wall, weak and dizzy, I pulled at the necklace around my neck. It felt like lead, though I'd been dragging around for hours. What did he mean, I'd understand soon enough? Frustrated, I tugged at the relic, only the cross split into two, scattering pearls across the cavern floor.

EPILOGUE

I sat casting on stitches in the chair beside the hospital bed as the Bermudan sun streamed through the windows. Despite the controlled environment, I managed to crack the window open an inch. The nurse would probably close it on his next rounds. I'd propped my leg on the bed frame, satisfied that today the bandage would finally come off. Every physical inch of me seemed determined to heal, regardless of what seethed inside.

It shocked me that I couldn't see signs of my festering heart when I looked in the mirror.

On the other hand, after two weeks of convalescence punctuated by police statements and multiple visits from the authorities, plus long-distance conversations with Nancy, my father, and even Julie, I'd finally managed to find time to get my stitches back on the needles. There was hope, after all.

"Don't understand how you can knit at a time like this," Max murmured from the bed. He lay propped up on pillows, gazing at the ceiling, still in traction for his fractured spine. He'd been wallowing in his own misery since they brought him in.

"This is the best time to knit," I said, concentrating on my work. The yarn had suffered on its travels, slubbed in parts and knotted in others. I'd cut off the badly tangled entrails to wind back into balls, each color now secured in baggies. "Along with every other kind of time, except maybe while bathing. I haven't figured that one out yet."

"I'm bloody pathetic, aren't I? A man who gets shafted by his own son and the woman he's lived with for 30 years. I never saw it coming; I never knew they were cooking this against me. How could I be so blind?"

"There's a few of us in that club. I'm thinking of running for honorary president, myself."

"I'm a damn bloody fool." He began making snuffling sounds, a man unused to crying. "I'm chicken shit. I didn't treat them well enough, never made myself dad enough for my son. He thought I was ashamed of him but I wasn't. I was ashamed of myself. His mom was a beaut, a real artist. I met her when I went bush in the Top End buying Aboriginal art for my shop and, yeah, it was a fling, but I didn't know she got pregnant until Noel showed up at my door."

Thinking of Noel now delivered a punch of emotions I had yet to sort through. Why did the one man I thought I could fall hard for have to be a crook?

"But Maggie, she was my girl," Max continued, sobbing now. "I always loved her. Gave her my credit cards, let her handle the stuff that interested her, but I should have married her. I'm a damn bludger."

"A dropkick, I think you called yourself yesterday. That fits. And, for the record, you were a rotten father, and an inadequate boyfriend. Oh, and a crummy godfather, who couldn't tell his goddaughter the truth about anything, including the existence of a son. So there it is. Now what?" I knit my first row back along the rescued stitches, reveling in the deep satisfaction of recreating those tiny knots. "Welcome to the human race. We're famous for our imperfections. The fact that you weren't the perfect father or the best man doesn't mean you deserved what they did to you. They're chicken shit, not you. You don't deserve it; I don't deserve it; and neither does Alistair."

"Do you forgive me, honey? I'll make it up to you, I promise."

"You're forgiven, and I'll settle for honesty over gifts any day." I plucked out a ball of turquoise silk from my carpet bag and held it up to the light. Yes, perfect. I'd invite Bermuda blue to play along my next row.

"Can't believe Wyndridge won't have us prosecuted after all this. I expected him to, thought he should. Maybe not you, but certainly me."

The turquoise stitches settled in beside the dark blue, alleviating the somber mood with luminescent currents. "But he won't. You're as much a victim as he is and he's setting the cavalry after the true villains. Alistair's a good man," I said, gaze still on my needles. "Too good for what that bastard did to him. And me. And Dad. And you."

"Noel?"

"Not Noel. Well, Noel, too, but Toby most of all. Toby's the mastermind." Damn. I worked the last 4 stitches so tightly, I could hardly move them off the needle. Taking a deep breath, I lowered the project back into my lap and turned to Max.

"You can't really believe that, sweetheart."

"How else do you explain how the jewels in Alistair's secret room turned out to be replicas and the real treasure stolen? Who but Toby knew about or had access to that room, let alone the skills necessary to strategically pull off a stunt like that? My brother, the master strategist, did a brilliant job of orchestrating this one."

"I can't believe it," Max muttered. "Noel, yes—that boy's got a chip on his shoulder the size of Uluru—but Toby?"

"Toby's the rogue wave. He came up behind us all and knocked us all to our knees. Love, apparently, doesn't matter. Only winning does."

"Toby loved you and your dad."

"Just not enough. He stabbed the man who loved him by using that love to snake into his sanctum. That's unforgiveable. And everything Noel said or hinted at implied Toby's involvement. '"Not my story to tell,'" he said. My own brother abandoned our father, used his lover, you, and me —everyone who loved him—to mechanize the heist of the century. What kind of person does that?"

In my agitation, my knitting slipped to the floor, forcing me to bend over, grunting, to fetch it. Once back in my lap, I stroked it apologetically. "What kind of person would do that?" I repeated, forcing back tears. I would never forgive him; I'd hold rage in my heart until the seas dried up.

"The same kind who robs his father and conspires with his father's girlfriend." Max began snuffling again. "Two peas in a pod. Three peas," he corrected.

"Right. So what are we going to do about it, Max?" I thought of Noel, wondering if he'd made it through the sea caves with a bullet wound and trying not to care one way or the other.

"Do about it? What can we do about it? They're gone. The police haven't tracked them down, so how can we? Noel knows a ton of tricks on how to fence precious goods on the world market, and you can bloody believe he'll used every one of them. And if it's true Toby's in on this, which I'm not buying yet, we're buggered. That boy's too bloody brilliant for his own good. They got away with it. End of story."

A mirthless laugh caught in my throat. "Like hell it's 'end of story,' Max. The story's just beginning. Do you think I'm going to let them get away with this?" I hoisted myself to standing, letting my knitting fall to the floor once again. "We're going after them, Max, you and me."

He looked up at me, startled, gaze fixed on me as if seeing me fully for the first time: "You've changed, sweetheart."

"Damn right I have. My heart's no longer sweet, if you haven't noticed. Did you hear what I said? We're going after them."

"How?"

"I'm going to work with you, be your 2IC."

"But I was going to close the business, Phoebe, honey; I haven't the heart for it now."

"I'll give you emotional CPR, but you're not closing Baker & Associates. We need your contacts and that operation to track down Alistair's treasure and our family of criminals. We owe it to our DNA. Besides, I think I'd love the work you do, providing I do it my way, as in legally."

"But what about your dad?"

I hobbled back to the chair and sat down. "I was going to say, but first I have to take care of Dad. I'll go home for as long as it takes. Nancy's with him now for a few days. She says he's confused and keeps crying. When I talk to him, he just tells me over and over again to come home. He blames himself, but the blessing is, he'll soon forget the details, or I think so. I'm just hoping he doesn't keep harboring the pain without knowledge of why he's feeling it. Anyway, I'll comfort him. He's my dad."

"Whatever you want, Phoebe. You're my only family now."

I stared unfocused on the floor, caught in the currents of love and loss, awash in grief and some powerful force I couldn't quite define. Eventually, the coil of blue yarn at my feet begged for attention. I leaned over, plucked up my needles, and began steadying my tension until the stitches realigned.

AUTHOR'S NOTE

Oak Island, Nova Scotia, is a real place and a real mystery. Recently new research came out in a book entitled *Oak Island and its Lost Treasures: the Untold Story of the British Military's Role in the Island Flood Tunnel* by civil engineers Graham Harris and Les MacPhie. This is only one of numerous book posing intriguing theories as to what truly lies at the bottom of the elaborately-engineered flood tunnel. Those who become entranced by the unsolved mystery continue to invest huge amounts of time and money on the quest. Recently, a show running of the History Channel, describes the latest treasure hunters. This group has even managed to find coconut fibers, presumably used for drainage purposes, near the site. The fibers have been carbon-dated at 1200 AD, bringing veracity to yet another theory surrounding the presumed treasure site: Templar gold.

Though I completely fictionalized the events connecting Nova Scotia to Bermuda, I encourage anyone interested in unsolved mysteries, to read further on this fascinating topic.

The second book in the Crime by Design Series, *The Warp in the Weave* will be published later this year. In the meantime, Ms. Thornley has another published novel, *Frozen Angel.* For more on the author, please visit her website Janethornley.com

Made in the USA
Middletown, DE
13 August 2016